A SHOCKING EXHIBITION

Dorothy McCluskie

CHAPTER ONE
Wild Dreams & Window-cleaners

Someone famous once said, "When you're tired of London, you're tired of life." How could anyone be tired of London on a fabulous day like today? I have just been woken by a blaze of glorious sunlight streaming into my bedroom. It's a new day, a fresh start. My boyfriend Jake has gone in a puff of Lynx deodorant.

This is weird. I'm to being alone. It's not bad, just different. Struggle up onto my elbows and peer out of the window. Spring has most definitely sprung. The park across the road is bulging with flowers and small squealing children. Even our imposing Victorian terrace in Highbury has an almost undignified gleam. Sunlight sparkles off walls showing all the colours of the stone. Windows are open, radios playing and the sky is as bright and blue as a holiday brochure. Wonderful. So what if I haven't got a boyfriend? I have still got a wonderful flat, fantastic friends, and health if not wealth ... yet. I, Carly Watson, have plenty to be thankful for. My figure is curvy but not worryingly so, I have long brown hair and blue eyes and look ok with the right makeup and outfit. And I get to do a job that I really enjoy, painting, usually portraits. I would be happy to do it for free, but unfortunately life is not free or it would be truly perfect.

Yesterday was my birthday. I am now the highly mature and almost granny-like age of thirty-bloody-four. And contrary to popular belief it doesn't hurt at all. Women's thirties are much maligned. We are constantly bombarded by claptrap about wrinkles, cellulite and clocks – the thirty-something woman's bogeymen. Ooh, I'm sooo scared! I'm not even sure what cellulite actually looks like. It is like the after death issue - interesting in a scientific sort of way. But the consequences of finding out render me less than eager to know… And on top of these alleged horrors, I hear there's a flabby arms thing? It appears to me like a sadistic prank by the almighty chap in the sky. Has God got a grudge against women? By George, I believe that he has. Imagine holding a grudge this long over a harmless orchard misdeed. Bloody blokes, sooo unreasonable.

Anyway, what do I care? If any of these horrors have affected me, I can't say I've noticed. Jake never said anything, and the king of tact he's not. I must still be fairly flaw-free. I shall only worry if they affect my main interests in life - painting, shopping and nookie. But not in that order of course. Though admittedly the latter has lately been just in my head, due to Jake turning quite unexpectedly into Sir Slobalot, King of the Couch Potatoes. Since sustaining a serious knee injury playing professional football Jake has been wallowing in self-pity, pizza and beer, not an attractive combination. I have tried to be supportive. I know that playing in the national league was a huge part of his life, but you can only listen to incessant whinging for so long. He was always out training before. Now he just lies on the sofa moaning. But he's gone now. It was his choice and there is no point dwelling on what might have been.

Turn and peruse the bedroom thoughtfully. For one thing it's very quiet. No unbearably loud snorking from a boyfriend-shaped duvet mountain. One that steals all the duvet while you sleep so that you wake up frozen. This is a definite plus.

So, what shall I do this morning? I don't have to be anywhere in particular for a change. No urgent portraits to finish. I could…relax. I could even go back to sleep and have a wild erotic fantasy about a non-snorking hunk of my choice. Oh yes, that's an excellent plan. I wonder if imaginary sex still releases the same happy chemicals into your brain as actual sex, chocolate or narcotics… or if it uses up any calories at all? Perhaps it does both. Hmm, it is worth a try.

…………...

2

Later... Much later... Aahh! That's better. Who needs reality anyway? I won't have to go to that step class now. Stretch my arms high above my head and have a wriggle about to wake up. Toss the duvet aside quickly before my willpower runs out. Roll sideways into a standing position in one overly ambitious fluid movement.

"Oomph!" Try to pat my bizarrely bouffant hair into place as I stagger kettlewards blindly. I am most definitely not a morning person. Morning people are crazy. Ooh, coffee, coffee, coffee...

Music on, kettle on, cereal out. Dance about a bit feeling funky.

"I'm every woman! I'm every ...oh!" Clutch my bowl of Frosties tight in sudden shock. I am being watched from the window by a somewhat surprised new window cleaner. He is poised mid-shammy wipe, impertinently observing my skimpy new knickers and vest. Well, hello there Mr Snoopy. No, no, you go right ahead and look all you want sucker. You are never going to get it.

"No, you're never gonna get it... My loving..." Shimmy off back to the bedroom singing and waving my spoon in an exaggerated, pseudo-seductive manner. Oh, who cares? I'll never see him again anyway. Besides, he was quite sexy. And at least I was wearing my nice, new silky knickers and not my ghastly old period pants.

....

Slightly later... I have decided to be ultra-decadent. If you're going to be decadent at all then it really must be done properly. I have got lots of DVDs and I am going to slob out on the thankfully Toad-free couch and watch them all during the day! I'm a total couch pomme de terre. I have Pride and Prejudice (the Colin Firth version, of course), Bridget Jones, Pirates of the Caribbean and something that had an aesthetically pleasing man on the cover. That ought to do the trick. All extremely good films, not too heavy, with at least a couple of supremely shag-worthy, ogle-able blokes in them. Well? Don't know about the last one, obviously. But by then I probably won't care. It's only an understudy DVD anyway, in case the others let me down in some unfathomable way.

Fan-bloody-tastic! I am totally ogled out. Lots of gorgeous men falling into lakes and oceans like some kind of male wet T-shirt Olympics. Now I know that there must be a God. However, it's just as well that the Bible does not clearly state *which* men were made in his image. There may be some early printing error. I could be tempted to rush out and join Exit … only for a disappointing eternal confrontation with some flaccid, smelly creep. Yeuch!

I didn't actually think Colin Firth was that nice before the lake scene in P& P. I wonder if he's only nice when soggy? It is really his middle that's appealing. His head isn't absolutely imperative? But then, he'd be entirely gross with no head at all? …Or perhaps the wrong head? …Or someone else's interchangeable head in the manner of Worzel Gummidge? …But obviously not John Pertwee's Worzel head? No, I just refuse to have that thought! Oh, O.K., fine. He can just keep his own. This is getting way too complex now… And he has got nice eyes after all.'

Casually flick off the T.V. and lie there studying some fascinating thin air above my head. Perhaps it's an actual body of water that has magical powers? Like a kind of fountain of sexiness? But which one? …And would it work on a random batch of half-decent guys if they were thrown into Windermere per se? A quick dook et voila! Nookie-on-legs? Yippee! …Or is it compulsory to be drop-dead unattainable first? Hmm? Interesting…

I am suddenly startled out of this deep and meaningful contemplation by my unnecessarily loud and inconvenient phone. Roll off the settee and crawl over to the receiver.

"Hello?" There is a hissy silence interspersed with wheezing gasps and groans a la some random pervert. I sigh and shake my head.

"Oh, go and jump in Windermere you sad git. See if it works. You sound like an ideal test subject. And if it doesn't at least you might drown and save the Vice Squad some trouble." I'm about to hang up when a wail echoes in my ear,

"Car-leeee!" It's my friend Angie [something in television]. She sounds like she has been traumatised yet again by Miles, her waste-of-space married lover.

"Carly, what am I going to doooo?" Erm, nope, too non-specific. Not a clue what the question is. I shall stab in the dark hopefully.

"Umm, find someone single who's nice to you?"

"Noooo! There isn't time!" Is she dying or something and I didn't even know? Aren't I just the worst friend in the world?

"Isn't time for what Ange?"

"It's the fourteenth already Carly?"

"The fourteenth what? Hole? Dimension? Time Miles has got on your wick? Come on Ange, be sporting. At least give me a clue."

"God, Carly. You are hopeless."

"Yeah, I know. Jake tells me all the time. So what?"

"It's the fourteenth of June. As in three days before the seventeenth of June. As in this Saturday. Carly? The Globe Of Britain awards? It's in three days time!"

"Er, ...and?"

"AND? And I am escort less! What the hell's that gonna look like in the tabloids for God's sake?" Tabloids? Jeez-us. She has lost it?

"Carly, can't you see the headlines already? Can you imagine what they'll say about me on the night.... And here's Angela Montrose now folks, and.... Will you look at that people? Gasp, shock, horror! The prune spinster queen of the airwaves has NO PARTNER tonight!" Oh-my-God! She's totally barking?

"Angie, no-one cares if you've got a partner. I mean, surely there's gonna be what, a squillion celebs there. Why would they choose to castigate you when there's going to be so many other, you know, more famous people there that they could be misrepresenting?"

"Carly, Carly, Carly. You just don't get how things work in this game, do you?..." Hell, no. I'm just a simpleton-peasant.

"...I'll either be branded a raving lesbo...." Well, raving's certainly fair.

"...or even worse, I'll have the 'poor old Ange. She can't get a man because she's got cellulite...and we have the photos to prove it'

5

accusations flung at me by the morning…AT THE LATEST! Carly, my career is OVER!" As I've never been entirely sure what Angie's career actually is I cannot dredge up a suitable platitude for this situation. It may well be a silly, naïve peasant question but I have to ask,

"Angie, can't you just take someone else? Like Jerry or somebody? I mean he is still a bloke, technically. Quite a presentable bloke. Wouldn't he do?"

"Oh, for Christ's sake Carly! Can you just imagine that? He would either turn up covered in pink sequins and upstage me completely…or else people would think we were an item and Miles would be furious."

As Miles is her married [to someone else] sleazebag lover, who let her and his phenomenally long-suffering spouse down in the first place…and the second, third, etc. place… I cannot find it in me to feel bad for him. Angie is clearly one pistachio short of a picnic and you cannot reason with a nutcase… Yet I always have to try.

"So what exactly Ange, do you want to do? You don't want to go alone. You don't want to take J. who, incidentally, adores dressing up, is the perfect gentleman and would really love to come. You'd rather be splashed all over the front pages with mega-bozo Miles, somebody else's frigging husband?" God! I was quite happy till she phoned.

"Don't call him that! … Look Carls, I just thought…. That maybe… maybe you might like to come?" Erm, why? Because I won't upstage you as much as a gay man? Thanks a lot.

"Er, Ange, sorry to state the obvious, but I thought you wanted an escort? A male escort?"

"Well of course I do. But if I did go with another man Miles would be sooo jealous... so you'll have to do. I know, we can pretend that you're someone important! We'll pretend that you're a successful artist!"

"Oh could we? Thanks for that."

"Yes, that's perfect. It still has some kudos if we're celebrity gal-pals. And Miles won't be upset. Unless you're already doing something, of course…" Uh-oh. Guilt trip alert.

"... with Mr Happy, like some boring old married couple? Watching Casualty or something riveting, huh?" Ooooh, great! Thank you for reminding me that I'm single. Four hours of medicinal DVDs wiped out in a fell tactless blow. Excellent.

"No Ange, we're not doing anything...because he left me last night!" Stick that in your ipod and smoke it, you self obsessed media slut.

A small silence ensues as this bombshell is absorbed. Angie is traumatised every other week. She doesn't expect it to happen to other people.... Well, except Jerry.

Shocked,

"Oh no Carls, you are kidding! Well, I mean, obviously, you're not kidding but.... You two have been together for years?"

"Centuries even."

"Oh don't worry Carls. He'll be back."

"God! Do you think? I'd better get the locks done."

"Don't be silly. You don't mean that? You don't want to be left on the shelf forever do you?"

"Frankly Ange, at this moment in time, a nice peaceful shelf for one sounds like heaven. If I ever see another man again it will be far too soon. Except for the imaginary ones of course. They're allowed. Being unattainable, they're safer than your pain-in-the-neck real guys."

Angie laughs nervously. She is not the celibate type, quite the reverse in fact.

"You're just upset. That's all. You're not thinking straight."

"I am Ange, for the first time in years. Men are more trouble than they're worth. I'm taking a vow of chastity. You ought to try it. It's fantastic... peaceful."

"Now you're just being silly. It'll be the shock. I know what you need Carls.... a good night out."

"No? Not really? You astound me. I can't imagine where this could be leading."

"So you'll definitely be there? Great Sweetie, knew you wouldn't let me down. Byeeeee!" There is a click as she hangs up. Hey, wait a minute? Did I agree? I don't remember saying yes? Oh well, no point moping about here on Saturday. I might start feeling sentimental and forgive Jake, if, God forbid, he did come back. And let's face it, he's always sorry afterwards.

Lie back on the sofa and shut my eyes, remembering the car-crash - in -motion that was the day before, my birthday.

I'd arrived home from a fabulous birthday lunch with my friends, feeling really happy, partly due to the liquid half of the lunch in question. I recall reaching the stone steps onto the street, opening the heavy front door with my back. My arms were full of presents and a box containing three-quarters of a stupendously gooey and alcoholic birthday cake. This was from the biggest sweetie on the planet, Jerry aka J. - fashion icon, philoso-poet and my favourite friend. I'd staggered awkwardly up the three flights of stairs humming to myself....

"Oomph. La-de-da." Nearly there, I wonder if my angel-come-boyfriend has done something amazing for me? Like, for example, got up?

Opening the front door with difficulty I'd dropped all my bags in the hall, deposited my huge cake on the kitchen counter and dashed excitedly through to the lounge to find... the beer-swilling, football-shirt layabout from hell. What? Where is my birthday surprise? I am living with Jabba the Hut.

Jake grunts as he registers my presence. He used to give me a kiss and cuddle as soon as I arrived. Now I don't even merit a hello.

"Oh, so you're back then. What did you get for dinner?"

"I thought that maybe we could go out Jake."

"No way Carls! The Gunners are playing tonight."

"You're snubbing my birthday for a football match?"

"What? It's the semi-final. We can go out anytime."

Narrow my eyes at him, astounded.

"Anytime is not my birthday. My birthday is tonight."

"Jesus Christ Carls. Listen to yourself, me, me, me. What age are you? Five?"

Gasp.

I hate it when he twists things round like that to make me the villain of the piece. He does it so expertly and with such conviction that, as usual, I'm almost convinced that I'm the one who is being unreasonable.

"Fine! Watch your stupid match if it means that much to you." He doesn't even bother to look round or reply.

Stomp back through to the kitchen in a huff. That little spat has put me right off the idea of eating dinner anyway. Rummage about and find a Kit-Kat and a bottle of juice. Shuffle back through quite deflated. I cuddle up in the big scruffy armchair as the couch is quite covered in stripy nylon toad. Toad-boy eyes my biscuit.

"You can't eat that Carls? You'll get fat." I can't eat it now? You have spoiled it. He casually indicates a crumpled envelope lying on the coffee table. I don't have to open it to see that its just some cheapo card. Glare at the card, biting my lip tensely. Jake raises an impatient eyebrow.

" Are you going to open it or what?" No, I can see that it sucks. Offhand,

"Maybe later." He sighs heavily, shrugs and turns back to the T.V.

He hasn't got me anything at all? I know he isn't working right now but a box of sweets would have done. It isn't the price, it's the effort involved. He clearly doesn't love me at all. I can feel my eyes burning. So I scuttle off back to the kitchen to hide. I am not going to cry over this.

"Stick the kettle on while you in there."

I'm distraught and you want a cup of tea? Grab hold of the kitchen worktop and try to concentrate on calming down. I can hear a gaspy sound. Oh, good grief. It's me? Wipe my face with the back of my hand and try to breathe deeply as advised in my yoga DVD. I'm not going to cry. He's not worth it. Glance down at my fabulous cake. This is what I get from my friends. At least they actually care about me. He's just a complete and utter toad. My eyes fill up and I blink hard and dab at them with some handy kitchen towel.

Peer out of the window. There's a couple holding hands in the park, heads close together as they chat. A horrible tight pain grips my chest. What have I done to deserve this? Even my miniscule biscuit pleasure has been swiped from right under my nose... by a beer-gut, meanie, football-twat. He does this every time. Every time I'm not eating a lettuce, or something else similarly yuck. My lovely cake swims back into focus. God help me if I try to eat that. Fat-Boy-Fat will berate me and I'll lose the will to live. Its not as if he is exactly slimmer of the year himself now... What a hypocrite.

"Carly! Come on, for God's sake. I'm dying of thirst out here." No you're not. I'm not that lucky... I know. I'll show him my cake. Even Jake can't fail to be impressed by it. Relationships need work. I must make an effort to be magnanimous and gracious and other saintly attributes. He is going through a major life crisis after all. He's bound to want a piece of this gorgeous cake and it'll put him in a better mood, like he used to be.

Pick the cake up carefully and teeter back through to the lounge. Jake is sprawled slurping out of a can - and burping. Oh my God, must you? He glances up impatiently and clocks my wonderful cake.

"What the hell is that Carly? And where is my tea?"

"It's a birthday cake. Jerry made it for me. Wouldn't you like a piece?" He sneers up at my cake in disdain.

"Oh, so Nancy-Boy can cook as well, can he? Ooh, well la-di-da! Has he got a little pink, flowery apron? I bet he has." Oh, you are so horrible now. Jerry has done nothing to you. ...No. I am going to be nice.

"Oh, go on Jake. You really ought to have some. It's really ..."

"Carly! Just bugger off with the cake. I don't bloody well want it! I just want a fucking cup of tea! Is that too much to ask?" Give him my most charming fake smile.

"Well, that is such a pity....because you are getting the cake." Splat it squidgy side down on his face.

"Argh! You fucking bitch!"

He leaps up all chocolate and cream. Oh God, that was almost orgasmic. First time he's achieved that in months. That was certainly my best present. I must remember to thank Jerry. Turn to make a dignified exit but find myself retrieved by a tight grip on my arm.

"Don't you dare walk away from me!" Uh-oh? Cake-boy is a little perturbed and is roughly one inch from my nose.

"Think that was funny do you?"

"Not only funny Jake but long overdue. Get off me." Tug at his hand in vain.

"Oh, is that right? Think you're too good for me, poncing about with your arty-smarty friends?" Oh God, he's gone totally crazy? He leers down with his cake-covered, beer-smelly face.

"Not so smart now, are you Carls, eh?"

"Jake, I'm warning you. Let me go. I don't want to hurt you. " He guffaws loudly at this.

"Yeah? Or what? You in no position to tell me…" Bring my leg up in an attempt to push him off with an old judo move. This goes a little wrong as he moves suddenly, causing me to hit him between the legs by mistake. He crumples into a stripy nylon heap.

"Oops, Jake I didn't mean that! Sorry." Edge back as he rises with spectacular speed and grabs both my arms, tighter this time.

"Sorry? You bloody will be!"

I must not have hit him that hard? Or perhaps he had little to lose? Lean back against the wall to catch my breath and distance myself from his rage. Should my life be flashing in front of my eyes? Shut them to check. No, must have been too damn boring. Jake is breathing stale lager fumes in my face and ranting furiously.

"You know your problem Carly, you think the whole fucking world revolves around you! Don't you *get* it? I might never play again… and all you care about is your stupid bloody birthday…"

"You have got to be kidding me? I have been running after you and putting up with your bad moods for months."

"Yeah? Good for you. Saint Carly of the Patronising Remarks. A man needs more than to be *tolerated*! Would it kill you to show a little womanly sympathy now and again? Nah, now that the big bucks have stopped rolling in, suddenly you can't be bothered. Do you think I don't see the way you look at me, like I'm worthless, disgusting? Who the fuck do you think you are, looking at me like that? "

11

He has completely lost it. The months of bottled-up frustration all spill out as he roars and barges around kicking the furniture and smacking the wall loudly near my head. Its clear he wants a response, something to kick against, someone, anyone to blame. I stand still, eyes squeezed shut, trying to blank everything out, hoping he will calm down and stop soon. Suddenly it is all too much. I will *not* be bullied. I don't deserve this. Open my eyes to see what he's up to. What's the worst he can do ... erm, kill me. Which will increase the value of my paintings no end - a boon to my family I'm sure.

"You know what Jake, I am sick of this." He raises his eyebrows in questioning derision.

"Oh no, poor you Carls. You seem to have conveniently forgotten that *I'm* the injured party here - literally."

"No, I'm serious Jake. I've had it. I'm really sorry about your knee and your place on the team and everything, but I can't take any more – the drinking, the temper, the shouting...and now this? You would actually raise your hand to me? No, this keeps happening and I will *not* be pushed around in my own home. I want you out of here right now."

Uh-oh? I've gone too far. I saw his temper snap in his face then. I think I am going to die. He goes up a gear into a deafening roar,

"YOU UNGRATEFUL LITTLE BITCH!" Hell's teeth, he really is out of his mind.

"…..And after everything I've done for you."

" Like what? Lying on my couch watching football and feeling sorry for yourself? Oh yeah, that was great. Thanks a lot."

"You sarcastic little bitch! You couldn't last five minutes without me. What are you going to live on, eh? The money from your stupid pictures?"

" That's what we're living on now? You haven't given me money for ages. You just give me abuse... and lots of extra tidying to do."

"Oh that's it. I get it. Now that the big paychecks have stopped, you really don't want to know. You bloody little gold-digger!"

"No! That wasn't what I meant at all. You know I've never cared about money. I liked you *despite* the football lifestyle, not because of it. But now, the way you're behaving …"

"The way I'*m* behaving? No I don't think…"

"Oh Jake, just go back to your mother's house. You're acting like a twelve year old anyway."

He's gone a nice shade of purple. Or perhaps it's alizarin crimson? Good! Serves him right.

"You are a total waste of space Carls. You don't even do the bloody ironing."

"What? Are you kidding me? I work. While you just lie on your batty watching the goddamn T.V.!"

"You call those crappy paintings work? At least my mother knows how to look after a man!"

"Oh, that is so disturbing. Just sod off Oedipus."

"But you Carls, have not got a fucking clue."

"Oh right. I see. It isn't a girlfriend you need? It's a housekeeper-come-nanny. I'm amazed you can ….Oh!" Pause to catch my breath as he shoves me back against the wall. Eek! He's going to kill me?

But no, he has stormed off in a rage. Oh, thank God for that. Slide slowly down onto the carpet and wrap my arms tightly round my knees. I feel a bit shaky and my teeth are rattling in my head. Why do I never know when to shut up? And what the hell is he doing? I can hear him banging about. Is he trashing the joint? It's probably best to keep out of his way. Rest my forehead on my arms and wait.

Twenty minutes later the crazed throwback lurches through the doorway.

"Right, that's it Carly! I'm off. Have a nice life you ungrateful little cow!"

"Oh charming. Well, that is just fine. I'd rather be alone forever than spend one more second with you!"

"Yeah? Well you probably will. Who would want you anyway, you crazy bitch? Incidentally, there was a voucher in that card for that fancy spa you said you wanted to go to. Happy gold-digging birthday. That's the last you are getting from me. Find yourself another sucker."

A colossal bang from the front door announces his departure. Oh dear God! I think I'll just lie here and die.

The full techni-colour memory spins round my brain making my head ache. Open my eyes but it doesn't make any difference, I can still see it in my head, still hear him shouting, all the cruel words. Put my hands over my eyes and moan, "I don't care how damn sorry he is this time. He is never ever coming back into this house... Men are absolutely full of it. Being on my own cannot possibly be any worse."

CHAPTER TWO
String Dress Fiasco

So - Saturday p.m. I'm at an exclusive media function full of exclusive media types - all terribly rich, famous and sophisticated. I am terribly none of the above. Predictably enough, I am here with Angie as a last minute substitute for her worthless boyfriend, creepy Miles, who has been unavoidably detained by his wife. I wonder if anyone can tell that I'm an impostor, as a media person, obviously. Not as a boyfriend?

"Remind me Ange, why are we here again? To party and ogle famous people, hmm?" I can't actually see any worth ogling, but I'm willing to persevere in a good cause. I have now been celibate for so long that my vital bits have healed right up ... despite having an alleged boyfriend till last week. I don't want a man, just a nice view of one to add to my mental library, for the purpose of entertaining romantic fantasies.

"I told you Carly. It's vital for my career to be seen in the right places. It's not what you know in this business, you know?"

"Oh right." Clearly not. As I seem to recall Ange left school with a grand total of three 'o' levels; Modern Studies, French and Secretarial. I have a disturbing suspicion that her success may be due more to something French than something secretarial. She always was quite amoral. But as she is my friend I'll give her the benefit of the rather large doubt. Glance around in amazement at the aircraft hanger sized hall filled with round tables. It is a vision in sparkly silver and gold material with ten million matching balloons.

"So this is one of the right places then?" Ye Gods!

"Well, of course Carls. This is one of the premier events of the film industries' calendar."

"Really?"

".… It's a perfect opportunity to do a bit of discreet networking Carly." Networking? What? Am I about to waste a perfectly good evening of my life watching Angie kiss some pervy old producer's butt?

"Fantastic Ange. Can't wait." Oh well. At least I got the opportunity to wear one of Angie's terrifyingly expensive dresses, which I could never afford. It's a stunning little halter-neck number apparently made of carefully knotted pale pink garden twine lined with a shiny material and split to mid-thigh. Obviously the ludicrously high price tag is because the dress has the magical ability to transform even elephantine porkers like myself into slim and seductive goddesses. Amazing! I am now Jessica Rabbit. I would have liked to be Marilyn Monroe but that would obviously be much more expensive.'

I try to slink towards our table in a manner befitting such an outfit but only succeed in stumbling in on Angie's glitzy stiletto torture shoes. Clearly more practice is required but there wasn't enough time. I settle for lounging in a sophisticated media-style pose on my spindly chair for a bit of sexy star spotting.

"Carly! Don't pull the material like that? You'll stretch it." Oh, that remark is so asking for a smack in the chops. I do not appreciate bitchy weightist comments. But as, to avoid visible panty line, I'm wearing only her dress I can't really fling it in her face and storm out. Anyway, it would be a shame to waste the chance to have a good pose while I'm all dolled up. It hasn't happened very often lately, not since Jake got injured.

"I was just wondering what it was made of, that's all."

"Its hand-spun Thai silk by Stella McCartney." Must have taken her a while to spin all that?

"I picked it up at her show in Milan for only three grand."

"What do you mean 'ONLY THREE GRAND'? I wouldn't have borrowed it if I'd known. My God! What if I spill something on it? I'll need a flipping bank loan."

"Well, you could hardly have come in one of your 'arty' outfits Carly." Bitch! Just because I'm an actual starving artist, it doesn't mean that I don't have feelings.

"They're not 'arty'. They're just reasonably priced. And in case you've forgotten, you asked me to come here tonight." To help you ponce about.

"I know. I know. I'm sorry. I didn't mean to be snooty. It's really Miles that I'm angry with." Huh! No comment. I have nothing pleasant to say about Miles. It's hard enough to believe that one woman could actually fancy him. He's not physically ugly, just repellent in a smug, two-timing sort of way. Besides, despite being a professional media tart, Angie is blonde, slim and a very nice person. She could do much better than creepy Miles, the Fulham Philanderer. Men really do mess with your head.

....

Well, we've been here for twenty minutes now and nothing exciting has happened. I've seen a couple of semi-famous presenters, a selection of East Enders and some bloke from Channel Five – how dull. It would seem that I have got all dolled up for nothing. Angie has found a colourless fat guy to suck up to a couple of tables away. Don't know who the hell he is but he has a very large cigar therefore he must be famous/ important/ a complete tosser. So I find myself abandoned at my own table with a variety of nondescript dinner suits. Chorus of "So Carly, what do you do?" Smile my best scary shark smile.

"Oh, you know, paint things, …pictures. I'm a proper artist, as opposed to 'piss' or 'con.'" Nope. They haven't heard of one of those. Didn't think so. The indifference is clearly mutual. I think I shall just stretch my leg out and relieve the incredible tedium by admiring my glamorous shoes. Hmm, they really do make my legs resemble a giraffe. Or is that a gazelle? Anyway, it's a huge improvement on my usual pale and stumpy look.

Unfortunately, as I'm engrossed in admiring myself, I completely fail to see someone approaching stage right till…oops, too late! I have a man at my feet at last. Not my intended scenario.

"God, I'm sorry. Are you ok?" I know my face is crimson. He struggles to his feet and brushes himself off. Hmm, quite attractive actually when vertical… Probably not un-attractive when horizontal, but as usual it was too quick to tell.

"No, really, it's fine. I wasn't looking." Ye Gods… tall, dark and quite unfeasibly shaggable…and American? Ooooh! I'm rendered speechless with lust and can only gape like a twit as he smiles politely and saunters off before I can wreak any further injury. Damn it! I didn't even get his name, never mind a flipping phone number.

Angie, back from Mission Suck-up, has clocked my clumsiness,

"Carly! What are you doing? Do you know who that *was* you nearly crippled just then? "

"No, but I imagine it would be a great loss to womankind if he were."

"If he were what?"

"Crippled. What a waste." 'What a waist, what a bum, what a …'

"Carly!"

"What?"

"We're supposed to be here to network, not to assault well-known people."

"Pity. Do you know him well enough to have his phone number at all?"

"No. Besides Carls, you've sworn off all men forever, remember?"

"Damn! That's right. So I have. It was a moment of weakness. It won't happen again. Concentrate Carly - all men are pigs, all men are pigs…except Jerry and my Dad, but all the rest are pigs."

Angie sighs heavily and turns away. The lights go up on the vast twinkly stage and a rotund, aesthetically-challenged dinner suit waddles on to the thunder of sycophantic applause. It is more than apparent that this is mostly inspired by the cameras panning over the audience in the hope of spotting a celeb, but the suit spreads his arms wide in appreciation and smiles a cheesy, showbiz , practiced-at-home-in-front-of-the-mirror smile. Yeuch! What a yutz.

"Thanks a lot folks, heh, heh…..Now I ain't gonna ramble on…." Yes, you are and everybody knows it.

"…cause I know it ain't me you're here to see…" 'Too right it ain't buddy.'

Half an hour later he is still rambling to a sea of politely comatose faces. Angie's smile has long since frozen but she's gamely paying attention in the vain hope that a camera might swing round in our direction. Not probable this far back firmly ensconced among the plebs. This admirable perseverance might just be the reason why she's rich and successful and I'm not? …Nah! It's because she's a tart.

…………...

I have wandered off into Fantasy Land due to the monolithic banality of it all. They really should have events like this for other lines of work like..umm? - plumbers and stuff. 'And this year's prestigious Golden Ballcock award for the category of 'Plunger Of The Year' goes to…. Archie McSquoogle of Lemington Spa for his memorable work on 'The U Bend'!

"HOORAY! HOORAY! HOOORAY!" Archie blushes and picks up his gleaming ballcock statuette, struggling to hold back the tears.

"Come on Archie, SPEECH!" But wait, maybe that is an acting category? - Plunger of the Year - for handsome male leads in romantic fiction perhaps? Hmmm, a professional plunger, ooh? Are any of these guys potential plungees?

Peruse the audience thoughtfully. Oh, Good Lord, I do hope not! If they are there's been some horrible mistake with the casting? It is a sadly disappointing turnout. Turn back to the table and assume my Clint Eastwood face, all the better for paying attention. The dinner suit is STILL saying blah-di-blah-di-blah… Oh, good grief. Do hurry up. This is most definitely above and beyond the call of any normal friendship. What I really need now is…a drink. So, where's the bar?

"Back in a moment Ange." Her fake smile doesn't even flicker as she hisses through clamped jaws,

"Vodka and coke - treble!"

Now, the last thing I want is for any of those rogue cameras to accidentally flash a view of my worst and unfortunately most noticeable angle into zillions of homes from behind my back, so I sidle backwards in an attempt at discretion through the minute gaps between the tables. Aim hopefully in what I presume is the general direction of the bar. Judging from the wall of backs facing me on arrival we are far from alone in our desperate need for medicinal aid. Taking a massive breath in order to shrink a couple of sizes or three I plunge into the fray at approximately shoulder height to the crowd. Can't see a bloody thing. Must be almost there now... Bit of a tight squeeze. OUCH! Wait a minute, I appear to be caught on something. Or more to the point, Angie's beautiful, very expensive dress appears to be caught on something? AAAAAARGH!

The dress is attached to the sleeve of someone's shirt. A strange hand is attached to my body somewhere in the vicinity of my behind. As you will already have ascertained, my behind is most definitely not my favourite body part. It is without doubt my Achilles heel. Could he not have attached himself to my shoulder, for God's sake? Bloody men, it's always boobs and bums. Realising his arm is being restrained the stranger turns to tower over me. Oh, my GOD! It is my previous victim. What is the chance of that happening?

"I'm so sorry but I appear to be stuck to your sleeve." 'Yes Carly, very impressive.

Looking a trifle surprised, the handsome stranger attempts to jiggle his hand free without actually touching my body at all, never mind my butt - an astounding degree of restraint for the male of the human species? Unfortunately, this proves to be quite difficult given the precise location of his entrapment,

"NO!!! YOU'LL RIP IT!" Where did that squeaky voice come from? I am morphing into Minnie Mouse at the least opportune of moments. People are starting to notice our predicament and are openly staring at my bum. This is my very worst nightmare. The stranger frowns in consternation,

"Ehrm….sorry. You know, maybe we should find somewhere quieter to untangle this." Excellent plan. It cannot be carried out soon enough for my liking. Both look round frantically.

I squeak,

"Where? Oh God! Oh God! I do not have the budget to replace this. Angie is going to kill me."

"Come on, this way. I'm Aaron, by the way, Aaron Stanford. I'd say pleased to meet you and all, but in the circumstances I don't expect you're too pleased to meet me huh?" Uhh, ok. I do not care if he is Jack the sodding Ripper. I am not staying here to await imminent public ridicule.

"Er, yes, quite. But I mean it's hardly your fault. If anything, I blame Stella McCartney. This dress is like a Venus flytrap. What was she thinking with the whole twine thing? …And I'm Carly Watson. You know, hi."

"Aah, yeah? Stella …? Is that who you're here with?"

"No. And just as well for her." Aaron raises his eyebrows in a politely bemused fashion and drapes his arm round me. Try to look as if we are a normal couple engaged in a perfectly normal casual stroll and not two freaky nutters glued together against our will by designer twine and buttons.

…………...

We have now been skulking round the deep red velvet walled corridors for ages, looking in vain for a discreet un-entangling spot. My face is scorching and may well be clashing most horribly with my dress. It's surprisingly hard to make small talk at this particular point. I've never been stuck to anyone that I didn't want to be stuck to before. As virgin stuckees go, his manners have so far been good. He bends down with an embarrassed smile,

"It's alright, you know. I don't think anyone noticed."

"Really? Do you think so?" He's quite nice for a phantom dress ripper? Of course, he is quite clearly a man, so he can't be that nice. All men are pigs. Some just hide it better than others.

"Aha! What about in here?" Aha? Do you have a cape? But no, he has found us a heavily curtained cubicle as in a box at the opera or a changing room in the better class of store. It's empty. Scuttle in before anyone can see us. Hmm, so now what? Doesn't appear from his expression that he knows either. ..And STOP staring at my butt!

"Well, er, Ma'am, perhaps we'd better have a look at it."

"Excuse me, it's not an injury? And I am quite capable of looking at my own bottom, thank-you very much!" Aaron looks taken aback. That must have been rude in American? And clearly he did not realise I was a nutter or he would have attached himself to someone else.

"Sure, sure. You go right ahead then." He studiously examines a handy wall.

"Erm, it's your shirt button that's caught. I can't get it out without ripping my dress." A muscle starts twitching in his jaw.

"Damn! What can we do? We can't wander about all night like Siamese twins?"

"Well, I don't know, do I? I've never been stuck to a man before!" Oh no! I did not say that! His face is pink as well but he is too polite to lower the tone any further. He gets a decisive look.

"O.K., let's be practical here."

"Yes, let's, why don't we? Great. You've thought of something?"

"We can't risk tearing the dress, right? So we'll have to get the button off somehow?"

"Good plan so far. I'm completely in favour of not tearing the dress."

"Have you got a pair of scissors on you or something?"

"Scissors? Why would I? Do I look like a flipping girl guide? Oh, you mean because I'm a woman? Well you're a bloody bloke, whip your Swiss army knife out."

"And why the hell would I have a knife?"

"Because, Mr Stanford, it fits your rugged manly gender stereotype... See! I rest my case." Oops! I've ticked him off now. He is doing that sneery face and has gone all, what's the word, brusque? I quite like cross men actually. Does that make me a pervert or not?

"Look Ma'am, I don't know what your problem is, but I don't have time for a debate on gender issues right now. Can we just deal with the problem at hand and get back to the show?"

"Oh!... Well, Fine!"

"Great. So...either we find a pair of goddamn scissors soon or one of us is going to have to get naked here." Eek! Fine if it's him. Not fine if it's me. A full scale disaster in fact!

Now his whole body is twitching about and his patience is obviously at an end. I know the danger signs well as I'm so good at accidentally provoking them.

"Well, Mr Stanford, it is certainly not going to be me so you'd better have a plan B up your sleeve...along with my dress. Could you not have worn cufflinks or kept your hands to yourself or something...and saved us all this trouble?"

His eyebrows reach the top of his forehead at this aspersion.

"Kept my...? What the hell do you take me for?"

"I'm not taking you! I'm trying my best to put you back!"

"Look Lady, I like to think I'm a gentleman... but keeping my hands to myself right now is taking all of my willpower. So I'll tell you what we'll do. I'm renting an apartment near here about ten minutes away in a cab. Let's just go there right now and sort this mess out and we'll come right back, huh? O.K.? How's that for a plan B? Unless you've got any better suggestions?"

"Erm, no, I.... Not really... But Angie? I can't just leave her here?"

"Leave her a message at the front desk. We'll cut the damn button off and be back before you know it. Come on, let's go already!" Seems reasonable so go for that plan. Give the joint a swift body swerve in a passing taxi. Should only take, what, twenty minutes? Half an hour at the most.

. . . .

Half an hour later - still in the taxi. The traffic is horrendous. Both of us are highly freaked out. As I'm still stuck to his hand sitting comfortably is out of the question. Both sit totally rigid, staring out of opposite windows. Why? Why me? This *never* happens in the films.

…………...

We arrive at his place at long last, a posh South Kensington flat. Well, lucky old him. He pays the taxi with the hand he has left and ushers me into the hall. I shall just brush past the embarrassment of us both squidging through the front door. The flat is quite modern inside, all pale greys and shiny tiled floors. Perhaps he's in interior design or something?

He flicks on a secret lighting switch and manhandles me into the lounge. As he busily rummages in a tiny drawer in a metal table I decide to lean against the wall.

"Scissors? Scissors? …Ah! Scissors! Right, come here woman."

"Pardon? What happened to calling me 'Ma'am'? "

He smirks annoyingly.

"I'm adhering to my manly gender stereotype. Now come on. Give it up already. … The button."

Fluster,

"I can manage thank you." He hands over the scissors fake-politely and smirks some more. Git!

Fiddle, fiddle, stretch right round. It turns out to be remarkably hard to see one's own back view. I can't reach and I'm terrified of a three thousand pound slip of the hand. Try to hold myself smaller and twist backwards.

"Uh, uuh, uh…." He is watching me with a fixed expression.

"Uh, Um, nearly….oh? Not quite…uhh."

"O.K., that's enough! Just give me the goddamn scissors?"

"Umm…no?" Unfortunately I don't really have a choice. Hand over the scissors reluctantly and turn round. He starts rummaging about and muttering under his breath. I shouldn't have to put up with this? I'm officially a spinster now Jake's gone. I shouldn't have to put up with strange men footering about behind me, being awkward and shouting indiscriminately? No, this definitely can't be right? If you don't get the nookie then you shouldn't get the hassle. Sheesh! Men! They're bloody unavoidable? Like death? And badly cut trousers. Still, it could have been worse, I suppose. I could have sat on a splinter or something. Now, that really would be embarrassing. No, this isn't working. I'm still totally mortified. And what the hell is he doing back there?

"Erm, haven't you got it out yet?" He is breathing all funny in frustration.

"What?... Oh yeah, the button. Uhh no. I can't get at it without ripping your dress. Sorry" He stands up suddenly and tosses the scissors back into the drawer.

"Eh? What are you doing?"

"It'll just have to come off." I have often dreamt of this calibre of man saying that to me but not in quite these circumstances.

"We can take it to some specialist menders. I'll lend you something to wear."

"I can't take it off. I'm not wearing any undies!" This shuts him up.

"Anyway, what about your shirt? Can't you take that off?" He talks slowly like I am a fool,

"I can't take my jacket off while my cuff is stuck to your dress." This is true. He can't. 'AAAAARGH! Help! Help! God?'

"There is no way in hell I am going to take this dress of in front of you. So you can just forget it!" But God is apparently on a lunch break and Mr Pervy refuses to wait.

"Oh, come ON. It's no big deal. I have seen naked women before."

"Not me, you haven't."

"So, have you got something different? I'm sure Darwin is spinning in his grave. But we can call the National History Museum later. Really, I'll look away. O.K.? I'm not doing this for kicks y'know? I have no desire at all to see you naked."

"Oh? How dare you? Why not? What's wrong with me? I mean, erm, good."

25

Find myself dragged through into a massive bedroom. The only thing in it appears to be the most gigantic bed I've ever seen. It's a masterpiece in shiny tubular metal, provocatively adorned with an expensive looking cobalt blue silk cover. Find myself towed remorselessly towards it by the crazy Yank. It suddenly occurs to me that as usual I'm missing the truly obvious. This might be a good point at which to get scared. But no, it seems my fears are totally unfounded. The bed is not the only thing in here. It has two discreetly matching cabinets, one of which he makes a determined beeline for... only to carry on with his favourite hobby, rummaging? So? He likes to rifle through drawers, does he? Well, you're not rifling about in mine, matey, even if I did have them on! He yanks a drawer further open and casually tosses a big jumper and shorts onto the gi-normous bed.

Thoughtful,

"My trousers would be too big for you."

"No, no, no, no, NO!"

"Well, can you suggest a viable alternative?"

"Umm yes! I could just kill you. And then you wouldn't see a thing!" Glare at each other, hoping for divine inspiration. Big pause... Huge enormous pause...... Nope, God is still on his tea-break. God, I'm warning you, if you don't do something RIGHT NOW then I'm never going to speak to you again! ...God? Oh right , that's it! I'm going to be a Buddhist or something. This is a 999 situation... or from the look of the mad horny American, possibly even a 666. And where are you God? Not here. Consider yourself fired. I'm obviously on my own. Glare defensively at my impatient captor,

"Well, you'll have to shut your eyes."

"Excuse me?"

"You will have to shut your frigging eyes!"

"Oh,.. Uh, ok."

I can NOT believe I am doing this.' Slip the troublesome dress gingerly down to my waist but it won't go past his hand. I feel a little bit exposed here. I don't even go topless on the beach, only for doctors and lovers. Seems I've found a new category now. He has his eyes shut but he is smirking. 'What a complete and utter git!

26

"Erm, you'll have to slide your hand down a bit so that I can get this off."

"Oh? Oh right, fine." Mr Smirky crouches down with a quite unnecessary amount of slidy hand contact. He really will have to die! Bastard! How dare he enjoy this? Grab the clothes from the bed and fling them on with the jumper on back to front. Hate him! Hate him! Hate him! Meanwhile he is lounging happily on the floor with my dress stuck to his arm.

"Can I open my eyes at all yet?"

Grudging,

"I suppose so." I can't look him in the face though. I am far too busy dying. His next smirk could well be his last.

"Right. I'll slide your dress up inside my sleeve and then I can take my jacket off." Sit down on the bed to watch him struggle - to precisely no avail. 'Well, ha ha ha ha HA! Serves him bloody well right.'

"It won't fit inside my sleeve? The material's too bulky."

"Well, we'll just put you into the specialist menders and have you surgically removed."

"Oh fuck it!" He storms off. I have that effect on men. Should I bother to get up and see what he's doing? This is a very comfortable bed. But maybe he's gone for the scissors? He's going to cut up the dress? Spring off the bed and bound through the hall in a single panic-stricken stride. The dastardly fiend is poised with his scissors in his hand.

"Don't you dare cut up my dress!"

"I wasn't damn well going to." He cuts the cuff off his shirt.

"What? You couldn't have done that before? You just let me humiliate myself? You sadistic bastard!" Run over and slap him.

"What the ...? What the hell was that for? Are you out of your Goddamn mind?"

"Why didn't you do that in the first place?"

"Because I didn't think of it! Why do you think?"

Scream,

27

"I think that you're a complete and utter sadistic pig. And that you were having a good old chortle at my expense!" Push him in the chest so that he staggers back against one of his posh sofas. Look round wildly for a suitable object to kill him with. Nope. Nothing. I'll have to use my bare hands. Shove him in the chest ineffectually. He's too tall to conveniently dispatch. His eyes flare with temper. Oops! Not again? Clearly annoying men is my forte? Oh, who cares? I'm still going to kill him. Find myself scooped up unceremoniously and tossed onto the nearest sofa.

"Oh? Put me down!"

Slide off onto the fluffy fireside rug. I am about to exact my revenge on behalf of all downtrodden womankind when he decides to pin me to the floor.

"Goddamit woman! You screw up my evening completely! None of this was my fault. I cut up my favourite shirt to keep you happy and save your stupid dress. What in God's name is wrong with you?"

"God's got nothing to do with it. He never takes my calls! And there's nothing wrong with ME! You're the raving pervert who torments innocent people for fun."

He gives a small, not amused laugh,

"Oh, so you're innocent now, are you? No, I don't think so sweetheart. Certainly not in that dress."

"What the hell is wrong with my dress exactly?"

"Well, it's hardly a Julie Andrews number now, is it? So don't give me that innocent abroad crap!"

"Oh how bloody well dare you! Are you saying that I'm some kind of tart?"

"If the cap fits... Which is more than the dress does incidentally. Don't you think it's a little bit…revealing?"

"Oh! You mean I'm fat! Right, that's it mate. You've gone too far." Wriggle one hand free and slap him again, not that hard, just enough to really wind him up. He turns a rather unfetching shade of purple. GOOD!

"O.K., That's IT Lady, come here!"

CHAPTER THREE
Cold Daylight Dawns

Umm…where am I? Feels very warm and snuggly. Don't want to get up… Wait a minute. What's that odd weight on my side? That's not usually there? …Oh my GOD, I am not alone! Memory floods back in hot, excruciating, I-wasn't-even-drunk waves. It's him from last night, Aaron thingy, the American. What was I thinking of? … Well, yeah, obviously. Oh no. No, no NO! Open one eye for a terrified recce. Oh! I'm still in his flat, in his bed to be precise. And the strange weight is a big, hairy naked arm pinning me down. AAAARGH! It is absolutely fine to have this scenario in my head for pleasant dreams and stuff. But this is real. This is most definitely a real man. And I am most definitely in a lot of trouble. Worse still, lovely as it undoubtedly was, I have accidentally shagged a complete stranger - on the same day as I met him. I am a slut of the first order. He cannot fail to think that I'm some trashy trollop from Tarts-Are-Us, who does this on a regular, perhaps even a financial basis? ARGH! ARRGHHH! I have to escape. Right now.

Sneak a peek under the duvet. I'm not actually in the buff. I'm wearing his shirt, his bastard shirt, which caused all the trouble in the first place. So, where are my clothes? Gently push his arm away as he is making tiny little asleep-breathing noises somewhere in the region of my head. I shall just sneak to the edge of the bed and locate my missing clobber. Eeeek! He makes a sudden little growly noise and pulls me back against his warm and memorably appealing body. I am consumed by a scalding mixture of rather belated shame and unbelievable lust. He really is gorgeous. He is gorgeous and right behind me! He's sort of rubbing his face into my ear. Oooh! Is he actually awake? Or just in that sort of half-awake, could still go back to sleep if he doesn't get too horny state? I'll lie very still and not provoke him any further with careless wriggliness.

....

Of course, he will most definitely wake up at some point in the future... And I really do not wish to be present when he does, as I am totally unfamiliar with the required social etiquette of this kind of occasion. I am going to have to try again... Do the arm-moving thing again and he rolls over onto his back. It worked! I find Angie's crumpled dress and hellish shoes on the floor beside the huge stranger's bed [huge bed - not stranger, obviously. Well? No, to be fair...really... quite huge.]

Make it to his bathroom. Its all shiny metal stuff, very modern and expensive looking. Aaron is clearly a quite impressively trendy stranger-molesting pervert. Get my dress back on with lighting speed. Decide to carry my shoes for a silent exit. Poke my head out of the bathroom doorway for a furtive check. It's all clear. I can see the massive white front door. Make a commando style dash for it. Damn! It's locked. It's locked in a highly complicated and unfathomable way? I do not have time to come up with a Prison Break kind of plan right now. That would take weeks? Bang my head gently on the door in impotent terror. It's Fort-flipping-Knox and he's holding me hostage to use in his kinky sex games ...Mmm, naughty man, oooh! But no, this is a real situation. I must get out. He could wake up any minute now. Help! Run into the lounge, as it isn't the bedroom. Hmm, a window. Excellent! I can't open the door but I can probably open the window. And it isn't too high up really. A quick furtive glance to the rear to check that Mr Crazy the Yankee Shag Monster hasn't escaped from the Land of Nod yet. Post-coital exhaustion, the git!

Push the window wide open, clamber up onto the ledge, make a speedy assessment of the least sore landing spot. Shut my eyes tight and jump. Oh-my-God that hurt! And it probably did my pink twine dress absolutely no good at all.

"All right there luv?"

"What?" Oh, it's a milkman. Not God with a weirdo cockney accent.

Go for a dignified tone,

"Fine thank you." Nope. He's still staring. Perhaps I ought to stand up? ... Why is there always a rogue tradesman about when most strictly not required? Clearly he thinks I am mad. I shall leave immediately before he decides that I am actually a pitifully inept cat-burglar, exiting my latest crime-scene and calls the cops on his milkman mobile. Hold onto a handy wall and stagger to my feet. O.K - Right. I'm up. Now, act normal. I am walking slowly away in a dignified manner. I can feel him watching me. I will NOT look round. ...And I'm walking slowly along the street. I'm almost round the corner...RIGHT! ... RUN-LIKE-HELL!

Chapter Four
Guava Berries & Cream

Late Sunday morning in Boots... the shop. We don't want any further confusion here. I am consoling myself after my traumatic week with tons of superfluous make-up...and perhaps the odd pot of [scientifically proven] miracle moisturizer? There's nothing like a bit of gratuitous self-delusion to cheer a girl up, I find. From now on I'm going to look after number one. I'm going to be young, sexy and... smelling of strawberry milkshake apparently? Peruse the pseudo-wooden toiletries stand in amazement. Strawberry? Chocolate? Vanilla? Clearly designed for those who wish to be licked somewhere or other? Huh! Too late!... Perhaps a little touch of guava berry body rub though? Guava berry and cream to be precise. Do I want to smell like a guava berry, whatever the hell that is? ...I don't know, do I? And more to the point, would anyone else want me to smell like one? I mean would it be appealing to say, an entirely random attractive man, in the unlikely event of that ever becoming a consideration again? I mean, well, obviously he'd be bound to find the cream bit appealing ...if applied to the appropriate regions. But guavas? Nope. I'm just not sure. This is way too complex for a Sunday.

Saunter along a bit humming happily to myself. Maybe things aren't so bad? After all, I've still got painting and shopping. I can live without the nookie for a while, especially after last night! Hmm, bubble bath? Well, O.K. Carry out a thorough inspection of the labels to prevent a potential guava re-occurrence. 'Let your problems drift away. Pamper yourself with a luxurious blah-di-blah soak and rejuvenate your senses with a sensual combination of jasmine, musk, sandalwood and orange blossom. What utter twaddle. Hey! Wait a minute... I used to do a bit of aromatherapy and this looks very familiar. It's a recipe for a particularly potent aphrodisiac, which I have actually tried out with disastrous success some time ago. My friend Siobhan and I drenched ourselves from head to foot in this aforementioned magic potion. We succeeded in attracting every repellent drunk in the entire known Universe and were damned lucky to escape from the pub un-shagged. Something with these properties clearly should not be used in such a cavalier fashion but should carry appropriate health, dosage and location warnings? I wonder if the bubble bath people are aware of the potentially disastrous consequences of its use? Probably not, it would be much more expensive. Or maybe it's a prank by an exceptionally bored, mad chemist in their labs who thought it would be funny in a strange, sadistic way?

Oh well, I'll take a couple. But I shall only use it in the appropriate circumstances. What would be better would be if it was in atomiser form, to be kept in one's handbag for emergencies; condoms, spare knickers, skooshy shag-inducing spray? The bubble bath pimps are missing a huge gap in the market.

Trundle casually up to the checkout with half of the shop in my little wire basket. It's like the Tardis. Amazing. Rifle awkwardly in my handbag for my purse with my credit and Boots cards, whilst still covetously clutching my booty basket. Sadly, it's a perverse law of the Universe that no matter which order you put things into a handbag, be it five hours or five milli-seconds later, when you look for something the said item will have vanished to the inaccessible bottom of your bag. This is such an occasion now and it's my turn at the till.

"Sorree!" Give my best apologetic smile to the stony-faced sales woman, whilst tipping the entire contents of my bag over the counter, to the tune of much disgruntled tutting from the queue behind me. My purse is not here? I've been robbed? And worse still, I'll have to pay...with money? I have five pounds and sixty pence. Not enough. Maybe my purse is not stolen. Maybe it's at home and has just fallen out of my bag. Dump all the wonderful me-changing stuff and make an extremely sharp exit from Boots. I'll go mad and get a taxi home. Speed is of the essence. There could already be some petty villain en route to Barbados with my plastic! Well? No, not really? Not with my plastic. Skegness perhaps?

"Taxi!"

Twenty minutes time - Home, no purse. I have phoned the bank and my new cards are coming soon. So, now what? I cannot indulge in my pre-planned beauty binge, as I am completely stuff-less. Things you already own do not have the same appeal. I know, I'll chill out and watch a little TV. Maybe there's a good film on. Flump onto the sofa. Find the remote cunningly hidden under a cushion, by J. no doubt. He watches my T.V. more than I do.

Have a quick flick through the channels. Boring, boring, bo.. Hoi, wait a minute! Quick reverse flick. I was going too fast. It's him! Aaron Whatsit from last night? On my T.V.? It is a very weird sensation to see someone you have just accidentally shagged suddenly appear unannounced on your own television set. It is a period drama and he is striding manfully around a poncy Edwardian bedroom, wearing actual britches no less. He is aiming a spectacularly realistic rant at some half-naked woman, who is lounging in a pro-slut fashion on a gi-normous four-poster.

What? This is just too weird. You've got to be kidding me? I am totally stunned and can only stare at the screen in mounting horror as, before you can say 'Egad Sir!' the fiend has jumped on her bones and is engaged in sucking her face off. This is clearly his raison d'etre. The scoundrel! How dare he suck naked women in front of me like that? Women who are quite blatantly not me! ... No! Er, I didn't mean that. I wouldn't touch him now with a very long pole. Unless it was for the strict purpose of inflicting as much G.B.H. as is humanly possible. Not that I wanted to touch him in the first place. I was a completely innocent bystander who just happened to be in his clutches. She is welcome to him. Pah! This confirms what I've said all along. Men are all about the trouser-urges - randy ratbags the lot of them.

I cannot believe it but I can't stop watching. It is a most horrible rabbit-in-headlights experience.

"BANG!" (My front door.) Don't bother to look. It must be Jerry as he is the only person with my key in the vicinity. He flounces in with a multitude of posh shopping bags, looking very pleased with himself, and proceeds to drape said self gracefully over the other end of my settee in a manner not unlike Greta Garbo.

"Hi Babes. What are we watching? Oh fuck me! What are they doing?" A bizarre onscreen game of rude twister is in progress. I can't speak. It's just too horrid for words. J., completely engrossed, has sprung up like a whippet and is now approximately one inch from the screen.

"The dirty fuckers? Oh, my God! Would you look at the buns on that? He is *gorgeous*. But what in the name of Johnny Depp is happening with his hair?" Oh my God? This is the end. My best friend is ogling my one night stand's butt? Oh horrors!

"Never knew you were into this kind of thing Carls?" Jerry pauses mid-drool as he finally clocks my talcum powder face and rigor-like grip on the remote.

"What? It's not that bad Carly? I mean, they've still got some clothes on. And there's no, like, animals involved. Turn it off if you don't want to watch it."

My voice doesn't seem to be working.

"It's him Jerry!"

"Who? Tongue Boy? That's Aaron Stanford Sweetie. He's in everything. "

"Well, clearly!"

"Even you must have seen him Carls?"

"Jerry you don't understand. I have seen him. I saw him last night in his bedroom actually." He sits up on the rug to guffaw.

"Oh har-de-harr, Carly! Yeah, like, right! You went out on Saturday night and , like, shagged him. Harrr. Holy Orlandos Carly, that's a good one. You couldn't just have joined his fan club like a normal person? Harrrr!" Someone here is going to have to die!

"I am not joking Jerry! ...And no, actually, I didn't know who he was! You know I don't watch much T.V." At this he jolts upright, eyeballs bulging.

"Oh, no way Carls! You're never serious? Oh my God, that's right. You were at Angie's T.V. butt kiss thing last night, weren't you? How the hell did you meet him, you lucky bitch? Did you, like, just walk up to him and say 'Hi there. I'm Carly. Would you care to get your kit off, you big stud, you?' Oh no, you're having me on?" It's clear by the stony silence that I'm not.

"You lucky thing! And to think that I could have gone…Were you really pissed? What was he like, you know?" Waves his weaselly eyebrows at me in a highly lewd and insinuating manner.

"Was he, like, *amazing*?"

"Well he damn well surprised me! And I do not want to discuss it."

The scene onscreen has changed and Lothario is now cuddled up in bed with his showbiz slut smoking a post-shag cigar. He looks like he has had a very good time. BASTARD! How dare he sleep with both of us? I am not lucky. I am fuming! I feel like some cheap, tacky trollop who has allowed herself to be accidentally podgered, in a moment of extreme weakness, by the infamous Podger King… who obviously podgers everyone in his path. I do not want to see him ever again! Flick the off button on the remote and fling it straight out of the open window.

"Take that Tongue Boy!"

"Carlee! For Depp's sake? This is the fourth floor? …And that might hit someone? …And now we'll have to, like, stand up and push the buttons?"

"I don't care! I am not sorry! I have gone off T.V. all of a sudden, oddly enough. I am a very hard-done-by person and I am most definitely NOT BLOODY WELL PLAYING!" Stomp off through to the bedroom and fling myself onto the bed face first... only to be pursued by J. in his most annoying agony aunt mode.

"Look darling, he is an ac-tor, you know? Not a bloody welder. I mean, he was only acting then. He didn't really bloody bonk her."

"Yeah? Right!" My voice is slightly muffled by the pillow.

"He kissed her! I saw him! He is a totally unforgivable tart!" I can hear Jerry rummaging distractedly through my jewellery and make-up on the dressing table.

"But Carly, that was just screen kissing. It's not real!"

"Yeah? Like Brad and Angelina weren't you mean?"

"No, that's different. That was just them, the exception. They gave it a bad name. Normally it's just like kissing your mother or something."

"If he kisses his mother like that he is an Oedipus of the very first water. He's a slut and I hate him!"

"Oh! .. So you won't be seeing him again then? Oh Carly, what a shame! You know he is such an improvement on Fat-Boy, erm I mean Jake. And I don't really think that there's anything to be jealous about. But then again....?"

"Jealous? What?" Spring up indignantly on the bed.

"I am not jealous! ...And what do you mean 'but then again'?"

Jerry does his ' I don't know how to tell you this' frown." Uh-oh?

"Weeell Carls, it's just that the girl in that film, Jennifer McLeish, well he has been linked with her quite a lot .... in certain publications."

"What?"

"I mean, I'm not saying there's anything in it Babe..... It's just that, well, it's better to know these things really, isn't it?"

"Uh, no? No it bloody well isn't! Two-timing scumbag. Well, I couldn't care less. I don't need him or Jake or anyone. I am a mature and dignified woman. Besides I'd only met him once."

"Yes, and look what bloody well happened."

"Smarty! Anyway J. it's purely incidental."

"With the emphasis on 'incident'."

"Gerald P. Green!"

"Eek! Don't Sunday name me Carls. I was only messing about."

"Well, stop it and pay attention to this newsflash. I don't want to have to say it again... I do not want a boyfriend. I am a complete woman who does not-need-a-man to make her happy. I have just split up with Jake and I don't need any old ac-tor tart who can't keep his bits to himself either. I am em-powered! ...So there!"

"Great speech Carls. Gotta say I liked the 'So there!' bit best. Imagine if Ghandhi or Mandela or Martin Luther King had finished their bon mots with 'So there!' Yeah, that would have been really OUCH! What? What did I say? Keep your cushions to yourself, you crazy broad."

"If anyone's crazy it's you Jerry. Me, I prefer empowered…. And I know I actually am you see, because I saw it on an Oprah know-yourself special. "

"Oh well, tablets of stone Babe… No, I'm pleased for you, really I am. Just calm down with the cushions already. And if you're sure you don't want a guy sweetie, then that's fine isn't it? If you're really, completely sure?"

"Absolutely POSITIVE! I'm going to be happy, celibate and aloof!"

"Quite right honey. If that's what lights your candle, you go ahead and be a loof. Your country always needs loofs."

CHAPTER FIVE
The Aftermath

Monday morning summit at my flat. Jerry and Siobhan have dropped by, on their way to work, to dissect and analyse my bizarre weekend [snoop]. I am not yet dressed, due mostly to the unwarranted early nature of their arrival, but also to J.'s complete indifference to my body. He has perched his irritatingly skinny backside on my kitchen table and adopted a psychiatrist stance, with shiny metal glasses balanced precariously on his forehead. He doesn't actually need them. They are a fashion accessory to make him look more intelligent and creative. They're not really working but I haven't the heart to tell him. He has a notebook in his hand and a biro pointed accusingly at my back as I rummage about making coffee. This is a must for post-disaster occasions. I cannot function without caffeine at the best of times…, which this is quite clearly not.

With Siobhan as reinforcements and cushion deflector, Jerry has a bit more to say about my new celibate stance. He fails to grasp the appeal of celibacy and is trying to change my mind for-my-own-good.

"So Carls, explain it to me again, because I really don't quite get it. You can't go out with one of the most attractive men on the planet why exactly?"

"God! Are you thick or what? Besides I didn't know you thought Jake was attractive."

"Not Jake, Aaron Stanford. Sheesh Carls! What's wrong with *him*?"

"Jerree! He's an ac-tor? Worse than that, he's a successful ac-tor. Du-uh?" Siobhan frowns in confusion,

39

"So … you'd want him if he was a nobody?"

"Why can't you both see? It's *obvious*. He only took me home because Keira Knightly was busy."

Jerry,

"He took you home because you were stuck to his jacket."

"You're just being deliberately obtuse J. He didn't have to ravish me, did he?" Jerry falls off the table snorting and holding his chest in derision,

"You're complaining about that? Oh pur-lease!"

Siobhan assumes a half-serious, worried expression. She is a prosecution lawyer and sometimes it affects her view of life,

"Carly, he didn't… you know, force you or anything, did he?"

Jerry snorts even more from his collapsed position on the rug,

"Har, har, like she'd mind." Siobhan leaps up from the couch and waves a prosecutorial arm in the air,

"Jerry! This is serious. Good Lord! The man's a danger to society. He can't go around molesting my friends against their will…. I WON'T HAVE IT!"

"Bloody hell Siobhan, Jerry didn't mean…Anyway he didn't. I'm fine… You really ought to be somebody's mother."

"Well good heavens Carly. It's obvious that you are far from 'fine'. So what did he do then?"

"Oh God, do I have to spell it out? I just don't want to be another flaming notch on his casting couch, O.K.?"

Jerry,

"Huh, too late. Anyway sweetie, isn't it producers and directors and stuff who have those? You know, like, old ugly past-it blokes who might actually need them, hmm?" I hate it when they are reasonable like that. Stomp over to the window with my coffee, arm flailing in an explanatory fashion,

"Well, he still didn't have to shag me just because I was there…like, like some convenience shag from the Tarts-R-Us takeaway? I don't want to be a convenience!" I know that I am ranting now but unfortunately I can't seem to stop. Siobhan stares at me, astounded. Jerry smiles sympathetically in his self-appointed medical capacity,

"Carly, far be it from me to point out the obvious but you must have liked him a bit or you wouldn't have done it?"

"Well, maybe I did, I suppose? Until I found out he wasn't a real person, just a big showbiz Lothario. That's what he is. I expect he shags everyone he meets. I know the score Jerry. I've read your Heat magazine and your National Enquirer. Well? I've looked at the pictures anyhow. Honestly, men!" Siobhan is speechless. Jerry screws up his face and shuts his eyes tight, in order to imagine this potential scenario. He raises his hand, palm forward like a traffic policeman,

"No, Carly, that's really not feasible. I mean, at least half the people he meets would be male, and sadly that doesn't't seem to be his thing. Some would be like, old, or ugly... or like children! God, Carly no! You can't just go round accusing people of illegal stuff like that!"

"What? I didn't say that?" Jerry waves both his hands wildly, eyes still shut,

"If you were a journo you'd be in court faster than you say Ian Hislop. I can see the judge now, 'That'll be another ten grand for casual and entirely unfounded accusations Miss Watson, thank you very much."

Sometimes I wonder who my real friends are. And why these ones are so totally mad. Stare defiantly at J.

"I like Ian Hislop."

"What? Really? Well he's rich and famous; I'll give you that? But you couldn't wear high heels... and I think he might be married Carls. You're not Angie."

"No, not like that. I mean he's one of the funniest men on T.V. ... No, well? That's not really all that hard though, is it? Well, he's quite a witty man anyway."

Jerry frowns thoughtfully,

"Funnier than Billy Connolly?"

"You're just being silly now J. No-one is funnier than Billy Connolly." Siobhan shrugs herself awake and rises, grabbing her briefcase and jacket en route to the front door.

"Well, if you're going to start with the Scotch humour again I'm off."

"For Gods sake Siobhan. For the last time, it's Scottish or Scots. Scotch is whisky!"

"Really? How riveting. Thanks for entertaining us with your weirdo life Carls. Sadly I do have to go. You know, proper job and all that? Incidentally, you're still wearing some wode. Bye." It is not unusual for me to have the odd smidgeon of oil paint on my person somewhere or other. Scuttle into the outside hall after her to the great consternation of an elderly neighbour. Lean right out over the woodworm-ridden banister to retaliate in my snootiest voice,

"It's pthalo blue actually. All the best people are wearing it!" Mutter to myself,

"I feel much better for that. I am a mature and dignified adult."

Siobhan's designer suit vanishes swiftly downstairs, ignoring my dignified barbs. She probably hears much worse at work. I sigh and shuffle back into the flat to find Jerry firmly ensconced on my couch, chomping the last of my grapes in a languid, desultory fashion,

"Great! Carly Sweetheart, Miss Jean Brodie has officially left the building - sooo, now you can tell Uncle Jerry what the real problem is, can't you?"

"Well, I could do, if I knew myself." Slump back against the grey worktop and stare sadly down at my fluffy Koala bear slippers. 'I don't believe that Uncle Jerry can help me this time.'

"She is right though Jerry. I have made a complete and utter fool of myself, haven't I, …. again?"

"Oh, you shouldn't worry so much about that Darling. I never do. What fun would life be if we were all Scary Sensibles? You don't want to listen to Siobhan. She's just a little better at hiding her insecurities than you, that's all. We've all got them. Anyway, who wants to be normal? Christ, imagine - two point five kids and a semi in the burbs? I don't think so! So…. What about Aaron then? What the hell is really wrong with successful ac-tors….except maybe their ego's?" Jerry is a lovely guy but he doesn't understand. And of course I do?

"You see J., it's just that, you know, casual sex, I don't really think I can do it."

"Ex-cuse me? One - it's not that difficult, and Two - forgive me for saying this… but I thought that you already had?"

"But it's not as if any fabulously rich, famous bloke would actually want me, is it? I mean, why would they? Look at me Jerry. Jake's right. I'm a failure, a non-entity, a blob!" Sink onto the pouffe in despair [furniture, not friend].

Jerry leans forward,

"Oh I see! Fat Boy strikes again. So it's not actually anything to do with the gorgeous Mr Stanford being a rampant slapper that would shag any old scrubber given half a chance then, is it?" Glance critically at myself in a nearby mirror. It would appear that he already has.

"What you've got Carly my dear, is an exceptional case of self-esteem. You haven't got any. You should have said something sooner. I shall stop being Uncle Jerry immediately. What you need is a helping hand from Doctor Jerry."

"No thanks. I know where those hands have been."

"Or wait! Fashion Jerry. Yes, the very man." Shake my head sadly in amazement. 'Absolutely barking.'

"Look Fashion Jerry, I know you're only trying to help… but I don't really think that my wardrobe is the problem."

"Oh Carly, you are sooo wrong! I'll let you into a little secret, shall I, hmm? Despite various myths put about by cheap, scummy third, fourth and other rate tabloids… under all that make-up and luvvie costume palaver, actors are, and I know this may shock you, *actually people*!"

J. stands up with a patronising cheesy smile, arms outstretched awaiting spontaneous applause at this astounding revelation. Raise my eyebrows in suitable pseudo-amazement.

"No way?"

"Ab-so-bloody-lutely way! And, like any male of the species, well, only male ac-tors obviously, are easily influenced by pre-sen-tation. You present yourself like Thelma out of Scooby Doo…."

"I don't!"

"….and what do you expect?"

"I'm nothing like Thelma!"

"I don't mean her precisely. God Carly, that was only an example to illustrate my point. Who would find a cartoon character sexy?"

"Umm? I forget their actual names…but they were in last week's Sunday papers."

"Anyway, you're not a blob. You're a lovely talented person with fabulous dress sense, whom anybody would be lucky to get. Right?"

"Right!" Oh, I do love Jerry. He is a wonderful philanthropist and my best friend.

"Good Carls, problem solved. Now, what about that free portrait you were going to do of little old me in this utterly divine top? And remember Carly, we are funky, happening people. We don't need any old egomaniacal tarts, famous or otherwise, in our lives to make us happy. Now, is this my best side? Hmmm, is it?"

CHAPTER SIX
Some People ... Are Very Hard To Help

Saturday morning - for a change Angie isn't working/ networking/ seeing Sleaze Boy so we are going to 'do lunch'. And maybe even a little bit of shopping as my new credit cards have arrived. We are presently perched on a couple of ludicrously high metal stools in a pretentiously chic coffee bar. I am perusing the mouth-watering menu. Ange is perusing her already perfect self in the tastefully trendy mirrored walls. She gives a dissatisfied little sigh and pokes at her lovely face in a self-critical fashion with one French-manicured finger. I look up from my drooling as her traumatised sighing finally penetrates my consciousness,

"What, for God's sake? You look fine."

She wrinkles her pert nose,

"Fine? I'm a collage of wrinkles and cellulite. I should be on display in the Tate Modern." She points melodramatically to the side of one heavily made-up eye,

"Look! Just look! Crow's feet? Already? I'm never out of that bloody beauty salon. I've been for eight of my anti-aging treatments, and I still look like I've got a map on my face." She leans even further over despite the obvious height related peril and peers masochistically at her reflection.

Shake my head,

"Well Ange, don't go for too many. You'll end up with the face of a five year old and a body that's thirty-three. How silly will that look?" O.K. - maybe a bit flippant, but it's difficult to know what to say. She never used to be like this, just since she met Mr Critical a year or so ago. We all try to tell her she looks fabulous [which she certainly does] but it's like trying to tell an anorexic they're not fat.

"But Carly, you *would* think that after *eight* treatments?" Shut my eyes and put on a stern voice in a last ditch effort to drag her out of her quagmire of self-doubt.

"Angie! You do NOT have crow's feet.... or cellulite.... or any of the ten million other non-existent things you pay a ruddy fortune for at that flipping place. I mean, they're hardly going to say 'Oh no madam, keep all your lovely money. You appear to be perfectly fine the way you are.' are they?

She twists her face up at me,

"It's all right for you Carly. You haven't *got* stress lines." I ought to have.

"That's because *I'm* not going out with Criticism Man."

"CARLY!" Uh-oh? I shouldn't have said that. She's gone all quivery. Oh please don't cry Ange.

"I'm sorry Ange. It's just that he seems to upset you so much?" Defensive,

"He doesn't't mean to. It's *me*. I just get too *emotional* about things. I over-react."

Raise a cynical eyebrow,

"Is that a direct quote? And no Ange, I don't think it is an over-reaction to defend yourself against a man who's always putting you down. I know you don't want to hear it but don't you think he might have a tiny issue with control? If he didn't like you the way you were, he wouldn't be seeing you, would he?"

She frowns nervously,

"I suppose? I suppose he wouldn't. He just wants me to make the best of myself. There's nothing wrong with that. He's just trying to be encouraging, that's all. You guys don't know him. If you'd just give him a chance?" The only thing I'd like to give him is a hard shove off a very high cliff. Tosser! Smile in an attempt to placate her. It's not her fault she's in love with a twat,

"Hmm, yes, I'm sure…"

Fortunately a handy waiter chooses this very moment to swagger up, whipping out his notepad with a professional flourish and a glint in his sexy Mediterranean eyes,

"And now, for the beautiful ladies, what can I get for you? Uh? You will try to-day's speciality, no? Fillet of salmon with a fresh herb salad and a piquant Hollandaise sauce? Hmm? I can recommend it."
...And so forth for at least five minutes.

Even the sadly crushed Angie peps up a bit after this invigorating burst of attention. She smiles soppily after the waiter's retreating crisply ironed shirt,

"Oh Carly, wasn't he gorgeous? Why can't British men be like that?"

"What? You mean sociable? I've no idea. I wish they were. I can't afford a flight to Greece."

Give the matter a moment's thought,

"The government should set up a network of charm schools - for the emotionally challenged. And blokes could be drafted to go to them if they fail a national charm test. You know - basic manners, conversational skills and rudimentary compliment giving. That kind of thing. And they shouldn't be let back out into the community till they show a reasonable aptitude for attentiveness and awareness of basic foreplay requirements. And other vital stuff."

Angie smiles despite herself.

"Excellent plan Carls but it'll never work. The schools would all be privatised in a week. There would be a tedious docu-soap out about the inmates struggle to fit into society. And of course, at least half of them would decide they wanted to become pop stars or T.V. presenters."

Snigger childishly.

Lunch arrives, courtesy of our tanned Adonis, Luigi, who gives Angie the full benefit of a particularly racy smile as he pours her wine. Ooh! Now why couldn't she pick someone like him? Angie simpers. Luigi retreats to lurk by the bar with a longing backward glance. Smile happily to see her so cheered up and dive into my humungous herb

47

salad. Rocket? Parsley? Mmm, this place goes straight to the top of my lunch list. Angie toys with hers. Look up in surprise.

"Come on Ange, eat up. It's lovely?" She frowns in a paranoid fashion,

"I don't want to overdo it. There are a lot of calories in this dressing you know? A moment on the lips and all that."

"Angie, it's salmon and salad? It couldn't be any more diet conscious. Now, for God's sake, eat it - or Luigi will be offended." She gives a hunted glance over her shoulder at Luigi, whose mind clearly isn't on the food.

"Umm, I suppose so. He is looking over? But don't you think I'm…"

"No! Whatever it is, no!" Wave a threatening forkful of French parsley under her nose.

"Just eat it. Because then we're having the chocolate fudge cake….*with* cream, before you vanish into thin air." Her eyes mist over at the thought of chocolate.

"Oh no Carly. I couldn't possibly." Shrug nonchalantly,

"Up to you. I'm going to order them. So you can eat it or wear it. The choice is entirely yours." She laughs nervously.

"You wouldn't."

Draw her an end-of-my-tether look.

"Oh yes. It would give me the utmost satisfaction. I could pretend you were somebody else…." No prizes for guessing who.

"…I shouldn't have done it to Jake. Now I know how therapeutic it is. I've opened a Pandora's box of custard pie-ing people. There's a lot to be said for the humble custard pie routine you know? I had no idea. It ought to be the latest form of therapy. You could just pretend it was someone you didn't like and 'splat!' -a big pie to the head. Fantastic! Very relaxing. You ought to try it. You don't needing Rejuvenesse Ange, you need custard. Besides, it's shopping fuel. It'll give you energy to burn some serious plastic."

She is too busy chortling at this pleasant image to notice that she's accidentally eaten her lunch. Chortle her straight through the chocolate course, the wine course and head off to ransack the shops.

....

After a couple of hours of trying on things that look fabulous on the hanger but sadly unfabulous on us, and wondering why we looked fine at home but grotesque in the changing room mirrors [are they distorting mirrors?], our shopping zeal has departed. We are sauntering along the local high street trying to decide between one last desperate bid to find a sexy outfit... or just giving up and going for a coffee instead. The latter is looking much more appealing as I cannot bear the idea of another tortuous Houdini routine in yet another cubicle cunningly lit to make you look your very worst. I'm depressed enough already. Masochism is not my bag, man. Coffee, however, really is.

Ange,

"So, is it Slix for a frock or Starbucks for a caffeine fix?"

"Well, I don't know about you but I really have had...."

"HONK! HONK-HONK!" Eh?

Our deliberations have been rudely cut short by a licentious honk from the horn of a flashy lime green Porsche. As it glides to an expensive standstill beside us Angie's face lights up with undisguised excitement,

"Oh look Carly, it's Miles!" Try and fail to keep the sarcasm out of my voice,

"Is it? Oh joy." The car window slides down and Miles' annoying rat-like visage leers out.

"Hey baby doll. What's happening?" He drawls in a poor cross between Lloyd Grossman and Austin Powers. He is, quite possibly, in fact hopefully, the only man in the country apart from Peter Stringfellow to still sport a mullet haircut. Admittedly, thanks to regular visits to his personal trainer at an exclusive city gym, he does have quite a good physique for a man fast approaching the big five-o, but I'm very much afraid that the orange sun-bed tan , the poncy golden highlights and the permanent cloud of Paco Rabanne about his person more than counteract this fact.

I think he sees himself as a Sean Connery sort of figure - mature, sophisticated and exciting, (if slightly younger and not the least bit Scottish). Oh, he could not be more wrong. His whole look says aging club singer to me, and that's if I'm feeling particularly benevolent. And I am afraid that his touchy-feely attempts to charm leave me less tantalized than actually nauseous. He is like a human diet pill. He never fails to put me off my dinner. Unfortunately, despite all the laws of logical reasoning, on Ange it has precisely the opposite effect. She verifies to the rumour that there's no accounting for taste by squeaking excitedly,

"Miles, what are you doing here?" and clicking hurriedly over to Flash Harry's penis-compensating chick-mobile. Giggling girlishly she bends down to the window for a kiss from the arch fiend himself. Blargh! Men like that ought not to have a tongue?

Finally coming up for air, Miles adopts a carefully studied casual pose and addresses himself directly to Angie's breasts, ignoring her face completely.

"So, what brings you to this part of town Angel Face?" Overlooking this colossal faux pas Angie gushes,

"Oh Carly and I were shopping..." She indicates me standing behind her, arms folded impatiently, a cynical glare of contempt welded to my face. Noticing me for the first time he goes into sleaze overdrive and assumes his best seductive leer.

"Carly, hi sweetheart..." He seems supremely confident in the pulling power of his latent animal magnetism. This confidence is sadly misplaced. I do not find the fact that he's mentally undressing me either charming or sexy. And the fact that he's doing it in front of the adoring Angie just makes it ten times more revolting.

"You're looking very ....foxy today Miss Watson. Have you done something different recently?" Eye him with singular contempt,

"Yes, I've dumped my sleazy, whinging boyfriend. I'd highly recommend it. Does wonders for a girl's self-esteem." Raise a meaningful eyebrow in Angie's direction to ram the point home. A small silence follows this unexpected response but Miles' ego recovers quickly. He treats me to a provocative Don Juan smile [absolutely the worst move he could have made].

"So? You're young, free and single again, are you, hmm? Don't worry Carly babe, with a figure like yours those young bloods will be beating down your door. You know, if this pretty lady hadn't already captured my heart, I might be looking for your phone number myself, heh, heh." Angie giggles coquettishly.

"Oh Miles, you are dreadful!" Oh dear God, yes he is.

Seldom has an offer left me quite so underwhelmed. I am almost struck dumb by the man's appalling conceit, but unfortunately, not quite,

"Really? I would have thought Miles, that in the circumstances, your phone book was *more* than full enough already."

He at least has the good grace to look slightly abashed as this dart hits home, but any satisfaction in this tiny point-scoring victory is immediately extinguished by the sight of Angie's face. Her huge eyes have fill up and her bottom lip is trembling ominously. She shoots me an 'Et tu Brutus' look - horrified and hurt [the truth does that sometimes].

"Carly!"

"Sorry Ange but I'm not hanging about to chat with Lothario. I'm going to Slix. I'll meet you inside."

Turn on my heel and leave them to it. I can hear Angie tearfully apologising to the slimy creep for *my* behaviour and blaming it on my split with Jake. It takes all my willpower to keep on walking and not run back and tell him what I really think of him in no uncertain terms, interspersed with severe slaps to his sleazy head. But this won't help matters in the slightest so I just stomp along raging to myself. Jesus! I cannot stand that man! How can someone as lovely and intelligent as Angie possibly fancy him? He is sooo transparent. I never met anyone who made me quite so angry in my life. As Jerry would say 'in the name of Johnny Depp and all the boy bands!'

Ten minutes later a slightly shaky Ange comes twitching up behind me as I'm languidly rifling through a rail of dresses. Raise a cynical eyebrow at her,

"Lover Boy gone then, in the Twat Mobile, off back to the Twat Cave?"

Angie ignores the cheap jibes and goes for an ironically self-righteous tone,

"Yes, Miles has gone, as a matter of fact. He knows when he's not wanted."

"You astound me. I'd no idea he was such a sensitive little flower. Thank God I didn't criticise his weight or something. But then, what kind of a thoughtless git would do something like that?"

She blusters defensively,

"Look, I know what you all think of him Carly, but you're wrong. He's just going through a really bad time right now. You've no idea."

"My heart bleeds. Go on then, enlighten me. I'm all ears. In which way precisely is he the injured party here? Surely that would be you…or his wife?"

She starts snivelling into a hanky. My fragile grip on my patience snaps.

"Oh for God's sake Ange! Not again. Look what he does to you? You're a nervous wreck. Come on. Come in here and sort yourself out."

Pull her into a handy changing room, grabbing a couple of dresses en route for effect. Plonk her down onto a built-in corner stool and swish the curtain shut behind us. She's still sniffing and dabbing carefully at her face.

"If you would only give him a chance Carls? He's been going through hell at home for years… sniff. His marriage is a sham. He wants a divorce but *she* says she won't let him see the kids. Carly he adores those kids. How *can* she be so cruel? He *will* sort it all out. He promised. It just takes a bit of time, that's all. You *must* see that?"

Try really hard to see this whole sorry mess from Miles' point of view. No matter how repellent I find him, he's Angie's choice. And if he treated her better I could surely manage to be civilised if not friendly, couldn't I?

"Right Ange, tell you what, I'll make a deal with you. The second Miles puts in for a divorce, I will happily eat my words. If he makes you happy and his intentions are actually honourable, that's absolutely fine by me. O.K.? You can't say fairer than that, can you?"

"Oh? But…. I mean…. I suppose so. It's just that……he's really suffering now." Resist the urge to say 'Good!' and settle for nodding in a non-committal fashion and making some nothingy remarks.

Decide to try the dresses on as we're in here anyway. Fortunately Angie and I are roughly the same size so we try on one each. Mine looks yeuchy. Hers looks fabulous. Typical! I do have the perfect body. What a pity that it's upside down.

CHAPTER SEVEN
V.Van Gogh

One week later – at my flat, as usual, having an orgasmic painting splurge. And there is no one here to complain about the mess. HOORAY! I am severely paint-splattered and happy.

"Tum-ti-tum, tum…" 'Just a little highlight here and…' Lean right back to check. That's IT! I'm finished! I-am-a-GENIUS! …Albeit with unfortunately debateable Van Gogh leanings in the sanity department. I would *much* prefer to resemble Da Vinci or Angelo, my multi-faceted art idols. But hey, so who's being fussy? I am still quite a huge bit wonderful.

I have just *totally* finished a somewhat elegant full body study in oil paints. *Usually* I think that I've finished several times before spotting tiny potential improvements. But I have *actually* TOTALLY finished. But is it good though? Yes, yes, YES! I can feel a Meg Ryan moment coming on. Have a little dance about.

"Yes, Yes, yes, yes, YES!" I wonder if I could actually explain if asked – for example by a non-painter or similar artistic virgin – the phenomenal buzz that completing a good painting gives you? I'm not very sure that I could. What on earth could you compare it with? Well, let's see now, it's like a zillion times better than drinking… My God! It's better than shopping! But is it better than sex? Hmmm? Would have to say…it depends on who you're having sex with. However, it does induce a similar desire to squeal and jiggle about. So, I shall just dance about the house. I can feel the painting watching me. This is good from a technical viewpoint and not just Van Gogh paranoia. All good portraits watch you. If they don't you are doing it wrong.

Dance into the kitchen. Open the fridge door. No? Don't think that I'm hungry? Slam the fridge door and dance back through to my studio come spare bedroom. YES! Yes. Still fantastic! Collapse onto my stomach across the spare bed all the better to view my own genius. Ogle my wonderful painting for ages and smugly congratulate myself. Who do I love? ME! As I have reached my maximum level of self-satisfaction, I think 'I'll just... have a small nap.'

....

"Bring! Bring! – Bring! Bring!"

"Uuh,uh?" Where am I? What's that? Uhh? I seem to be still on the spare bed and that noise is? That noise is my phone.

"BRING! – BRING! – BRING!" That phone just has no patience! Scramble off the bed and though to the lounge.

"Uum, umm, hello?" I have not completely woken up yet.

"Heeello! May I speak to Miss Carly Watson, please?" Well, don't you sound just like Leslie Phillips? Don't remember giving my number to some middle-aged cad? Not sure at all about this person.

"Yes, that's right, that's me?"

"Oh, heeello!" Oh, my God! It is him. Is he twiddling his moustache?

"Ay'm sooo pleased to get a hold of you at last!"

"Oh, really?" I'm getting a tiny bit scared.

"Oh, yeees! I'm Edgah Shrimpton-Boswick..." No WAY! No one is really called that?

".... I saw your work at the McLennan Gellery last week. It's just ex-zectly what ay need." Oh, YES! Please have a great big wallet?

"Oh, really? Do go on, Mr, er, Shrimpton-Boswick." I feel very silly saying that. This had better not be one of Jerry's mad friends phoning up just to extract the you-know-what.

"I'm heving a little show at my gellery next month. D'you know it, the Eglinton Hall?" Oh, my-GOD! You are kidding? Mega-bucks Central for sales!

"Yes, yes, of course, I know it."

"D'you think you could do me a few pieces, my deah? Whatevah subject y'like. Y'know, just a dozen or so?" Oh! I've died and gone to painting heaven.

"Em, yes, yes, I think that that would be fine."

"Splendid! Ay'll get my secretawy to send you the details. Naice to do business, my deah." Likewise.

"Thank-you Mr Shrimpton-Boswick, er…um…good-bye." Good! I can stop doing my quite-polite telephone voice now.

"Yes, yes, yes, yes! Aaargh!" Potential ecstasy overload. Sex has gone right down in the charts. Painting has gone up.

…………..

It is the evening of my day of success. I have uncorked my lethal bubble bath mixture. I don't actually want a man, but it may be amusing to torment one. I am splooshing about in the tub. As a celebration is clearly in order I am going out to be silly with Siobhan, if that is not actually a contradiction in terms. Siobhan has way too much guilt for someone who isn't a catholic. And she can't really let her hair down as she hasn't got quite enough of it. Perhaps she could just ruffle her helmet-like bob?

Period of very deep thought.

Oh, well, she can just get blitzed on one shandy. I expect it might do her some good. Sploosh out of the bath and cuddle into a huge fluffy towel. Toddle through to the bedroom to peruse my extensive wardrobe. Cupboards open, drawers open. My God! Is that it? Just a trifle limited, if only counting items without paint or holes, which might just still be in fashion. So, what shall we go for tonight? Short and sexy Bridget Bardot? Nope, I would need a blonde wig. Sleek and slinky? I do like this dress but don't know where we're going to go. I would look like a total numpty if we go to a downmarket pub. O.K., we'll go for sexy! I *have* got my bubble bath on. I might as well go all the way. …Though *that* is extremely unlikely. Oh, well. A girl can look. It's really quite fun being single.

Slink about to a raunchy Rolling Stones CD that Jake left, to get in the party mood.

"Yeah, yeah, I'm gonna tart me up! And make a grown man cry-y-y Ooh! Ooh! I'm gonna..." Dress on, make-up on...all of it at the same time. Practise my best prostitute pout in the mirror. Yes, fine. That'll do. Now, where did I put my necklace? Hmm, it's usually on here? Quick rummage on the dressing table. No? It appears to have gone? Oh God!

I'm starting to panic now. That necklace belonged to my Gran. I can't have lost it? I CAN'T!...Now, just calm down and think, Carly. When did you see it last?...I wore it on? On Saturday night, to go with the pink twine dress. Oh, no! I feel quite sick. It's probably at that Aaron guy's house. It must have come off when...? Aargh! It can't be true? Oh, holy Christ, NOOO! I can hardly just pop back and get it.

"AAARGH!" So I shall run about screaming instead.

"Aaargh! Aargh! Aaaargh!" No? No, wait, hold on. What *should* one do in such a crisis? I know, I'll phone a friend. I wonder if J. is home yet? Trundle off through to the phone. Jerry is in. Thank God!

He grasps the full horror with immediate empathy.

"Oh, my GOD! Carly, how *awful*!"

"I KNOW! What am I going to do?" Silence while J. is considering options.

"We-ell, as I see it, babe, there only are two options here."

"Yes? Yes?" Great! He's thought of a solution.

"One – you just go round there and ask him?" NEVER! Never! NO!

"No way before hell freezes over!"

"Hmm, rather thought you might say that. So, option two, we will have to break in." Break in? Break into his house? As in commit a crime?'

"Jerry! We can't do that!"

"Well, really, Carls! Do you want the necklace back or not?"

"Of course! It was my Gran's. I've GOT to get it back."

"And you absolutely don't want to speak to him?"

"No! I...I just CAN'T!"

"So fine! We'll just do his place over." I think he's being a bit complacent about this. We can't just go out and commit a crime. I don't know how to?

"Oh, Jerry, I don't know?"

"God Carly! It is *your* necklace. It's not like we're going to rob him or anything. We're only going to get your own property back. And anyway, it can't be that hard. There are zillions of break-ins in London alone, *all* the time, all perpetrated by yobs with, like, two 'O' levels or something. It's hardly rocket science."

"But what if he notices that the necklace is missing? He'll know I've been back in his house?"

"Oh, fuck, Carly, he probably hasn't even noticed it was there in the first place... And even in the unlikely event that he had: One, he doesn't know where you live to come and get you, and Two, he might just think he's had a normal burglary. He isn't going to know it was you."

"But, but how would we go about it? I mean, how would we actually get in? I don't want to break a window or anything. It's not really fair to cause any damage."

"Don't know. Let me think about it for a bit. I'm sure we can come up with something. I'll pick you up first thing in the morning and we'll nip round crack the joint. Byeee!"

"Jerry! Jerry?" Too late. He's gone. Oh, well. I'll worry about it tomorrow. It's not as if he's going to have pawned it already. So, party on!

....

I am meeting Siobhan in a new wine bar. She says it's supposed to be good. I do hope she's right for a change. I could do with a distraction from life. Jangles? Jangles? Ah, here it is. Hmm, looks quite snazzy from the outside, all wriggly wrought iron railings and stuff. Oh, well then, let's have a look.

Open the door to a horrendous sight. Oh, sweet Jesus, I am in a creche? Where is the grown-up bit? Spot Siobhan huddled in a corner trying to just disappear. She is looking very conspicuous though. She has got at least half her clothes on. I'm so glad that I went for the short dress or I might look like somebody's mum. Hustle over quickly knocking children aside to rescue Siobhan from herself. I am followed by a saucy waft of my bubble bath stuff. Oh, no! If the potion works on anyone here I shall go straight to jail, without passing go en route. But maybe it doesn't work on pre-pubescent chaps? Oh, Good Lord, I really hope not!

I am being smirked at by schoolboys, as opposed to just the same mental age, which is the usual depressing scenario. This is just freaky as hell. Squeeze into a corner seat and ruthlessly push Siobhan to the front [in manner of throwing lambs to the wolves.] If they get us they're getting her first. She's squealing,

"Carly! DON'T!"

"Siobhan, what the hell were you thinking of coming in here? They're the tallest kids in the world. Look, they're like baby piranhas. We're going to be eaten alive."

"Oh, hell, Carly, you're right. They do seem to be looking this way. Why do you think they're staring at us?"

"We're the only ones here who have breasts! Except for that big horrid man at the bar. They can't be on solid food yet?"

"Oh ignore them. They might just go away then?" Glare at the baby perverts.

"They ought to. It's well past their bedtimes. And they might have homework and stuff." A rogue baby weasels on up to out table.

"Can I get you ladies a drink?" EEK!

"No, your voice hasn't broken. So run along home to your mum." Uh, maybe a little mean. But you have to be quite firm with kids. The adult-molesting sprog-thing scuttles off back to his gibbering troupe.

"Oh, Carly! That wasn't very nice. He was only trying to be friendly." What the hell planet are you on?

"Siobhan, I don't *want* to be friendly with anyone I could have given birth to. Jesus! How horrid is that?"

"So, O.K. Where do *you* want to go then?"

"Somewhere that the grown-up people drink." Leave the bar in search of grown-up men. They are much more fun to torment.

....

We have found a more adult location – a trendy pub by the river.

"Let's try this place, Siobhan. I haven't been in here yet. It's supposed to be really, …what?" Why has Siobhan grabbed my arm?

"Siobhan?" She's looking totally horrified? Oh no, don't tell me, not another den of puberty? I have seen enough illegal spawn for one night.

"Oh, no! Carly, let's go."

"What?" What's she looking at for heaven's sake? They look more than old enough in here to me? Turn my head quickly to see…

"Oh my God!" It's him, with his tongue down someone else's throat. I think I feel a bit sick. Siobhan is still tugging at my arm but I seem to be unable to move.

"CARLY! Just leave it! Let's go." At the sound of her voice he looks up and sees us. Jake is kissing some other woman, a skimpily dressed voluptuous blonde who looks about twenty-five. Oh how could he? That's too vile for words, like being kicked in the stomach by a large horse… I think I might be about to lose my dinner.

Jake jumps up, equally horrified.

"Carly! Shit! What are you doing here? I didn't see you come in."

"No, you're obviously busy. Siobhan and I were just leaving. Excuse me."

Grab hold of Siobhan's sleeve and hiss.

"Get me out of here!" We turn back towards the door, but I can't leave. Someone's got a very firm grip of my arm. Glance round at… a total stranger?

"Excuse me, but that's a lovely perfume you're wearing…. Could I maybe buy you a…"

"It's NOT perfume. It's my bubble bath! So put me down and buy your own." Tug my arm back in fury and make a snooty sharp exit from the pub.

We have gone to ground in a thankfully quiet and almost empty wine bar roughly three streets away. Siobhan is at the bar for restoratives and I'm holding my face in my hands. That was one of the most disgusting things I've ever seen in my life. God help the poor buggers who actually catch their partners in complete inflagrante. It doesn't bear thinking about. I know that we're separated and considering my own behaviour recently, I'm in no position to criticise Jake …but I feel awful. I must still love him. After all, we were together for years…Oh, my God! What if I've made a mistake? What have I done?

There's a slight clink as Siobhan puts a glass down gently in front of me.

"Carly, speak to me…Are you O.K.?" Shake my head from inside my hands. I can hear a little moany noise? Oh, my God! It's me? Again? Siobhan sits down and puts an arm round my shoulders. She really is a very good friend.

"Come on, Carls. He's not worth it. You know he isn't, don't you?"

"Well, he did behave quite badly at times but…."

"Quite badly? The man's a self-obsessed, egomaniacal bully! If it's one of those you want we'll just ask Angie. Maybe Miles has got a friend?" Oh, ouch, that hurt. Not Queensbury at all. I am *not* like Angie, am I?

Pull myself together and sit up. This isn't fair on Siobhan. I'm behaving like some pre-pubescent fool. I'm a grown woman. I'm fine. Give Siobhan a wry grin.

"Sorry! Don't know what came over me…you must think I'm a total sap."

Siobhan does a small relieved smile.

"No, I don't. Don't be stupid. That would have freaked me out too. If Giles did that I'd kill him…Oh! Carly, no, I'm sorry."

"No, really. It's fine, I'm O.K…I was bound to bump into him sooner or later. Might as well get used to it, I suppose" She gives my hand a reassuring pat.

"Anyway, you don't need the likes of him. There are plenty of other men in the world."

"Oh, thank-you, Siobhan, for not saying fish. I've heard that about ten times this week. Besides, the last thing I need, right now or ever, is another man to mess up my head." Siobhan looks totally horror-struck.

"Oh, Carly! You don't mean that. I know how you feel about kids. You're thirty-four already. Don't you *want* to have a baby?"

"Well, given my present circumstances, it might prove a little tricky to achieve. Unless I want to have a holy baby and I don't think you can do that on request. Anyway, what I most certainly *don't* want to do is just grab the first sperm donor who happens to be passing in case my body clock runs out, like some horrible game of musical chairs. No, Siobhan. No way! If I can't have someone that I can imagine spending the rest of my life with then I don't want anything else. Someone who could actually make me happy even, or I shall just make myself happy alone... I am going to take control of my own life for a change. I don't need anyone's permission to be myself or anyone's approval of what I want to do or be. I can have anything I want. And I can get it by myself! I *don't* need anyone to get it for me.... And most certainly NOT HIM!"

"So, didn't Jake make you happy then?" I frown. I'm not sure? Did he?

"We-ell? To start with he did, you know, while they're still making an effort. Then just occasionally, then I suppose it just got too much like hard work, especially since his accident. And it shouldn't be like that, should it? Not so much of the time?"

"No Carly, it shouldn't. I know that you all think my Giles is a bit dull."

Oh, my God! She knows? Oh horrors!

"Oh, no, Siobhan, we don't."

"Yes, you do. And maybe in some ways he is. But he *does* make me happy and in the end that's the bottom line, isn't it? That's what really counts, Carly. And if Jake didn't do that for you, let it go. You can do better than that."

"But can I though? As everyone is so keen to remind me, I *am* thirty-bloody-four and so therefore *must* be a dried up old prune? It would seem that the days to my sell-by date are numbered and I ought to be profoundly grateful to be asked out by any potentially nabbable husband, however repellent, before it's too bloody late?" There is a highly celibate pause as we consider this.

"I think I may kill myself now."

"So you're thirty-four. Who cares? And too late for what, for heaven's sake? The rest of your life? You could live to be ninety years old. What are you going to do? Sacrifice the next sixty years to terminal boredom with some git that doesn't even know how to treat you, just because you feel sorry for him over a busted knee and the vague possibility that he might have to change his career? Oh right, that's an excellent plan. I'll go and get your pipe and slippers now... Carly, wake-up! You don't have to do anything you don't want to, just because your friends or your family or society in general thinks you should... Get a grip, why don't you? This isn't the Carly I know. When *did* you become such a muppet?"

Christ, Siobhan, just you say what you think. Don't hold back on my account.

"You are actually right though Siobhan, I don't want to spend the rest of my life in an emotional coma. And I certainly don't want to feel like *this* ever again. If it wasn't for my biological clock this might never have happened. Well, it *won't* be happening again! I am not giving up everything I care about to be a drudge for some boring twat who rates making love to me as less important than beer or getting tickets to see the bloody Gunners!" It is a revelation of biblical proportions.

"Oh Lord, Carls! Please be kidding?"

"I wish... We were making love on the rug once and he actually stopped to look at the T.V. because Arsenal scored a goal? I'm surprised he didn't go out for a pie and Bovril!" Siobhan does a high-pitched nervous horror laugh.

"Oh, God! You are *lying*?" No, really! I wish that I were. Shake my head slowly. I cannot believe it myself.

"Compared to that Giles is Rasputin himself. Oh, my God! You poor thing."

I can't stop laughing at that idea, Giles-Rasputin-Cardigan Man, the biggest shagger in town. He probably has a selection of little hand-knitted woollen condoms – ribbed, but of course, for your pleasure…Aaargh. Oh, no, that's too gross for words.

Siobhan smiles in relief. She clearly has no idea why I'm laughing but decides to join in anyway. Perhaps she is humouring me. Fine. So we'll go with mass hysteria, shall we, if we can be a mass with two people? Maybe only in a Catholic Church?

CHAPTER EIGHT
Small Time Villains

Early morning [too early by half!] J screeches to a halt outside of my house. He's in getaway driver mode already. This would have been much more effective if he didn't drive a bright yellow Volkswagen Beetle with huge daisies painted on the side. The horn trumpets an impatient 'Paarpp!' as I'm still scuttling down all the stairs.

"Hi babes. Are you ready for the heist?" J. has donned his best camouflage gear and is having the time of his life.

"Jerry! This is a serious matter. And what's with all the camouflage stuff? We're in Highbury, not darkest Peru."

"Oh, don't *worry* Carly! I'm not going to wear these for the actual *job*. I've got us both something better for that!" Us? Us both? – Uh-oh! Jerry whizzes Miss Daisy [the Beetle] into the oncoming traffic to a furious chorus of horns. I'm going to die before I even get there!

Ten minutes and we're here (Not where I expected to be either). We are parked in the car park of a huge B&Q. Hmm, well, you know - now what?

"Right, Carly, out we jolly well pop. This'll be the very place to get it."

Eh? To get what? Struggle out of the awkward door and hustle to keep up with the extremely fast-moving Jerry.

Inside, Jerry rubs his pointy chin thoughtfully and scans the shop.

"Right! Now…. where do you think it might be?" *Eh?*

"Jerry, what am I looking for?" J. shakes his head like I'm some kind of imbecile.

"Well, Carly! You *know*? The *stuff*, the stuff for doing a break in. I mean they're *bound* to have it in here! It'll be like - tools of some sort or other." What?

"Well J., they're not just going to have a big sign up are they- Gardening, Lighting and Burglary? ...And it's not as if we can ask someone, 'Excuse me, but do you have a crowbar?" J.'s faces lights up at that remark.

"Carly, you clever girl. That's it! A crowbar! Or as us *pro's* like to call them, a jeemy."

"Jemmy!"

"What Sweetie?"

"Not Jerry, Jemmy! That's what they are called."

"Oh ye-es. Oh, I'd completely forgotten about those. I saw them on D.I.Y. Challenge." I am in *so* much trouble. But Jerry is undeterred.

"Well, we'll just have to start at one end of the shop and keep looking until we find them."

. . . .

Twenty minutes later.

"Jerry! I think that this might be the thing that we want?" J. rushes over to look.

"Yes, that's definitely the thingy, Carls. But *really* darling! *Black*? Don't they come in *any* better colours?"

Take the jemmy to the checkout and whiz back to Miss Daisy. If this is to be done, it is, as they say, better to be done quickly, very quickly. Then I can just go home and die.

. . . .

Outside Aaron's flat. Good thing that it's on the ground floor. Jerry has discreetly parked Miss Daisy on the far side of the street, as discreetly as one can ever park in this car. We are both slouched right down in our seats and J. keeps popping his head up for a look. I cannot believe I agreed to this. We are waiting for our victim to exit and leave the coast clear for our plan. But he might not go anywhere for hours?

"Jerry, I don't think that this is going to work. What if he doesn't want to go out? We could be sitting here all day."

"Oh, Carly! Don't be so ungrateful. I'm putting my ass on the line for you here. I could end up as some thug's bitch in prison. Mmmm! But well, then again…"

Oh, well, as long as somebody's happy. As I'm lying almost flat on the floor of the car due to a dodgy passenger seat I turn round and glance in the back.

"Jerry, why have you got two buckets and some old clothes in here?" This can't be a new fashion statement, the peasant boy look? J. is absorbed in his spying.

"Oh, that. Oh, no. That's our disguise." What? Am I to put a bucket on my head so that no-one will recognize me?

"*Wouldn't* a stocking have done?"

"Eh? We're going to be window cleaners darling. You know? In case he's got a very low fence." Shake my head in horrified amazement.

"Uh, uh!" No, no I don't think so. I think I'll just stay here and die.

"OHH! Carly! Something's happening. The door is opening and… it's him!"

"Who did you expect to come out of *his* front door?" Oh, please God! Please, don't let him see me! Jerry is practically wetting himself with excitement.

"Oooh, Carly! I can't believe this is happening. A stakeout! It's just like on 'The Bill'." Oh, take me now, Lord.

"And he's come out of the house. He's getting into his car. God! That's his car? Flashy bastard." Jerry shoots down in his seat, turns round to face me and hisses.

"He's looking over this way!" Oh-my-GOD! We both crouch on the car floor rigid, totally scared out of our wits till, as a powerful engine purrs past, J. plucks up the courage to peek.

"Oh, thank fuck. He's gone. Thought it was the slammer for sure, Babe."

"On what charge, exactly? Lurking with the intent to make a complete tit of yourself? We haven't actually *done* anything yet.

"No, well? I suppose that we haven't but that is just about to change. That big Yankee slut isn't keeping your granny's necklace. Carly, buckets...HO!

....

We are in Aaron's back garden after a highly undignified clamber over his extremely high fence. We have donned big shirts, cloth caps and waistcoats and look like no window cleaner on Earth. Jerry has a scarlet cravat tied in a cheeky manner under his chin. He really needs to do more costume-research. We look like Victorian orphans? He has produced a weird expanding ladder, which falls slightly short of the high kitchen window.

"Where on Earth did you get that thing, Jerry?"

"Oh, I got it from one of those through-the-door-catalogues that you usually throw in the bin. I quite like to flick through them, Carly. It's amazing what weird stuff they sell."

"What were you actually going to use it for?"

"Oh, I don't know. It was so mad that I just fancied having one. You know?" No, I don't. I am way too poor to waste my hard earned pennies on weird expanding things of no consequence. Jerry weasels up the tiny ladder and perches jauntily on top of a green wheely bin.

"Righto, Carly up you come, then." NO! no-no-NOOO!

Suddenly a piercingly nasal voice rings out rudely over the unfortunately low middle fence. It is a very large woman in a hairnet and full make-up.

"Hey! You there! Yes-you on the dustbin. ...What ex-zectlay do you thenk you are up to? We *do* hev a neighbourhood watch!"

Jerry, unfazed leans to whisper.

"Don't worry. I'll settle her hash. Watch this." He waves an overly familiar shammy at the snooty neighbour in a disturbingly cheap T.V. way.

"Wotcha! Ow-do-de-doday there, Missus? Could I see to your buttons and bows.? Give em' a good going over wiv me shammy?

Ear' darlin, wot-d'you say?" Oh-my-God! The woman is quite clearly horrified.

"You'll do no such thing you *unspeakable* little man! Remove yourself this second!" She exits with a loud window-slam. I am totally gob smacked.

"Jerry! Who the hell were you trying to be? Dick Van-Bloody-Dyke?" Jerry is standing there preening.

"We-ell, Yes, I really *was* rather good."

"Dick Van Dyke was a frigging chimney sweep! NOT a window cleaner. For God's *sake* get the character right."

"Carly you *are SO* fussy. I mean, they're both, like, you know, still *trade.*"

J. turns, poised to make free with his jemmy when we realise that the window is open. He frowns in disappointment,

"Well.... bugger me."

"There's no need to sound so disappointed. At least it's just 'entering' now."

Jerry does not look convinced. He gives a disconsolate wave of his crowbar,

"Oh, well, then. Just go ahead in."

"What! ME? Why not you? You are still the man around here."

"Oh, Car-lee, I can't. I'm the lookout."

"Don't remember when that was arranged?"

"Come ON now, Carly babes...HUPP!"

"Oh, O.K. I suppose I might as well. But I am not happy, not happy at all."

I grab onto the kitchen window ledge and heave myself over the sink, head first onto the expensively tiled floor.

"Oops! Oww that hurt. It's as hard to get in here as out."

"Are you alright, Carly?" A quick scrabbling and J.s head appears.

"Oooh! Snazz-ee kitchen. Are you *sure* that you really don't want him? He's obviously worth a few bucks."

"No! I just want my necklace." Stomp off in a huff. Now where did I leave it? Must be either the lounge or the bedroom. Toddle in and rumple his cushions.

Nope. Not under here. And it's not on the rug either apparently. My necklace is not to be seen. Don't really have time to waste snooping … but maybe a quick peek at these? Stretch up onto my toes to peer at some photos on the very high mantelpiece. Hmmm… sort of parents, perhaps? Him on the beach in just shorts ... ummm! And…

"Carlee! Hurry UP!" O.K. O.K. I was only having a quick look. Trundle at top shuffle into the major scene of the crime. The huge bed has been made but is still eyeing me in a derisory ha-ha fashion. Hit it a kick on the way past. My necklace does not leap out and shout 'I'm here!' unfortunately. Bedside table? No. On the carpet? No. Maybe it's underneath the bed? Scramble down onto my knees and lift up the side of the duvet. Nope, nothing but fluff. There's a sudden 'flick' noise behind me. What the blue blazes was that? Look over my shoulder nervously.

"Flick!" A tiny pebble is bounces off the window. Oh, no! It can't be? Scuttle over to the window and check. Down below Jerry is shouting with all the effect of a goldfish. Damn! Didn't allow for triple glazing. He's pointing madly towards the house. Oh God! Aaron must be back and I can't jump down from here? I would break at least one leg for sure. I'm not an ac-tor, so I don't want to do that. I'll run back through to the kitchen…

BANG! Uh-oh? Front door? I'm too late! Under the bed? No, too yucky. Right then, I'll hide in here. Open the only other door in the bedroom. It's the most massive walk-in wardrobe in the world. Don't have time to think as I can hear him whistling about the house. Aaargh! Dive into the wardrobe room and cower behind the furthest rail of suits. No wonder he could afford to cut up good shirts willy-nilly. He's got half of John Lewis in here?

The whistling is getting much closer. Slide down the wall in pure terror and bunch myself into a ball. Now? What could I possibly say if he catches me? ….If? …Or even when? Hmmm , I can see his feet now…and his legs? He in mooching about in the bedroom and has flung a casual T-shirt on the floor. He is coming towards the wardrobe… He is coming into the wardrobe and rifling through the other end of the rail. Aaargh! Aaargh! Double Aargh!

"Dum-di dum,dum!" He is humming? My life is nearly over and he's bloody well humming? I am done for!

BANG-BANG-BANG-BANG-BANG! What on earth?

"Huh? What the … ?" He mooches away to investigate. Oh, my-God, another ten years off my life. A very familiar voice echoes through from the hallway.

"Good morning Sir! I'm Father Green from the Church of the Latter Day Frumpians." Hooray! It's Jerry, my saviour! I can hear him desperately ad-libbing at the front door in his best diversion mode. Creep out of the wardrobe and peek round the bedroom doorframe. Aaron is lounging against the front door in a casual, half-naked fashion saying,

"Hi. What exactly can I do for you, Father?" I know exactly what he is doing for J. from the front viewpoint as he is doing the same for me from behind. His dark hair is sexily disarrayed, curling slightly into the nape of his neck, his biceps are toned and his back is all rippling muscles. Uuuummm. Turn my head sideways to get a better view. No! What am I doing? I must sneak past to the kitchen now and escape. Fortunately it is a very long hallway. Use my best imaginary commando manoeuvre. I can see J. eyeing me wildly in his peripheral vision, past Aaron's shoulder. He is clearly trying hard not to draw Aaron's attention by looking directly at me and it is obviously killing him not to. He gives Aaron a sincere look and clasps his hands dramatically,

"So, tell me, Sir?….Are you happy in your life?" My hero. Talking utter but very realistic rubbish.. Scuttle into the kitchen, clamber back over the sink and fall down the weirdo ladder on my suddenly jelly-like legs.

"Ooomph!"

Once again I am in a heap outside this bloody house. Fortunately, for once it's tradesman-free. Scoot over the fence with newly-aquired super-human strength. (Amazing what fear can do for you!). Hustle speedily back to Miss Daisy and collapse in a bright red gaspy heap on the pavement behind her. Ten seconds later I'm joined by Getaway Jerry in a similarly traumatised condition.

"Oh, fuck me, Carly. That was close! I thought that he had you for sure." Can't speak. I'm too busy breathing.

"Did you see me, Carly? Did you? Wasn't I fantastic? I was just like a real Jehovah. I thought I was going to convert him..!"

"Please tell me that you mean to God."

"Well, really, Carls! If you don't want him?"

"Just GET ME OUT OF HERE!" Crawl into Miss Daisy from the passenger side and exit to safety, thankfully minus the buckets. As we drive off I remember,

"Incidentally Jerry, Father Green is Pere Vert in French."

"Pervert? That can't be right Carls?"

"Fraid so. If you join the French Clergy you'll have to change your name." J. considers this option for a moment, then shakes his head briskly.

"Not for me Carls, I'm too fashion-conscious … way too many bad habits."

…………..

Back home after the non-heist – thank God! And without a criminal record. But no thanks to some people here. J. is crouched on the settee in a kind of yoga position wittering and watching T.V. Perhaps I should have a calming drink [for strictly medicinal purposes]. Wonder what's in the cupboard?

"D'you fancy a cocktail Jerry?" Stops wittering for a second to decide.

"Um, don't know, Carls. What have you got?"

Shuffle off into the kitchen to look. On investigation I find that I possess the wherewithal for a long and comfortable screw. Well, isn't that ironic? I wish that I'd known that before.

"What about a screw then, Jerry?"

"Oh, darling! You're just not my type."

"Oh, ha ha. Well, that's what we've got so that's what you're getting." Think I'll just make it pretty with some fruit on the side and stuff. Presentation is all. Return to the lounge to the sight of J. drooling over some greasy old fool. Hand him his drink with a sigh.

"Budge your butt up, Jerry. I want to read my magazine." Moves his bum along the settee but his face is still stuck in mid-drool.

"Oh God, Carls! He's gorgeous!" Glance up from my reading to check.

"Nope! I've never met him. And I don't think that I'd want to at that." A bit slick for my liking. J.'s taste really is in his butt. I can feel him glaring at the side of my head but decide I can't be bothered to look. I just want to finish this page.

"Sorree Your Ladyship! I forgot. You only like rugged and smouldery... and worth about ten zillion quid!" Miaow!

"Shut up, J. I'm not listening." He's just trying to wind me up. I shall not rise to the bait."

"Of course, it's all right for some of us..." Eh? Forget the plan and look up.

"What? I wasn't listening." Yes, that's Jerry's wind-me-up face.

"Tell me, Carls, just out of interest, what's it like to sleep with a thesp? You being such an expert and all." Oh, MIAOW! – That hurt!

"Jerry! Don't be such a bitch!" But it's too late. He's on a roll now.

"...You know, like, once he's finished, do you have to clap and stuff?"

What? Oh, sod off you git ...I'll ignore him. He'll get bored in a bit. Turn back to my abandoned magazine.

"...Or did you just lie there saying 'bravo' a lot and hoping for an encore? Like? - like, would you give him a good review? Oh, har-har-haar-haar!"

"Just shut up J. or I'll have to stab you. Then you'll never get to meet Jude Law."

"Did you fling things during the performance? You know, like your knickers and stuff?" Pause to consider this point.

"That's not acting J. That's Tom Jones. I think people usually fling flowers at actors but I could be confusing it with skating."

"Ooh! Scorecards Carly! 6-4? 6-5? .... 6-10? How much for artistic interpretation? Oh, har-de-har, har, har!" Put my head down on my knees and shut my eyes really tight. Why me, Lord? What have I done? J. is exultant to have gotten a reaction at last and is crowing happily at the other end of the settee.

"Skating on thin ice as usual. Ooh, Carly, you are a naughty girl." Perhaps I could just strangle him? Or worse still take his remote? I think it has now reached the point in the evening when it really is time for my screw.

CHAPTER NINE
Should She Stay Or Should She Go Now?

I'm meeting Siobhan for a lunchtime rendezvous after a very cryptic mid-morning phone call. For the first time in thirty odd years, she actually sounded rattled. Apparently she needs to talk but can't discuss it over the phone. How hum, now what? Wander aimlessly along the shop-lined street as I am twenty minutes early and therefore Siobhan will still be in the office. Due to the somewhat erratic nature of London's public transport system, it is almost impossible to just be on time. You have to choose between very early or very, very late. Being a considerate sort of person I have plumped for early, thus the aimless trailing about. If you sit alone in a restaurant for twenty minutes, not only are you bored witless, everyone thinks you've been stood up. 'I'm waiting for a friend' indeed.

Stop for a minute outside W.H. Smith's to peruse a colourful display of new best sellers. Hmm, perhaps that's what I need, now that I've got the peace to read it. Surely reading is a more fruitful intellectual exercise than vegging out in front of the T.V.? And none of your old paperback snash. If they've bothered to make it into a hardback then it must be good, right? Let's have a look then. Wander in for a nosey about. Make a bee-line for the huge display at the front of the shop. Unfortunately a quick rummage and a flick of some fly-leafs reveals the sad truth that today's offering is either too gory or too depressing sounding to be particularly to my taste. I am not good with gore, I'm afraid. And terribly poignant tear-jerkers I can do without. I have a bank statement for that. Drat! I just wanted something interesting or funny. Is that really too much to ask? Oh well, maybe there's some better ones on the shelf? I shall go and investigate forthwith. I'm more in the mood for something light-hearted - something of the Jill Mansell, Catherine Alliot ilk, something to chill out with. Down here maybe? This shop is massive.

Wander down a handy aisle in search of humour [non-black]. I am just passing the magazine shelf when something odd catches my eye. Glance down at the shelf. Oh dear God! It's Mr Poky the dress ripper? Is he everywhere? Aaron's annoyingly rugged features adorn the entire front cover of a prominent celeb gossip magazine. There's a charming corner insert of a candid shot of him and some girl on a beach, somewhere exotic and patently unaffordable looking. It could be the same girl as before...or not. It is impossible to tell as she's wearing shades, she isn't in turn of the century bodice and bloomers and it's not a very good shot. Good enough to show off her tremendous assets in a miniscule white bikini though. I feel a mortified flush flood my cheeks.

Look round nervously, in case some of the passers by might somehow be psychic and know that I've slept with him. Oh God, the shame! I've not only been used by a total git but by someone who is apparently legendary for it? God alone knows how many women he's slept with? And we didn't even take precautions? I could have Aids? I could have anything? Oh how could I have been so stupid? Screw my fists into tight balls at my sides to prevent me from ripping the magazine display to shreds. Turn on my shabbily sand-shoed heel and stomp outside again. Lean against a handy lamp-post breathing heavily. Should I get an Aids test? Or a something else test? Oh God no! Take a deep breath and shut my eyes in a supreme effort to calm down. Right, now, there is very little chance that I've caught anything. I shall just need to go to the doctor or a clinic and ask. But it's fine. I'm fine. Now calm down and go and meet Siobhan. Open my eyes to glance at my watch. Only ten minutes. Near enough. Turn and make tracks for the appointed rendezvous, a tastefully discreet little wine bar just off the high street.

Take a calming breath and push the glass door open. There's no sign of Siobhan but I'm still early. Take a seat beside a tiny mullioned window. There's a nice view of the pretty little mews outside - flowery tubs everywhere, very 'Homes & Gardens'. Settle down to look at the menu till cryptic Siobhan arrives. Wonder what the big secret is? Must be pretty important if it couldn't wait till tonight. Hmm? Scampi or tikka masala? Decisions, decisions. I am notoriously slow at making up my mind in restaurants so it's nice to get a head start. I have just about cut the choice down to a couple of things when Siobhan flusters in through the door. I have never seen her less than calm before. Wave and smile. Push out a welcoming chair,

"Hi Siobhan. Sit down. Take the weight off your briefcase."

"Hello Carls. Thanks for coming."

Shrug,

"No problemo. It's hardly an imposition to come here. You're not going to force me to eat chocolate fudge cake or anything unspeakably dreadful like that, are you?" She laughs,

"When have you ever needed forcing?" Wrinkle my nose,

"So I'm the pot and you're the kettle, right? Anyway, come on, spill the beans. What's the big secret?" This stops her laughing immediately. *Oops?*

"Well Carls, I can't quite believe it myself yet. I just found out this morning. I really don't know what I ought to do."

"What? Are you o.k.?" She starts playing with her napkin distractedly,

"Yes, I'm fine. It's just that, well, I've been offered a promotion at last, after all these years."

"But that's fantastic? Well done. Oh that's great." Stop short as she doesn't look quite how someone who's just been offered a plum job ought to look. i.e. happy, excited, irritatingly smug -blah, blah.

"Siobhan, what is it?" She looks up from he napkin and frowns,

"It's exactly the job I want.... but it's in Melbourne." Stare blankly,

"Melbourne?" She nods,

"Yes Carly, Melbourne as in Australia?"

"I know where ruddy Melbourne is! I'm not a complete idiot. I just don't know what to say."

"I know. Precisely. It's initially a year's contract with the option of staying on." It's extremely difficult to know what to say here. Obviously, it's the chance of a lifetime for Siobhan. And obviously, I don't want her to go. I've known her since we were about seven years old. I can't imagine her not being around. But it's the chance of a lifetime. The chance she's worked towards for the last fifteen years.

"What does Giles think?" She looks away guiltily.

"I haven't told him yet. I couldn't phone from the office. I'm seeing him tonight. I haven't accepted it yet Carls. I mean, Giles' career is here. And it's not as if I could pop back at the week-end." Stare dismally down at my hands. Despite my concern for Siobhan's awful predicament, self-pity rears its ugly head. First no boyfriend and now my oldest friends are vanishing to the ends of the Earth. Oh, this sucks. But I have to think what's best for Siobhan. Besides, it might not be forever. Attempt to lighten the funereal atmosphere,

"So, we're alright for an Aussie holiday then? We'll all come and kip on your couch. Jerry'll be ecstatic. All those hunky bronzed surfers. He'll be straight out to buy a new pair of flip-flops and a big tasteless Hawaiian shirt." Siobhan smiles,

"So you'd come and see me then?"

"Course we would. I'll just have to sell a couple of paintings, that's all. You know, big paintings. And J. can sell his body or something. Ange can put it on her expense account. Sure. It'll be fine." Siobhan smiles bravely.

"I still don't know if I ought to take it you know." Try for a sensible face in keeping with the gravity of the situation.

"Well what are your options? What happens if you say no? Will it count against you career-wise?"

"Probably. It'll show lack of commitment - a cardinal sin. I might well never be offered a job like this again."

"Do you care?"

"Yes, I damn well do. It's really hard for women to work their way up. Everyone expects you to pop off and get pregnant any second. We have to work much harder to get the same money as the men for doing exactly the same thing when we've got exactly the same qualifications. And I didn't arrive half-way up the corporate ladder courtesy of some posh public school or the old-boy network. I've worked bloody hard for this. I've had to graft for years. And some of the shit you have to put up with is unbelievable. If I don't take this post I'll be confirming the myth that women aren't up to the job. But if I take it, even for a year, my future would be totally secure. Giles and I could afford to buy a nice house in a nice area - without a crippling mortgage. I'd be stupid not to take it. The money's amazing. And I've always wanted to see Australia. It's just Giles... And you guys."

"Well, I think you've answered your own question, don't you? And we'll still be here when you get back. And as for Giles, maybe he'd like to come with you?"

"Giles? Leave London?"

"Why don't you ask him? He might surprise you."

"I don't know if he could get a job out there. And he wouldn't want to live off me."

"Well, before you make any decisions, I should find out what all your options are. The two of you could have a fabulous time out there. At least give him a chance. How long before you have to give them an answer?"

"Till Friday. Five days." We are interrupted by the arrival of a waitress at this juncture, after which the conversation turns to other matters.

"So Carls, what have you been up to? Molested any famous people this week?"

"Oh ha ha, very funny. No I haven't and I won't be for a very long time. Anyone, that is, not famous people in particular. In fact, not famous people ever again. What an arse!" Siobhan sniggers,

"I know. Jerry said he had a nice one." Just glare at her. I've had enough of this tack from J. Remember something.

"Actually, I saw him in Smith's before I met you." Her jaw drops onto the white linen tablecloth. She screeches,

"What? What did he say? You did speak to him? Carly he is gorgeous." *Oh no? not you too?*

"No, no, no, not in person. On the cover of a magazine. With his girlfriend. He's even worse than Jake. At least he waited till we broke up to go out with somebody else. He wasn't a serial philanderer. Mind you, he'd hardly enough energy for me, never mind a string of floosies. Nope, that's it Siobhan. I'm off men for good. They're more trouble than they're worth."

"Carly, you don't mean that? They're not all bad. Look at Giles."

"O.K., fair enough. I'll concede that small point. Giles is a sweetie. But it seems that he is in the minority. The men I end up with, or not with, are not. I'm going to concentrate on my painting. It ought to be much easier now that I've got peace and quiet. Besides, I've got a tiny little exhibition to do, remember? That should take up all my time and then some for the foreseeable future at least. Celibacy and painting - that's the plan." Siobhan is shocked,

"But Carly? No nookie?"

"Yes, that is a bit unfortunate. But I can't do the casual sex thing. But on the bright side…."

"Oh? Is there one of those?"

"Oh yes! By the time I've painted fifty pictures for Shrimpton-Boswick I will be way too knackered to care. I think I might have some chocolate to console myself though. So? Where's my ruddy fudge cake?"

CHAPTER TEN
Painting By Musical Numbers Baby

Tuesday – 10a.m., at my flat. I am working on a life-size portrait from a precarious position on top of a shaky old stool. I'm wearing my paint-spattered denim shorts and a manky old bin-fodder t-shirt. My hair is struggling gamely to stay in a clumsily constructed knot. I am a complete and utter babe. I am singing along to a very funky song on the radio by I–don't-know-who and having a little wiggle in time so far as my teetering position will allow.

"I'm just a teenage dirtbag, baby. Listens to Iron Maiden maybe? La da di dada dirtbag baby, like you." Sudden throat-clearing noise from behind. Eeeek!

"Er, hi Carly. The door was open so…., What are you doing?" Oh, God! It's him, Aaron the ac-tor tart! I'm falling, that's what it would seem that I'm doing?

"I'm being a teenage dirtbag, baby. Why? What are you doing? And more precisely to the point, why are you doing it here? How did you know where I live?" Hmm, not one of my more gracious retorts but what the hell is he doing here anyway? Make a belated attempt at dignity from the top of my stool. He is staring in amazement at my yucky shorts. What a flaming nerve?

"Oh, you left this necklace and this wallet when you, when… erm, you left them at my place. Your address is in the wallet. Thought you'd want to have them back. I'd have brought them round sooner only something came up." So what's new? And I know what came up, you toad, or rather whom!

"Oh, right! Thanks." This is horribly embarrassing. He thinks I'm a floosy and he knows that I climb out of windows. Also, it would be much easier to be polite if he wasn't so damn sexy! This is doing nothing for my new celibate resolutions. But I must be polite as he did bring my wallet back after being snubbed. I shall just be mature and ultra-aloof.

"Coffee?"

"Er,... Fine. Yes, please." Manners too, huh? Well, you needn't think I'm impressed that easily. Jump down and saunter through to the kitchen in a couldn't-care-less fashion leaving the sex-god to follow in my wake. Unfortunately I am unable to stop my mouth. It kicks in after roughly ten seconds.

"So…how's Jennifer?" He is looks a bit confused.

"Jennifer?"

"You know? Jenn-ifer, your girlfriend?" Now he looks decidedly pissed off. Good! Mission accomplished.

"She is not my girlfriend!" God, he's gorgeous! Nope, don't like you! Don't like you! You can't make me like you. Spin round and point an accusing splattery paintbrush at his sparkling white shirt. I have decided that he is the shirt man from hell.

"Don't give me that! Jerry told me everything! And you've been all over the papers!" Now he is absolutely furious. Great! Fan-bloody-tastic! Why should I be pissed off by myself?

"Firstly Carly, who the fuck is Jerry? And secondly, just because some scandalmonger prints a cheap rumour in the gossip columns *doesn't* mean that it's bloody well true! I am *not* going out with her. I never *was* going out with her." Derisive,

"Really? If you say so."

"And *you*, Carly, you jumped-out-of–my-window so *don't* give me a fucking hard time about who I'm *not* going out with!" Oooohhhh! Sex-ee! I cannot think of an adequate reply so turn back to the kettle and sulk.

" Fine!" Fine? Is that it, Carly? Your best cutting response? Pathetic! I'm in a double sulk. Fold my arms in a huff and glare out of the window. I can't remember whether the kettle has boiled or not but

I'm not going to admit it. So I will just ignore him till he goes away - as he surely must do soon after my astounding rudeness? But no... I don't believe it! He has snuck up behind me and put both hands on the worktop so that I'm trapped in between? Oooohh! Doesn't he know when he's being ignored or something? What the hell is he up to? He should be gone by now? I can feel his face approx. one inch from my ear. I am *not* going to look. He is putting both hands round my waist and snuggling my ear? WHAT?

"Car...lee." I do not believe it! He's bloody well insatiable?

"Caar-lee? C'mon, I didn't come here to fight...Mmmm?" Eh? What did you come for then? NO! No, ab-sol-utely bloody not! He thinks I'm a total trollop? I am OUTRAGED!

"*Put me* DOWN! I do actually *possess* knickers you know! How *dare* you come round here making indecent assumptions all over the place? Get out!" Push him away and run into into the bathroom like the mature, self-possessed adult that I am.

"Carly! Come out of there." Humph! That told him. You can't get me now, you tart! The door is bloody locked.

"And, ...and don't come back, you slapper!"

…………...

Quite a long time later - Expect it's safe to come out now. Haven't heard a thing for ages. He *must* have gone? Open the lock really quietly and peer round the door. The front door is now shut so he has gone. [Sadly] Expect he thinks that I am a raving mental case now. Trudge round the flat just to check. Then, as it is clearly a man-free zone, lock the front door and cuddle up on the settee with my duvet to feel sorry for myself. Don't feel that much like painting anymore.

Approximately ten minutes later - A sudden crazed knocking on the front door. Bloody hell! You have *got* to be kidding? The man's like a ruddy boomerang! Well, I am *not* going to put up with this! Storm to the door, fling it open and prepare to deliver a discouraging smack: Oh! It's only Jerry. Oh? I should be pleased it's only Jerry?

"Well, about time too! Carly, Darling? What the bloody hell's the matter? Thought you were going to do your old Tyson bit on me there, Babe.

Oh, oh? What is wrong with me?

"Oh, Jerreee, Uh-uh, snuff, snuff." I need a cuddle. Fortunately, I can cuddle Jerry at will without fear of any kind of repercussions.

"Carly? What's wrong? Has Jake been back here upsetting you, because I have friends, you know, that could settle his hash for a very reasonable price." Let Jerry usher me into my own house and decide to tell him all. J. is an extremely smart person. He will know exactly what I should do.

CHAPTER ELEVEN
Life, Love & Electrical Cupboards

Angie's swish new loft warehouse conversion – a house this empty screams 'cash'. But it doesn't appear to be making her happy because Miles is still being a shit. Of course, this may well be genetic and might not be the poor bugger's fault. But somehow I doubt it. I think he has just had an inordinate amount of 'how-to-be-a-shit' training and the practice of many a year.

J. and Siobhan have gone out for booze leaving me in an Angie-sitting capacity. It's becoming clear as the seconds tick by that for this role I am sadly unfit. Angie is striding about her gargantuan 'living space' and her nerves are clearly in shreds. If they weren't she might just sit down? I dread to think how developers describe the other rooms in this joint? If not a 'living space' then *what* is it for? But silly old me, of course, there *are* no other rooms in here – except for the bathroom, I hope? But if the bathroom is not part of the 'living space' then what the hell is in there? Probably best not to know.

Our friend the Fulham Philanderer has buggered off to Spain with his wife. And for some reason which I can't fathom out, Angie seems to think this is a cheek. I would not make a very good mistress. It seems there's no logic involved. And I am quite a logical person when I'm not led astray by my pants... but maybe then that's Angie's problem? When your brain moves into your knicker region you really have not got a chance. But from a purely logical viewpoint, I can see no benefit in this for her, and plenty for Miles the Git. So why the hell does she do it? Has she got no self-respect? Angie is still striding about like an extremely well dressed Sergeant Major Well? Transvestite Sergeant Major, perhaps? No, no, they have female ones.

"I can't believe that he'd do this to me." Eh?

"How could he go away with that bitch?" What? His wife, do you mean? Hope it's a rhetorical question.

"He promised me he would tell her...about the divorce and all that." HORRORS! I don't want to know this?

"Of course, their marriage has been over for YEARS!" Oh, hells handbags! Please guys, hurry UP! This is too grisly for words.

"Well, there's no way I'm going to stand for this! No, Carly, no way at all!" Good. Fine. So dump him.

"So, Ange, what are you going to do?" Oops! She has stopped striding. I must have interrupted her flow.

She answers in a quavery voice.

"Well, I.... I don't...really know?" She collapses beside me onto her black leather couch and bursts into big scary tears. Oh, no! Oh, no! I'm sorry. I should have gone for the drink and left J. He's far more in touch with his feelings. Oh, God! Please hurry up. Whatever I do I must not slag him off. It will have a reverse psychological effect. Also, it's one thing to slag your own boyfriend off but someone else's? That wouldn't be right. So I just give Angie a cuddle and make some nothingy remarks.

"There, there, Angie. Don't worry. Everything will be fine, you'll see."

"Waaaah!" Oh dear, she has gone very snotty?

"I'll just get you some tissues. Hang on."

"Yoo-hoo! Girlies! We're ba-ck!" Oh, thank Christ! Please help me! Rush over to them and tactfully whisper,

"Erm, Angie's a little upset." Unfortunately, sometimes Jerry has all the tact of a large brick landing from a height on your head. He bellows encouragingly across the shed.

"Well, of course she is. That Miles is a shit."

"Waah! Waah! Waaah!" Siobhan shakes her head in amazement. Having met Giles in third year at school she has never been single her whole adult life and knows not what real trauma is.

"Angie, why in God's name don't you ditch him? He's clearly a bastard from hell!" Oh God, Siobhan, NOOO! Grab her sleeve and hiss right in her ear.

"*What* are you trying to do here? You can't just *say* things like that!" Siobhan turns in disbelief from Angie to me.

"Why ever not when it's true?"

"It's not! It's NOT! He *loves* me!" Angie is shrieking in tears on the floor. Oh no! She will make herself ill. We all bustle forward in medical mode and scoop her back onto the couch. Jerry assumes command,

"Quick! Give me 10mls of vodka here, please!" He's been watching those hospital programmes again. There's no way he's getting a scalpel. I'm sorry but I've just got to ask,

"So what's your prognosis, Dr Jerry? Do you think anything can be done?"

Siobhan is still waving her eyebrows as Jerry swings round to pronounce in his very best surgical manner,

"What this girl needs is a screw!"

…………...

Several screws and the odd peach schnapps later - we are all in a heap on the floor, talking absolute rubbish. Angie leans up on her elbows and shoogles her cocktail at me.

"Don't know why you're so smug, Carls. You've spent, what, three years with a toad." Oh, cheers mate. *Now* I feel better. But I cannot be bothered to retaliate. I am very happy lying on the rug with my feet propped up on the couch. Jerry is struggling to sit up. He never can resist a good fight.

"Well, at least *she* had the nonce to dump him at last!" Oh, thank-you, Jerry ...I think? Siobhan, totally bladdered, is sleeping curled up in a ball. Angie is making a foolhardy attempt to stand up and go to the loo, flinging insults over her shoulder as she clatters back onto the floor.

"There's none of you haven't been out with geeks, and *you*, Jerry, you are the worst." Jerry spins round in the Lotus position and mouths across at me,

"ME?"

Angie clambers up, holding onto the back of the couch and fumbles off towards the bathroom.

"Yes, YOU! Don't think I can't see you. You've been out with at least half of W.1. [this is a London district – not a band]. J. gasps in impotent indignance. I just lie and snigger on the floor. Angie's voice floats through from the 'non-living' bathroom.

"Remember that total weirdo last year? *What* was his name again – Klaus?" Snigger even louder. Oh I'd forgotten about him, Klaus from darkest Hamburg, the German accountant from hell. Jerry thought that he was God in a designer suit, till his custard fetish was revealed. Jerry is now squealing.

"Oh! That's hardly fair! He looked, like, perfectly normal. How the hell was I supposed to know?" He is only making it more funny. I'm getting a stitch in my side. Roll over to sit up and ask him.

"And who was after the custard guy?" He's tries to fob me off.

"Well, I *really* can't remember."

"Oh, Jerry! I think that you can. Remember the country and western dude? And you bought all the matching gear? Remember your little silver spurs?" Fall back down onto the floor helpless with mirth and alcohol. Jerry is far from amused. He is doing a little hen's bum with his mouth. Angie collapses beside us.

"Alright, what's so funny?"

"Jerry! In his Stetson and wee pointy boots." Angie guffaws and Jerry crawls off in a huff.

"You're just a couple of bitches! I hope that your hair all falls out!" He crawls off to sulk by the hi-fi and is rifles through some C.D.s Why do men like to rifle so much? Is it something to do with their genes? He is muttering away to himself. Oh! Now I feel a bit bad.

"Oh, come on, Jerry. We're sorry. You know we're only fooling around." J. slots in a random dance C.D. and shoogles about on the floor [far safer than messing with gravity now]. He waves a tipsy finger in the air,

"Well, let's face it, darlings, we've all been out with some quite dubious men." Think about this for a moment. No, not all of us have

"J. you're forgetting Siobhan. There's nothing strange about Giles?" J. does a dance with his eyebrows,

"He's not a man. He's a cardigan. I don't think, Carly, that counts." *Fair enough.* Angie is studying the sleeping Siobhan with a speculative drunken-bum eye.

"D'you think that they actually *have* sex?" WHAT? Jerry and I are aghast. Ooh, yuck! I don't want to think about this. But unfortunately Angie does. She has screwed up her eyes to consider the logistics.

"D'you think he takes his cardigan off or does he just, like, slowly unravel the wool?" *Aaargh!* J. has covered his face with his hands. [won't help you– the thought's inside your head]... He is squeaking at Angie in horror.

"Oh, Angie, stop it! That's YUCK!" I am suddenly distracted by a random depressing thought appearing like a light bulb in my head.

"So does this mean, and please tell me it doesn't, that there are only just two types of men?" I've got their full attention now. They both have 'Eh?' faces on. Jerry, intrigued,

"Why Carly, what do you mean?"

"Well, it seems in my experience..."

"And you've certainly done the research." Angie smacks him on my behalf.

"Shut up. I want to hear this."

"....that guys fall into two quite distinctive groups – profoundly shaggable bastards or the knitting patterns from hell? Please tell me that there is a third group and I've just been unlucky so far?" Jerry just shakes his head sadly.

"Erm...I don't think that I can...What do you think, Angie?" Angie is racking her brain.

"No, I would say that covers it. You're the Isaac Newton of sex. And all along it was obvious. So, now what the hell do we do?" I don't know. I don't want either of those? Jerry has had an idea.

"We could pop along to the Ann Summers shop. There must be something in there!" Oh, yuck! No. That is just horrid!

"I don't want a big plastic penis, thanks. Or one of those rubber doll things." Angie laughs.

"Carly, I *think* they're for men." Are they? So, then, isn't there both? How very sexist! Jerry is waving a C.D. at me. You can just about see his brain tick,

"You know though, you might have something there, babes – male rubber dolls might be good. It'd be just like using a condom...." Aaarrrgh!

"....and you could get them in all different characters, like those tiny little action man dolls of pop stars and stuff only ....*bigger!*" His eyes glaze over at that. Angie is getting the idea now.

"Oh, yeah. You could have all different categories – the slutty action man range, ..with the faces of famous singers or, or....?"

"Ac-tors!...Oops! sorry Carls – I forgot!" Hit him with reachable cushion.

"You are both truly disgusting! Those little dolls are for kids? Besides, they're like little voodoo thingies – creepy." Jerry smiles up from his spot in the corner in a patronising sort of a way.

"But Carly, admit it. You know it's true. All the guys we fancy are weird!" Angie waves a heart-felt tumbler.

"Or *mean*! What's the meanest thing Jake ever did?" Pause for a moment to think.

"Well, he did once ask me how much toilet roll I used because he thought it was costing too much." Both friends fall back in hissing in horror. Angie recovers first,

"Fuck me! Has he never had a period?"

Jerry frowns,

"Invasion of privacy. Yes, that's quite a serious crime. What about you, Ange? What's the worst thing Miles has ever done? Apart from the wife thing, of course."

"We-ll, once I went to eat a chocolate biscuit and he said that it would make me fat." Eek! Instant empathy!

"What a pig!" Jerry sighs at the wrongs of the world,

"Yes, that's clearly a hanging offence."

Angie snorts,

"Yes, but not by his neck!" I'm getting all over excited now.

"Right, Jerry what about you? And the bondage thing doesn't count. The category's mental cruelty. What's the worst thing that's happened to you?" He ponders on this for a moment.

"Now, let's see, who's the meanest boyfriend I've had? Oh, I know! Norman!" *Norman? Norman Normal?*

"Remember when I lived with him?"

"Uh huh? But he was a total mouse, with sensible glasses and stuff?"

Angie guffaws,

"Norman? What the hell did *he* do?" We are both completely intrigued.

"Well, you know how I love the odd coffee?"

"Uh huh." Jerry has caffeine for blood.

"Well, when I was filling the kettle Norman would come up and snoop to check how much water I'd put in." No. You have got me there?

"So he has a kettle fetish. That's weird but *how* is it mean? "

"Car-lee! I'm *getting* to that!"

"Oh! Sorry!" Resumes his story-telling stance.

"We-ll, *Norman* said that if you put too much water in the kettle, like more than enough for one cup, there's a little wheel in the electrical cupboard…" Is there?

Angie and I are non-plussed.

"..and it makes it spin round really fast." No, I just have to ask.

"How could he possibly know that? I mean, really, how could you accidentally find that out? You'd have to be in two places at once?" Angie is starting to snigger,

"Was he sitting in the closet with a torch? Just keeping an eye on his wheel?"

"Well, anyway, *Norman said* that if the little wheel thing goes faster, it costs about eight zillion quid!" Both clap and cheer at this finale.

"Oh Jerry! You win!" Who would have thought it of that mousy Norman?

Angie snorts,

"Norman the Geek! The meanest bastard in town. They do say, y'know Jerry, that the quiet ones are the worst." All fall about squealing. Jerry is pleased to have won.

"Do I get a prize or something?"

Sit up,

"Well, what would you like? A year's supply of valium, perhaps? Oh, no, sorry. That would be way too expensive."

We have all cheered up quite a lot now so we have another drink. Siobhan has started snoring. Jerry gives her a benign sort of look.

"You know girlies, I don't think I'd like to be Siobhan." Glance up from my head on his shoulder position.

"Why? Don't you approve of her dress sense? Can't you imagine yourself in a suit?" Shakes his hand drunkenly in her general direction.

"God no! I can't really. But no, Carls it just isn't that. I mean, you'd have to sleep with Giles, the most boring git on the planet? How awful. It doesn't bear thinking about." I have to agree on that point. Ange has stopped listening. She is getting far too drunk. I think we should put her to bed and perhaps we should take Siobhan home. She'll be drunk enough now to shag cardigan-man. J., obviously thinking along the same lines, nods at Angie and we both start to crawl across the floor. I shall try really hard not to drop her on her head. Jerry frowns at me thoughtfully,

"So Carly, are you happy? You know, being single and all?"

"Yes, J. I really, really am. It just feels kind of peaceful, like I've turned back into myself. I'm quite happy with my painting and I've got you guys. Why would I want to mess everything up?" Jerry gives me deep searching glance. I AM happy! I'm very happy. No beer, no mess, no horrible vibes. I don't want to fight anymore. Why, my home is completely transformed. I can even see my own floor. I know that Jerry means well, but I wish he'd stop thinking so much

CHAPTER TWELVE
Introducing Shrimpton-Boswick...

A very portentous occasion – I'm meeting with Edgar Shrimpton-Boswick, potential purveyor of money and dreams. I have decided to get a taxi to his gallery, The Eglinton Hall, as I do not want to be rained on and have all of my make-up removed. The bedraggled rat look may well be 'arty' but it is not what I'm aiming for today.

Alight from the exorbitant taxi in front of ... The Coliseum apparently? I had no idea of its scale. Of course, I've seen it on television but it was much smaller on the screen. If I had a huge HD widescreen then I might have been better prepared. Swallow my rising trepidation I ascend the enormous stone steps to the ancient double doors. The façade has lots of columns and statues and so on. I go in quickly before I can bottle out of this. The huge marble floored entrance hall echoes when you walk- very impressive. Wonder where Leslie Phillips will be? I shall just ask someone. That big snooty chap there will do. Approach a discreetly expensive grey suit lurking in the corner, in my best elegant arty-type walk.

"Excuse me, Could you possibly help me? I'm looking for Mr Shrimpton-Boswick, please?" If this is a wind-up I'll die, but not before Jerry does.

But no, Shrimpton-Boswick is a real person. I find myself ushered up to his office by the snooty man. But bizarrely enough, he does look a lot like a young Leslie Phillips.

"Ay –he-ello theyah, Cahlee, my deah. Dooo come in. Ay've been waiting for you." He grasps my hands in a clammy grip and leers down into my face. Ooh-er?

"Hello, Mr,..er Shrimpton-Boswick."

"Oh, no, do call me Edgah!" Ed-gah? He is waving a damp mitt at the tall guy.

"Niles! Fetch the lady a chair." I am *not* going to laugh at his accent. There is squillions of money at stake.

"My deah, you look eb-solyutely charming. What a de-lightful little ensemble that is. Now, you must let me give you the full guided tour. I can't wait to get you downstairs." ??? I can assure you right now, Leslie, that you won't be giving me anything else – upstairs, downstairs or anywhere else! Not even in the big entrance. So don't even dare go there. Rise from my chair with my best fake smile and skirt speedily round his outstretched hand en route to the door.

"Oh yes, Edgar, that would be lovely." I'll just keep out of reach of his hands.

"Cahlee, would you care to walk this way?" Oh, great, I'm with cliché man.

Allow myself to be escorted by the highly attentive Edgar around cavernous Gallery 2, my potential location for wealth, fame... and more wealth, hopefully. So, is this how Mick felt when checking out the Sistine ceiling? Probably. If I want to fill just one of these walls I'll be painting for twenty years at least.

....

Home at last and completely traumatised. I have accepted an impossible Rumplestiltskin-like task whilst temporarily out of my mind. I cannot believe that I agreed to do this exhibition. It will wipe out all other areas of my life... But perhaps though that is a good thing just now. And it is a fantastic opportunity after all. Besides, if I am totally absorbed in my work then I won't have time to get into more trouble.

....

Later on - I am painting in a Trojanesque mode with my deadline looming over my head like some artistic sword of Damocles. I may well be cut off in my prime. Jerry has come round to sulk in my house because I am too busy to come out to due to this unexpected Herculean task. He really is being a pain. It's amazing how hard it is to concentrate with a very bored friend in your house. He keeps peeking round the door frame whining like a bored and demanding child.

"Aren't you nearly finished yet, Carls?"

"No, I am not." I can hear him sighing behind me in melodramatic, hard-done-to way. He weasels in furtively and flumps over the spare bed, all the better to distract me presumably.

"Oh, Carlee! I am so bored." Answer over my shoulder. Have just got to finish this bit.

"Why? Is there nothing on telly?"

"Nooo. It's just a lot of crap."

"Look Jerry, you're my best friend in the world and I love you lots."

"Oh, Carly. That's sooo sweet."

"But I am in the process of becoming a famous artist here and you are dribbling on my parade. So please, please just go AWAY!"

"Ooooh! Oh, you total BITCH! Well, I know when I'm not wanted." J. flounces off through to the lounge. Turn back to my painting breathing heavily with sudden friend-induced stress. Oh, no! I don't believe it? My concentration has gone.

Fling down my brush in disgust. The muse has apparently buggered right off the minute I turned my back. Damn! Damn! Knickers! I'm never going to get this done. Slouch through to the bathroom to clean myself up. I can see Jerry sitting on my bedroom floor wearing his prune-raisin face. He seems to be rummaging through some old photographs that I found after Jake had gone. Amazing what was under all of his junk. Lord Lucan could have been here for years. I feel quite bad about being snippy to J. He really does look quite upset. Stick my head round the door into bedroom.

"Oh Jerry, you know I didn't mean it. I hate it when you sulk." Turns a disdainful sneer towards me.

"Oooh! We're talking now, are we? Oh, I'm sooo honoured!" Fling a handy slipper at his head and trundle off through to get washed. I can hear him trundling after me pretending that he doesn't care.

"So, has the muse left you then, darling?"

"Yes, thank-you, J. It has now. It has buggered right off out of here and has probably gone to the pub." He's skulking about at the bathroom door with a guilty look on his face.

"Oops. Like, um, sorry. Was it, you know, all my fault?" He looks stricken.

"Jerry, it doesn't matter. Do you want to go out?" His weaselly face lights up.

"Ooh, God yes. "

"Fine. Just let me have a bath and I'll be with you in a bit. You can think about what you want to do; club, pub, cinema or show? I'll be back in a jiffy." Oh! He's already gone? He has scuttled off to look for the listings. Now, do I need bubble bath or pure turps?

…………..

In the bath and nearly sleeping with suds right up to my eyes,

"BANG! BANG! BANG! BANG!" It's J. on the bathroom door.

"Carlee! Angie's on the phone."

"O.K. – I'll be right out." Snuggle up in a blanket-sized towel and drip through hall to the lounge.

"Hi Angie. How do you feel today?" She must be in hangover city by now.

"Oh, you know, much better Carls. The pulsating headache and jelly insides have distracted me from Miles." I imagine that both have quite a similar effect.

"Oh good. I'm pleased to hear it. Lesser of two evils I'd say."

"Anyway, that's not why I'm phoning." Uh-oh! So what does she want?

"You remember the other Saturday when we went to the Globe Awards?"

I'm hardly likely to forget it. It is etched on tablets of stone.

"Uh-huh, What about it?" Is she *still* in the huff because I left her and kind of forgot to come back?

"Do you remember Nigel McFarlane? He was sitting with us at the meal." Is anyone really called Nigel?

"No not really. Why? Which one was he?"

"For God's sake, Carly! The tall, blonde, fit-looking one." Oh. One of the nondescript guys.

"Umm?"

"Well, anyway, Nigel was asking me where that charming eccentric artist girl went." What? Eccentric? CHARMING?

"The ruddy cheeky toad!"

"I think he meant it as a compliment, Carls. He wanted to know where you'd gone."

"Look Ange, he really does not want to know that, and quite frankly neither do I. What's it to him where I went anyway? Who is he– the fast exit police?" I can hear Angie losing her patience. She has gone up by an octave or two.

"Carly, he wanted your phone number to ask you out to dinner. I said that I'd give you a call." Eek! No *way!*

"Ange I'm really not interested..."

"But Carly, he is *loaded.* And let me tell you, he is going places career-wise... Half the women here would kill to get his number... You'd never have to work again. Besides, he's a really nice guy, not the least bit up himself... and even *you* must admit, he's pretty damn hot ... "

"Angie, just stop, please! How can I put this to you clearly, in terms that you might understand? At this precise moment in time I don't even want to see anyone who's got a penis, never mind go out to dinner with a man who so transparently is one." Oh! Forgot! Turn my head.

"Sorry Jerry!" Jerry starts twitching on couch and addressing himself to the coffee table in simulated offence.

"Did she just call me a penis? Why, yes, I believe that she did!"

Sigh heavily and turn my attention back to the phone.

"Ange, I know that you're only trying to help, but if you really want to do that just stop trying to pimp me to every stiff in a suit that you happen to meet. If I ever get that desperate I will go to the Ann Summers shop! O.K.? Comprendez? GOOD!" Slam the receiver down into the little receiver hole. J. raises his eyebrows a notch. Eccentric? Charming? PAH! Stomp, stomp-stompitty-STOMP!

"Getting good at the stomping Carly."

"Shut UP!" And his face, it was shut.

. . . .

I am dressed and putting on make-up as J. shuffles back into my room. I can see him in the mirror as he flops down onto my bed.

"You know, I've been thinking Carly."

"Oh, no! You don't want to do that."

"The girls and I have been talking." So what's new? I am not impressed.

"It's not just that Nigel chappie, you know. There's lots of others as well." What? You mean, lots of Nigels? Put a finishing touch of lip gloss on.

"Other whats Jerry? Geeks? Are you trying to frighten me? Are they all swarming outside the door?" See Jerry point at my back in the mirror. His other hand is under his head.

"Carly I'm being serious here. For God's sake pay attention! Haven't you got the slightest idea how many guys are besotted with you?" Oh yeah? That's very funny? Wave a derisory hand in the air.

"I they could just form an disorderly queue in the hall you can tell them that I'll be right out." Jerry sits up in frustration.

"Now listen to your Uncle Jerry you ridiculous little Celt. You can't leave the poor buggers dangling like that. And anyway, life isn't supposed to be all work, work, work. Would it really be so bad to have some nice guy take you out to dinner, make a fuss of you, - maybe you might even enjoy yourself... There are *loads* of decent men in London, for God's sake at least try a few." He is unbelievable. Make-up finished. Turn round to answer,

"They're men Jerry, not pick and mix. You can't just have a quick nibble then decide to put them all back." J. gives up on being my Agony Uncle and does his innuendo sneer.

"Oh, but Carly you could. You could have something sweet and creamy perhaps, or, oh God no! A hard one. Oh, Har! Haar! Haar!"

"Jerry! For God's sake *grow up!*"

…………..

Later - At a snazzy local wine bar - Oh yes, this is the life! We have met with Siobhan for a gossip as we haven't seen her for a whole day. We have covered the usual subjects so far – work, men, money, men and sex….with occasional inserts of make-up and clothes and other fascinating, high-brow-type stuff. Jerry is giving Siobhan the low-down on the fact that I didn't want Nigel- the-suit.

"…And then she just called me a penis."

"Jerry! I didn't say that! I only meant that you'd got one. I'd made a penis-offending remark." Siobhan screws up her face in concentration.

"But why Carly? What's wrong with this one? Was he rich, sexy, famous or successful? Or something else equally repellent?"

"No, I just didn't like him, that's all. Why do I have to see anyone?" Jerry puts an avuncular arm round my shoulders,

"You don't have to. It's not like compulsory. It's just a bit strange that you don't seem to want to, that's all. Don't you want to have a baby?"

"Well, Jerry that's a very kind offer. But a Babycham will be fine."

"Oh, ho-ho-ho Miss Smarty." He weasels off up to the bar. Siobhan leans forward and pats my hand in a bereavement counsellor way. Eh?

"Carly, you don't have to pretend with us you know. We know that you're just in denial..." I AM NOT!

"And we know that Fat-Boy, erm Jake, really upset you and all….but you can't cut your nose off for spite."

"If that's a Van Gogh parallel thing I believe that it was his ear. And then where would I put my earrings?" Siobhan smiles in a highly irritating humour-her sort of way. I really *do* want to strike you Siobhan! Oh good! Jerry is back.

"There we go now, girlies – comfortable screws all round." Jerry has the biggest cocktails in the world, with gi-normous paper umbrellas and fruit and streamers and stuff. Take a huge gulp.

"Oh my God! That is heaven." All take a synchronised slurp.

Shortly - It's apparently quite impossible to drink these and talk any sense. I thought we were talking about literature but J. has somehow moved onto children's books. He is expounding some ridiculous theory to Siobhan?

"What Carly here needs is a prince. Eh? Vision of a small purple pop star person. No! No! NO! Surely not?

"She's been kissing all of these toads for years." Double eh?? Siobhan is nodding wisely so what he just said must make sense?

"Excuse me, who is it that I need?" Jerry shakes his head in amazement.

"Du-uh   ? Carly. Prince C."

"Prince Charles? Eh? Besides, he's married to Camilla?" Siobhan is doing that hand-patting thing? Please do *not* patronise me.

"No Carly, he meant Prince Charming, like in the fairy tale?" Oh! But he isn't real? Is he? Jerry,

"Yes, yes, that's the right chap. Mythical character of some notoriety, wealthy, goes out with lots of women. Is this sounding familiar at all?" Um, no, no, that's not right?

" Prince Charming didn't go out with lots of women J.?"

"Oh, but Carly he did though! The dirty fucker! Cinderella, Sleeping Beauty, Snow White – or *not* so snow white once he'd paid her a call." Nods knowingly and sucks his face in.

"No wonder he needed a horse to get about. I bet *sometimes* he could hardly even walk."

"It wasn't the same guy J. It was a different prince in every story."

"Oh no! That's what he'd like you to think."

The voice of reason. – Siobhan.

"Excuse-me, you two. He isn't real."

Jerry – quite the opposite voice.

"But Siobhan darling, Carly's prince is real! Rich, sexy… and interested. I'm just trying to make her see sense."

"But I don't want someone who goes out with other women. Who do you think I am? Angie?"

"I didn't mean *he* did Carly, sweetheart. I was kidding about the prince."

"Oh, but *he* does! *You* told me, remember?" Jerry does his hen's bum mouth.

"I didn't tell you any such thing. I just said that it was in the press. That isn't the same thing at all. Anyway, you were already off him when I told you that so you can't put the blame onto me." No, I don't believe that I can so I shall just have to sulk. Didn't want a prince anyway. They *will* always wear those big tights.

CHAPTER THIRTEEN
More Bad Advice & Lucky Pants

I am having a break and seeing a film with Angie tonight. It's a very long walk to the cinema but Angie wants to lose weight so, hey, why not? It's a lovely night for a stroll. Angie opens the batting,

"So Carls, where's Jerry tonight?"

"Oh, he's out with some guy called Renaldo."

"What? Like the footballer guy?"

"I would imagine that's quite unlikely, Ange. I think he's somebody from work." J. allegedly works for the Tourist Board. He bumps into lots of weird folk – does wonders for international relations, but not quite in the way that he ought. He would like to be a full time philosopher/ poet. But until his gems of prose make some dosh the tourist board it is.

"Oh! Some greasy spic then, huh?" You are so un-P.C.?

"Angie! You can't say things like that." That's not the image you present on the box. Good thing that there are no raincoats in here. Journos always wear shabby old macs – and sleep in the park on a bench. Or maybe that's dossers and perverts? Well, it's something of that dubious ilk. Maybe the coat is regulation undercover wear? Their Dictaphone is in the brown paper bag. A brilliant idea really. Who'd want to check it to see?

I've just noticed that Angie is walking all funny? And it's not just her strange shoes? She's doing a bum-wiggle-waggling thing, as if she has peed in her pants?

"Erm, Angie, why are you walking like that?" She turns round with a horrified glare. Oops! Have I put my foot in my mouth?

"I didn't realise that I was!" *Oh dear! Oh dear!*

"Sorree!" Ange looks furtively round just to check – yes, nobody near. ???

"I'm wearing a size too small knickers. They're cutting my body in half."

Erm, why?"

"Well, you know how I've been on this diet?"

"What for? You are a twig?"

"Miles thought I could lose half a stone." If anybody said that to me they'd be losing both of their stones.

"Um, really? So what's with the far too small pants? Are they constricting your body to squeeze out the fat? Like in a fast-weight-loss wrap?" Oh dear, I can see her considering that. No, please Angie, don't do it.

"No. Carly, do they actually work?"

"I've never been sad enough to try one. Anyway, you're NOT FAT! Miles is talking out of his hat." Or, as usual, his butt! She screws up her face in an unconvinced look.

"So Angie, what do they do?"

"What?"

"You know, your knickers?"

"Oh, I just thought that they might help my willpower." What? Like some kind of diet mascot? Lucky knickers? Ye Gods!

"How?"

"I thought they might encourage me to fit into them. You know, the discomfort might help me to get into the right mental state." Oh no comment!

"Angie, before you go through with this ridiculous, masochistic plan, there really is something you ought to be told in advance." She's looking really worried now. And has every reason to be.

"If you go on a diet your boobs are the first thing to go. Not your stomach and certainly not your bum. You will start off with Galia melons and end up with boobs like fried eggs."

"Aaargh! Aaargh! Oh CARLY!"

"I'm sorry Ange, but it's true. And it may well affect your balance as well. Your centre of gravity will be lower down." I feel quite guilty. She looks thunder-struck. But she really had to be told. Speak to me Angie. Oh dear! She must be in shock.

"Angie, is he actually worth all the trauma you put yourself through? He's always trying to mess with your head. The guy is an utter control freak." And don't shake your head in that way.

"He isn't, Carly. He's trying to help. He just does it for my own good." Uh-huh? Oh, Really? Cobblers!

"No, Ange, he doesn't. He's tripping on power again. Just, you know, ignore him." Hopefully he'll go away. Oh, good, we are at the cinema at last. That's quite enough Miles talk for one day. He's doing my blood pressure harm.

Trail into the foyer and start stocking up with sweets and stuff till I notice the look on her face.

"What? What now, already?"

"That's like, a zillion calories, Carls. You'll be at the gym for years." No, I won't. I'm not a sad poser.

"Oh, it's all right Angie, don't worry. I've already burned them all off in advance. I've O.D.'d on trauma and sex." And most of the trauma wasn't mine?

"Carly! Someone will hear you!"

"Oh, will they really?" Who cares?

....

Inside – seated in the dark bit. I am trapped in a definitive hell – the film trailer twilight zone. And I am totally sweetie-less. Ange insisted that I put them all back? This is what the damned sweeties were for! My brain will just curl up and die! Slouch down in our seats to wait till the tedium passes. Decide I will just shut my eyes... but Angie has gone into snoopy-snoop mode.

"Siobhan told me who you slept with last week. –We all think you're crazy, you know." Oh, really? Thank-you for sharing that fact. Open one eye to retaliate. She's giving me a beady look now.

"I didn't sleep with him on purpose you know. I just had a little mishap." Don't wave your eyebrows at me!

"Carly, a mishap is when you break a fingernail." Attempt to shrug in my seat. I am not listening to you. You are just a repeat of Siobhan. Leave me alone. I am happy.

"Didn't you even take his phone number?"

"Why? Did you want it? Go on Angie, I dare you. Go round there and network his pants." Oh God! She is so funny. Must be tedious to be on the make.

"But why Carly? What's wrong with you? He's rich sexy and…"

"Going out with someone else…." Oops. Tactless. Forgot about Miles.

"…somebody else rich and famous, as is the natural order of things. So please just get off of my case. Incidentally, I notice that in your priorities there, the first thing you went for was rich?"

"Well, a girl's gotta live." Turn round in my seat to explain.

"Have you seen Fatal Attraction, Angie?"

"Ye-es. But he's not Michael Douglas?"

"No, but it's just the same thing. A guy like that must have dozens of crazy fans, all waiting behind you to stab you and stick your rabbit in a pan."

"Carly you haven't got a rabbit?" I think she is missing my point.

"And he's absolutely bloody gorgeous. You're mad as a milliner, girl. But at least *you're* attractive, Carly." *Oh yeah? Oh yeah, RIGHT!*

"I attract horrible men and trouble? Oh, hell yes, I'm over the moon. And you're *not* unattractive. You're just having an affair with a slug. For God's sake get your facts straight. Now shut up. The film's going to start."

A very sexy ac-tor appears onscreen – my sole reason for coming to the film. I am not sexist at all. Eek! He is *lovely!* And I haven't got my usual candy stick. You can buy these highly amusing sticks at all decent cinemas… and probably other places as well. They are slightly smaller than a ruler in length and usually bright green or pink. Pink is my particular favourite. It is a brilliant multi-purpose entertainment device. You can play with it during boring trailers – like conducting an imaginary orchestra and stuff. It is very good for pointing at annoying people [like Angie] during heated debates. But best of all is very, VERY good for biting at a climax with big sexy men [the climax in a film, obviously. It would not be a seductive or appropriate thing to do with a big sexy man at other times.]. Well, here is just such a moment... And here am I totally stick-less? *How* am I supposed not to scream without it? Quite impossible, I'm afraid. Aaaaarrrgghh!

CHAPTER FOURTEEN
Culture Vultures

7.20p.m. - home alone, but not for long. I am about to experience something that I never in my wildest dreamt I'd want to do. Tonight, in the absence of a more suitably well-versed poetry companion, Jerry is taking me [me?] to a poetry evening at a trendy local café bar. Apparently lots of would-be poetry buffs stand up in the middle of the café and spout their erstwhile gems to the general café-going public. Frankly, poetry does not light my candle. In fact I am struggling to think of something I'd less rather do. But Jerry is my friend and it would be churlish to refuse. Maybe it'll be a laugh?

The great advantage of my own occupation is that it is very rare for anyone to watch you at work. Well, except for whoever you're painting of course, but they can't actually see what you're doing till you have finished so that doesn't really count, does it? Standing up in a public venue and intentionally drawing mass attention to yourself by proclaiming pearls of homespun verse sounds to me like a fate worse than snogging Shrimpton-Boswick. I am personally an extremely private person and the very idea of announcing your innermost thoughts from a podium whilst adopting a creatively meaningful pose fills me with a chill of horrified fear coupled with the odd churn of secondary nausea. And J. does this for amusement? His own amusement? He must be out of his tiny little tree? But oh yeah, we knew that already - silly me.

A deafening "Paarrrp!" from far below announces J.'s arrival in Miss Daisy. Pick up my bag and click off downstairs in my new kitten-heeled boots. Unsure of what one ought to wear to a poetry evening I have opted for the dreamy gypsy-style look - floaty skirt and a ruffled chiffon top. The boots aren't perfectly in keeping with the overall look but they were the only cream coloured footwear I possessed. No-one will notice them from under my ankle-length skirt anyway.

Clamber gracelessly into Miss Daisy, rumpling yards of skirt up to fit into the tiny passenger seat space without shutting my outfit in the car door. And also, of course, so that the nice new material doesn't catch on anything - sticky out bits of metal or plastic or stuff - quite probable in this car. Jerry casts an approving eye over my ensemble as he drives off with a screech of burning rubber. I do wish that he'd look at the road.

"Oh, very nice Carls. Very Cadbury's flake." Raise a facetious eyebrow. He's wearing a huge flouncy white shirt with a big bow at the neck a la Shelley, Byron or somebody's gran.

"There's only one flake in this car, J."

"Ooh! Mi-ow! She looks so demure. And yet she's a total bitch. You're supposed to be supporting my morals, not crushing them." Snort derisively,

"What morals? " He shakes his highly gelled artistic head,

"Carly! How many times? Which morals! Not what, which." Laugh,

"Aha! So you admit it then, do you? You couldn't support them with scaffolding."

"God, you are such a philistine. *Why* did I bring you?"

"Dunno. You were feeling particularly sadistic? Anyway, are you all ready for your big debut? Have you got your vocal chords honed?"

"Yeah, yeah. Just let me at that audience. The Café Luca doesn't know what it's in for tonight."

"What're you going to do? 'Liberator'? 'Mr Blue'? 'Sock It To Me Socrates'?"

"Oh no, no, no Carls. I've written a new piece. Just you wait. It'll totally blow them away." Uh-oh? That sounds a little worrying? Jerry's gems can be just a tad controversial. Like the time we went to a high society dinner party courtesy of Angie's work connections and J.

chose to regale the blue-blooded week-end fox murderers with 'Suffer The Little Creatures' - An Ode To Animal Rights.

"Jerry, it's not going to be anything too provocative, is it? I really don't want to end up in either casualty or the local nick if that's quite O.K. with you?"

"What? No! Well? Look you'll just have to wait and see. Like the rest of my adoring public." Oh God! Now I really am worried. Please Jerry, not 'Bend The Rules'?

"Ah here we are Carls. Can you see a parking space?"

"Uh? Nope. You'll have to go round the block."

"Don't be silly, this'll do fine."

"Erm, Jerry, I don't really think … oh!" J. swooshes Miss Daisy to a badly parked standstill in a miniscule half-space, one front wheel on the pavement, half her back bumper sticking out into the road. Dear God! We'll be clamped for sure.

"Jerry! You can't leave her like this? We'll have to find a proper space." He waves a dismissive frilly sleeve at me,

"Oh don't fuss so. It'll be fine. We won't be that long. Just an hour or so."

"Well, out of your wallet be it J. Don't come crying to me when you're destitute."

Hustle inside. The café is lovely - pale duck-egg blue rag-rolled walls, tasteful round marble topped tables and spindly wrought iron chairs - very continental. Most of the chairs have bums on them already, unfortunately. Or fortunately if you're a particularly exhibitionist poet and like lots of people staring at you. J. does.

"Ooh Carly, what a turnout! Isn't it fab?"

"Brilliant. Let's find a seat."

"O.K. - I need to prepare." Settle down at an inconspicuous corner table and order a couple of cappuccino's while we wait. We are a little bit early - on purpose, may I add. J. wanted to absorb the atmosphere of the place or some such twaddle. Oh well, as long as he's happy - which he certainly seems to be. He is rifling ostentatiously through some of his poems which are spread all over the tabletop and he keeps looking round furtively to see if the punters are impressed by his poetic celebrity status. Nobody is paying the slightest bit of attention, except a thin chap conservatively dressed in a blue round necked jumper and neat beige cords. He looks like someone has ironed him specially for the occasion. I can never understand such innate tidiness, being myself of quite the opposite persuasion - Scruffs R Us. Mr Tidy smiles nervously across at us from his perch on a high stool at the bar. Jerry doesn't notice. He's busily scanning the rest of the room [the table people] and having a last-minute bout of pre-poem nerves.

"Oh Carly, what if they don't like it? I'll be booed off the stage. They might even fling things at me?" Try for reasonable and reassuring,

"No they won't. One, there is no stage and two, it's £2.50 for a muffin in here. It'd cost a fortune to bombard anyone. Besides, of course they'll like it. I admire anyone who's got the nerve to speak in public. I couldn't."

"But you speak in public all the time? You're doing it now?"

"No J. In front of an audience."

"Oh right. Yes, well, it is a bit scary. But these ones look quite civilised I suppose." Indicates the cafe-goers with a nervous nod of his hair gel. They do actually look like quite a well-mannered bunch. But then, this is an upmarket West End café bar, not The Red Lion in Basingstoke or some such place. The crowd looks too well-bred to be abusive - I hope. No, it'll be fine. The compeer for the evening, a dapper little grey haired man in a suit that squeals Saville Row, steps up to the little space in front of the bar left empty to accommodate the 'acts'.

"Good evening ladies and gentlemen. Welcome to Café Luca's first poetry evening. I'm happy to announce that tonight we have five poets who have most kindly agreed to share their work with us." He politely indicates each poet at their various seats with an understated wave of one expensively-clad arm.

"Miss Cynthia Crawford." Small burst of applause,

"Mr Clive Hanson." More clapping,

"Mr Gerald P. Green." Jerry beams and nods at his appreciative public.

"Mrs Angela McPhee and Mr Robert Davies. Ladies and gentlemen, I give you.... The poets!" A huge round of enthusiastic clapping ensues. And nobody's even done anything yet? I think we'll be safe enough here. The compeer consults a small official looking piece of paper he's holding,

"Now first up I believe we have.... Mr Clive Hanson." A pompous-looking fat bloke in a bright purple silk shirt and matching cravat squeezes his way forward. He adopts an impressively operatic stance, one pudgy hand outstretched towards the ceiling, the other hanging limply at his side. Taking a massive breath he shuts his eyes. The tension builds. Suddenly he's off - a deep booming baritone tirade,

"An Ode To Lucinda.' He intones sorrowfully,

"Lucinda, how could you leave me thus?

You have wrenched my world apart,

Lucinda, Lucinda, Lucinda,

I see you still in my mind's eye,

Yea, tho' time has run out for us,

Your emerald eyes, your tender heart,

Your soft silky touch Lucinda,

In my memory shall not die."

More in this vein for oh? - ten minutes which feels more like two hours. Poetry is **so** not my bag. Here is this poor bereaved man pouring out his heart-felt anguish over the death of the love of his life and what do I feel? - empathy, sympathy, anything? Um, no. I just want it to be over - preferably this year. Jerry however is sitting, eyes screwed up, brow wrinkled in wrapt attention. Whisper discreetly in his ear,

"J, are you sure that's poetry? I've never heard a poem like that?"

"Well, it's not in any standard format Carls - most unorthodox. But I think it works as an artistic vehicle, don't you?"

"Erm, oh yes, very, uh? - touching."

Finally, looking as breathless as if he'd run the London Marathon, Clive snaps his eyes open and stares belligerently around at the dumbstruck audience. Struck by the depth of his bereavement they burst into spontaneous applause, some older ladies dabbing a lace edged hanky to their eyes. The poet bows deeply but doesn't smile.

"Ah, the poor man," They murmur. The compeer reappears from the sidelines clapping politely,

"Clive Hanson ladies and gentlemen. Thank you Clive. I think you'll all agree that was a truly wonderful piece. Clive Hanson. " Clive stomps off back to his seat.

"And now…." Checks his list once more,

"Miss Cynthia Crawford…" A super-skinny hippy chick, tie-dyed and heavily beaded makes her way languidly up to the front. The compeer smiles politely as she pulls out a crumpled scrap of paper from the ripped pocket of her unfeasibly flared jeans.

"And what will you be reciting for us this evening Miss Crawford?" Miss Crawford tosses him a supremely laid-back look,

"It's called 'When?'"

"Oh? Jolly good. Do carry on. Ladies and gentleman, Cynthia Crawford," Clap, clap, clap…. Running a beringed hand through her heavy mop of mousy curls she begins. She sounds half stoned and wholly petulant,

"When?

When? - when will it end?

The lies, the soul-destroying mediocrity?

This banal charade of democracy?

When will the truth ever out?

When? - when will we stand tall?

Tall in the sunshine of freedom?

Free at last from their heinous scheming?

When shall we victorious shout?

When? - when will we ask ourselves?

Whom amongst us has the bravery,

To spare us from political slavery?

Till then we must ask ourselves…. *When?*

The conservative little compeer's smile is becoming more fixed by the minute. He claps his way up beside her,

"Cynthia Crawford everyone. Thank you so much Miss Crawford. Very profound. Thank you…" Cynthia, indignantly aggressive,

"But I'm not finished? I haven't done 'Suburban Nightmare' yet?"

"Oh, I'm *so* sorry. Only time for one reading from each poet. Got to keep to schedule, give everyone a chance and all that." Ushers her off hastily in a placatory Basil Fawlty manner. Miss Crawford, it seems, is far from impressed,

"Stuff your schedules where the sun don't shine you fucking fascist wanker! I'm outta here! C'mon guys."

"Well really!" Miss Crawford departs the premises closely followed by her entourage of three manky looking suburban anarchists of debateable gender. The compeer pulls himself together with a visible effort,

"Well, I can only apologise for that most unfortunate incident, ladies and gentleman. I'm afraid that, as you will be no doubt well aware, the medium of poetry tends to raise somewhat heated emotions in many a breast. No doubt Miss Crawford's better judgement was momentarily blinded by the force of her passion." Either that or she's just an ignorant cow. Personally, if someone called me a fascist wanker I doubt that I'd be quite so generous about it.

"And now… Mr Gerald P. Green. Mr Green?" J. stands up hurriedly, clutching his poetic notes to his chest in a fervour of excitement,

"Ah, here he is. Do come up Mr Green." The compeer looks highly relieved by Jerry's less than butch appearance - certainly a hell of a lot less butch than his fiery predecessor.

"Wish me luck Carly. This could be my big break."

"Go on then J. Break a leg, or a pen , or whatever's appropriate." He minces off upstage, trying his best to look creatively aloof.

"Good evening ladies and gentleman, fellow poetry lovers. I'm Gerald Green and tonight I shall be performing for your enjoyment my latest work - 'Arise My Fair Herald.' Thank you." Everyone claps. The compeer mops his brow with a silk handkerchief and looks highly relieved by the uncontentious title. Clearly J. has turned over a new poetic leaf. This sounds like some romanticised historical thingy. He must have been watching 'Timewatch' again. Sucking his cheeks in, J. adopts a thoughtful high-brow demeanour, one index finger resting coquettishly on his pointy chin, the other clutching a skinny elbow.

'Arise My Fair Herald.' by Gerald P. Green." He declaims in a piercing soprano,

"Arise, arise my fair herald of love,

The moment is now at hand,

The long-awaited invasion is imminent,

Destiny draws you on to play your part." The compeer nods and smiles. The audience are totally focused on J. as he warbles on,

"I tremble at the sight above,

Inspiring awe, erect you stand.

Inevitable passion abounds,

Branding your claim on my heart."

The compeer is looking a trifle confused now and the public are politely murmuring,

"*Which* battle is this?"

"I'm not sure?" Etc, etc… Jerry is unperturbed, lost in his moment of glory,

"Deaf to my pleas you thrust and shove,

Running me through, yet still you expand,

With tender, sweetly murmured sounds,

Piercing my soul with your powerful dart."

I glance over at the compeer. It's quite clear from his rising-high-blood-pressure expression that the awful truth is sinking in. This historical saga is from slightly more recent times than we first all presumed. The audience however seem quite happy and are gamely paying attention as J. shrills into poetic overdrive for the… [if you'll excuse the phrase] climax.

"Till at last, gentle as a dove,

I hold you in my hand,

And finish you off with a couple of rounds.

Lo, time and passion spent….we part.

"Thank you, thank you so much."

The place is in uproar. The punters go wild cheering and clapping for more than they're worth. The compeer has collapsed on a spindly chair in a fit of homophobia and a young waiter is vainly fanning him with a napkin. Jerry is ebullient at his overwhelming success. He keeps bowing as if we're in a theatre,

"Oh, you're too kind. Thank you so much." A voice rings out from the back of the room,

"Encore!" he crowd takes up the chant.

"Encore!"

"Encore!" Jerry blushes furiously,

"Oh, I'd love to but I'm only allowed to do one. That other girl…." The faceless voice quashes his protests,

"That other girl was crap! Encore!" Jerry preens under all the admiration. Bounce up and down in my seat, now *this* is entertainment. Shout encouragingly,

"Go Jerry! Give us a quick burst of 'Liberator'. Go on!" The purple-faced compeer is in no fit state to stop him so J. hastily consults his notes and waves the groupies down to a dull roar.

"O.K.! O.K. If you really insist…"

"HURRAY!"

"I'm going to do an old favourite of mine… This is for my friend Carly, for truly, she is my scaffolding. This one's for you babes…"

Half an hour later - the last two poetic contenders have treated us to a couple of instantly forgettable odes but then, to be fair, Jerry was an impossible act to follow. He is still basking in the free-flowing admiration of miscellaneous strange people when I spot a familiar face. It's Mr Tidy, the pullover man from the bar. He's mooching about on the outskirts of Jerry's mob of groupies , a politely interested look on his nondescript face. I give him a friendly encouraging smile.

"Hi there. Did you enjoy the readings?" He gives a surprised smile,

"Oh yes, I did indeed - Mr Peagreen's in particular."

"Mr Who?"

"Mr Peagreen. Aren't you with him? I thought you must be his agent."

"Oh, you mean Jerry? But his surname's Green. Jerry P. Green. His middle name's Peter." J.'s admirer takes on a sundried tomato hue,

"Oh I see. How very stupid of me." I feel rather sorry for him. He's clearly mortified.

"Oh, I shouldn't worry if I were you. I only wish that was the most embarrassing thing I'd ever got wrong." If only.

"I'm Carly by the way, Carly Watson. I'm a friend of Jerry's. Are you a poet too then?"

He flusters,

"Oh no, no. I'm in publishing. Raymond Elkstone. How do you do? Tell me, who is Mr, er, Green's agent?"

"Oh, he hasn't got one. Why?"

"Really?" He's watching Jerry intently. How odd? I hope he's not a stalker or something, with a peculiar poetry fetish? If anyone could attract a strange admirer it's J. He doesn't even have to try. Must be an attraction of similars or something. Oblivious to Raymond's intense and vaguely worrying scrutiny, Jerry is loudly blabbing to a portly middle-aged lady in a flowery sweater and polyester 'slacks'.

"Yes, yes, I do agree Mr Green."

"Oh, call me Jerry."

"Oh. Yes, well, Jerry, I do think, don't you, that without question the finest poet of our time must be Shelley. Don't you just adore the way he wrenches your heartstrings with every single line? Such passion.... Rather like your own work, if I may be so bold" J. rests a thoughtful skinny digit on his pointy chin to ponder this interesting dilemma,

"Well, ac-tu-ally Hester, may I call you Hester? Oh yes, thank you Actually Hester, if I had to choose just one poet, I personally would have to swing towards Wilfred Owen myself." Hester raises a polite middle-class eyebrow,

"Really? You do surprise me Jerry.... Wilfred Owen you say?" Jerry nods, a poignant look on his face,

"Oh yes. I just find the war poets sooo moving. Wilfred Owen, Rupert Brookes...they would break your heart. When I read Owen in particular, I'm there in the trenches. I can see it all. The deep brooding intensity of his verse just turns me all a-quiver. Don't you agree?" Hester is nodding enthusiastically,

"Oh well yes. Of course."

"I mean, I'll grant you that Shelley is one of *the* great masters. But for me, Owen does it every time. "Hester nods intensely, hanging on his every word, as are the other dozen or so newly converted Jerry-ites clustered round him agog at his creative brilliance. As Jerry shows no signs of slowing up his uninterruptible pace Raymond Elkstone draws out a neat silver business card holder. Proffering a card in my general direction he murmurs politely,

"Perhaps you wouldn't mind passing my card on to Mr Green. I really must go. I have another engagement to attend."

"Oh. Of course. Certainly. No problem. Nice to meet you Mr Elkstone." He nods courteously,

"Oh Raymond, please. And the pleasure was mine. Good evening Miss Watson."

"Erm, bye." He exits stage left leaving me momentarily abandoned.

"Car-lee!" Turn to see Jerry waving me over. Oh good! He must be finished. I want to go home. I'm all poetried out. Mooch over to where J.'s holding court. Only a few stragglers are left now. One of them looks familiar.

"Carly, this is Clive. Remember, he was on earlier? Clive, Carly Watson, a friend of mine."

"Hi Clive. Nice to meet you."

"How do you do Miss Watson? Tell me, how do *you* view modern verse?" Resist the urge to say from as far away as possible and smile politely, feigning interest.

"Oh well, I think it's entirely subjective, don't you?" That ought to work - suitably vague yet covers most subjects. Better than the truth, that I haven't got a clue - about modern verse, old fashioned verse or anything even remotely of that ilk. I'm embarrassed to admit that my entire foray into the world of poetry began and ended in third year at secondary school when as an impressionable teenager I was subjected *to* Philip Larkin's popular epic on mortality 'Ambulances' which has no doubt inspired many a wrist-slitting incident. And also the wartime poets including Brookes and Owen which had rather a different effect on me than on Jerry. This somewhat dubious study allocation would certainly account for my subconscious categorisation of poetry with doom and gloom subjects, best avoided if at all possible. But fortunately Clive seems quite happy with my answer and pulling his ample stomach in he rattles off on an in depth analysis of latter day works by people I've never heard of and their fundamental pro and cons. Smile and nod gamely murmuring,

"Oh really? I had no idea. How fascinating."

Whenever he paused and looked expectantly at me - [as before, a multipurpose strategy suitable for an infinite variety of occasions.] During one such pause Jerry's new buddy Hester makes an unfortunate gaffe by enquiring loudly on the subject of Clive's earlier piece,

So tell me Clive, may I call you Clive?"This could get a bit repetitive?

"Oh, thank you. Tell me Clive, if you don't mind my asking, I was sooo moved by your piece, was it recent?" Clive draws his bushy dark brows together in query,

"I beg your pardon Madam, was what recent?" Hester pats his bulky sleeve consolingly and adopts a sensitive, bereavement counsellor tone,

"You know? - Your .... Loss? Lucinda?" His sallow face clouds over at the mention of her name,

"Aah. My little Lucinda. Yes, yes, it was a great shock. A great sadness to my heart, you understand?" Hester nods sympathetically and murmurs,

"Had you been together very long?" Bravely Clive goes for a wan smile and rubs one chunky palm over his eyes which are brimming with unshed tears,

"Oh yes indeed, dear lady. A matter of nine years last June. And every day we were together. I cannot believe that she has truly gone." A volley of concerned murmurs greet this sad revelation,

"Of course, of course, how dreadful. Have you any children? Children can be such a consolation at these times." Hester continues.

Clive starts a little, confused, his mind clearly lost in a melancholy reverie of the past,

"Children? No, I have no children. I never married. I always thought.... And now it is too late."

"Oh, no, no..." The attentive Hester insists,

"You mustn't think like that. It's very sad, I know, to lose a loved one. I'm a widow myself" I think I can see where she's going with this...

"But you mustn't give up hope Clive. You simply mustn't." Clive grasps her hand and smiles through his pain,

"You're very kind."

"And of course it's very difficult to let the past go, move on. It doesn't mean that you've forgotten her, you know?" She smiles encouragingly. Clive shakes his leonine head,

"Forget my Lucinda? Impossible. I shall never have another like she! - Her beauty, her elegance, her unflinching love. She was... beyond compare!" By now everyone is sniffling into their hankies at the heartrending tale ...Wrapt in his misery Clive continues,

"I held her as she passed away. As she slipped into her final rest a part of me died too... I cannot describe..." Now everyone is openly howling....

"If only I'd realised what pain she was in. She was so brave. If only I'd called the vet sooner " *Eh?* Chorus of 'eh's?' Hester, as we all are, is dumbfounded. I have to ask.

"Erm, Clive? Don't you mean the doctor? You called the doctor, didn't you?"Clive regards me in amazement as if I am some kind of imbecile.

"Doctor? Why would I call a doctor? What would they know about cats?"

Hester murmurs faintly,

"Cats, Clive? Lucinda was...?"

"The finest cat that ever lived."

After that shocking finale, conversation being impossible, there was nothing to do but leave. So we did. Quickly. Murmuring our respectful goodbyes to Clive and embarrassed to Hester and the gang,

Jerry and I shuffle off back to Miss Daisy, who is remarkably un-parking ticketed and unclamped. Scoot off home, home at last to a hot bath, a cosy bed and a well, very well deserved sleep.

CHAPTER FIFTEEN
The Absolutely Last Straw

As I am a new, aloof single person, I have decided to take Fashion Jerry's advice and treat myself to new and un-Thelma-like knickers. It is a well-known fact that wearing gorgeous, slinky undies will do wonders for your personal esteem, and as I apparently don't have any I am buying the entire stock of Knickerbox. Nope! Forgot. I am not buying the entire shop as I am destitute. I'll just purchase one, extremely exotic, super-sexy pair to die for instead. That ought to work equally well and I can just wash them every night till I have money. Hmmm? It is a toss-up between scarlet and silky or black and ever so slightly see-through - a very hard decision. Put the contenders for my chosen knicker awards on the display stand by the shop door and lean back to get better look at the colours in the correct daylight lighting conditions.

"Take them both." Aaaargh! It's him, Aaron, the sadistic American slut? I didn't see him coming. And what is he doing in Knickerbox? It's only for ladies and perverts! Immediately hide my new knickers behind my back, as I do not want him to see them. He has clearly seen quite enough of those already. He is smiling. Do *not* smile at me!

"I was just passing and I saw you…. Look, Carly, we really need to talk." No we ruddy well DON'T!

"Can I help you at all sir?" Oh! It's the scary shark sales-bitch. She has crept up on her prey from behind. How sneaky? There should at least be some music of Jaws theme variety to give victims a small sporting chance.

"Can I get you anything?" That translates quite roughly as 'Buy something now or get out, I know that you-are-a-deviant.' He is not even the slightest bit embarrassed? He must be a regular Knickerbox patron? Suddenly, with the approximate speed of lightning, he leans forward, puts his hands round my back, grabs my knickers and gives them to the sales-shark woman. The sales-bitch leers like a satisfied vampire. No! He saw my knickers?

"We'll take them both, thank-you!" No, we WON'T! How dare he? How dare he look at my knickers? And totally un-invited! Try ineffectually to grab them back.

"NO!" Oh, no! I'm Mickey-flipping-Mouse again? Too late. The woman has snuck off and bagged them before we have a chance to escape.

"And how would Madam like to pay for that?" Haven't got enough money? Oh-nooo!

"Eerrm…I...umm..." He whips out a bulging wallet and flings down a casual pink note.

"Er...what do you think you're doing with my underwear?" He gives me an extremely naughty smile.

"Well, sweetheart it's the least I can do. After all, I did rip the last ones."

"Shut up! Shut up! She'll hear you!" My face is absolutely scorching. He is just the cheekiest man in the world! The sales woman pockets his cash with a quite un-necessarily helpful smirk whilst casually ignoring me completely?

"Well, thank-you, Sir!"

"Fine, thanks! Bye." Mr Impertinent grabs me round the waist and my knickers bag from the counter and proceeds to leave the premises with both of us? What? Ooh!

"Excuse-me, but I don't believe that I've actually been paid for?" Oh! Oh! Entirely the wrong thing to say? He might think I actually want re-imbursement from the other night, as I am a fully paid up member of the tart squad?

He is walking at a very high rate of knots into the street, along the street and round a handy corner. I am having a slight bit of a problem keeping up and yet again have him welded to my waist expressly against my wishes. Well, really! He stops at last beside his flashy sports car and casually flings my pants straight onto the back seat. Well, could be worse. At least I wasn't in them. I am extremely out of breath now and have slumped back against a convenient lamppost. He has opened the passenger door and is waiting in a gentlemanly fashion for me to recover my a.w.o.l. composure. Uh,-oh? He is coming over to get me?

"Carly, get into the car!" No way! You can't kidnap me for the price of a pair of undies!

"No,..I can't, I.... I've really got to be somewhere." He doesn't look very pleased? He is a obviously man who doesn't much like to be crossed? He has grabbed my arms and is pinning me to the lamppost with the more interesting end of his denims. Ooooh? Look round in desperation for assistance. There is not a soul in sight. In the middle of London? At this time? Not really a normal occurrence. This is clearly a street for the sole purpose of muggings?

"Carly! We really do need to talk." No, we don't! Stop saying that! I don't like you. And I really want to go home now where I can be sure that my underwear is safe.

"So, get-into-the car!" No-no-no-no-never! You can't make me, buddy!

"No!" He makes a tiny little noise of extreme exasperation, leans back and scoops me up off my feet. What? Well, apparently he can? This can not be legal? This is a person-snatching offence of the very highest order!

"Put me down!"

"Certainly, madam." Find myself deposited quite unceremoniously in the passenger seat. Humph? How extremely unseemly! Aaron gets in, leans over and fastens my seatbelt with a quite unnecessary amount of fiddling. My seatbelt is the least of my worries? Flashes me the most impertinent of grins.

"Clunk-click, Carly." I'll clunk you if you even think of trying that again! I am speechless. He has whipped out a pair of snazzy shades and driven off without any information as to where-the-hell he's taking me. I am utterly bloody-well kidnapped?

So, it would seem that I have discovered yet another social occasion for which I am unclear on the acceptable behaviour. Is one required to speak to one's captor at all? Am I making some colossal social gaffe? Sneak a sly peek sideways at the demon mischief maker. He looks perfectly happy. Maybe he does this type of thing all the time? In town for a few essentials. Got some socks, got some beer. Oh look, a passing woman? Yup, I'll just take one of those. Has he no idea of the correct British procedures? Well, obviously not. He doesn't look the least bit sorry. Well, really! He just keeps glancing round and smirking. Does he know something I don't know? Like, for instance, where the hell we are? Nope! I've never been here before. We are driving along an extremely picturesque country road – all Olde Worlde houses and lots of trees and grass and miscellaneous green stuff. It's really very pretty. Oh! We appear to be stopping? We have swung into the cobbled car park of a quaint old-fashioned restaurant, all mullioned windows and big old oak doors with a charming little courtyard at the back leading right down to the edge of the river. Seems to be an exceptionally peaceful bit of river with floaty willow trees swinging down into the water and swans and ducks and…I've just realised that he's turned the engine off and is staring at me.

"What? What now?" Don't do that smirky thing!

"Do you like it, then?" Ex-cuse me?

"Pardon? Do I like what exactly?"

"Do you like it here? You, know? For dinner?" Dinner? What dinner? I most certainly did not agree to have dinner with you! I cannot dredge up a suitably cutting reply. And I'm not particularly sure of the appropriate facial expression to assume either…so do nothing.

"I'll take that as a yes then, shall I?" He slinks round the bonnet like the weasel he quite clearly is and opens my door. He's proffers a helpful and perhaps necessary hand to get out of his extremely low car. Oh! That's quite nice really. Don't know anyone who does stuff like that…except Jerry and that doesn't really count. I have to get out as there's no other option. He has the car keys. Suppose it's only dinner. Hey! Wait a minute!

"I can't! I'm not in the right outfit!" Aaron is looking sorely confused,

"Eh?" Well, really? This is clearly a very posh place and it is almost the evening so obviously, to go in here one should be wearing evening clothes or one will undoubtedly look like a total fanny.

"I can't go in there wearing this?" Gesture helplessly at my ultra-casual flowery sundress. DON'T laugh at me!

"Carly, it doesn't matter what you're wearing. You look fine." I don't want to look *fine*. I want to look fantastic… and preferably not ridiculous. He clearly does NOT understand! But I don't have any choice in the matter as he has tugged me towards the huge front entrance and is ushering me inside like a cross between a butler and a prison guard. I just can't decide if he is really quite sweet or just absolutely bonkers. And it's nice to be taken out to dinner by a good-looking man who doesn't want anything. Wait a minute! Straight men who are not related to you do not just take ladies out to dinner… unless they want into your pants? Oh, God! I am so stupid!

"You know Aaron, I don't really think we ought to. I don't think…." He has puts his arm round me and leans forward to murmur in his best growly voice. Wonder if that's his real voice or if he's still in character?

"Carly! It's only dinner. I'm not going to ravish you, so please stop looking like some old-fashioned heroine who's about to be tied to a railway track. I'm not some kind of monster you know." Hmm? Fair enough… Hey! Wait a minute. Why don't you want to ravish me? Is there something wrong with me? I was good enough to be ravished last week. Huh! How insulting!

"Now what, Carly? Why are you glaring at me? What have I done now?"

"Nothing! I'm not glaring! I'm… I'm…" floundering to think of what I actually am.

"I'm…?"

125

"Hungry? Good! So am I. So let's just go in, huh?" Umm? O.K. I suppose so?

"Oh, alright then," I am a bit hungry and if I say no he might go off in a huff and just leave me here. And I have no idea where I am. And a taxi home would probably cost about a squillion quid and I've got, ooh? – Somewhere about twenty? Besides, I want to see inside. Might not be here again. Mmm, it is very pretty. I might even enjoy this...

…………...

We've had a wonderful dinner in the gorgeous courtyard right beside the water. It's gotten dark and we've got candlelight and twinkling lights strung up from the trees all round the courtyard and…and…I am completely happy. I don't want to think about anything serious, like for instance tomorrow or five minutes time, or anything. There's soft smoochy music floating out from inside the open French doors. Oooh – lovely! I am almost asleep.

"Are you enjoying yourself, Carly?" Oh, forgot about him for a moment. He hasn't said much. He just stares a lot- one of these intense brooding types. Maybe he wants to leave now? I don't think that I want to. It's really quite lovely here.

"Hmm?" He's leaning forward so that I can hear him better.

"I said are you enjoying yourself? You look kind of…. kind of…" What? Kind of what?

"You look …very beautiful."

"Oh!" Don't know what to say. I'm not used to proper compliments. Jake thought s'pose you look O.K. was the ultimate accolade. Beautiful? No, that's a new one on me? Getting embarrassed, I lean back in my chair and fiddle nervously with my bracelet and try to change the subject,

"Thank you. Look Aaron, if you're in a hurry to leave, I mean to get back?"

"No, I kinda thought we could stay for a bit and have a drink or a dance or something?" What? Oh no! He wants his dessert? 'Beautiful' was just leading up to it.

126

Look round, a little panic-stricken. Admittedly, other people are dancing, but it's a slow dance? I'd have to, umm, …touch him? No way! But he slinks round the table and removes me expertly from my chair, so I really don't have much choice. Oh? Oh dear? I find myself pulled gently into the dancing bit of the courtyard. It's dark all beyond the courtyard wall, as only the countryside can be. The stars sparkle distantly and the twinkling fairy lights and the candles on the tables make a warm glow all around us, reflecting softly in the nearby river. I'm pressed up against his shirt. Hmm, he's quite warm and cuddly really? Not too cuddly, of course, that would be icky. I'm quite enjoying this actually. I'll just have one little dance. No harm in that… Put my head against his shoulder and shut my eyes.

…………...

Some time later - Hmm, that was very nice. But I really shall have to go to the loo. Must be inside somewhere? Obviously.

"I'll just be back in a minute Aaron." I'm still la-la ing inside my head. Pretty myself up a bit, because even though I don't actually want him, I want to look stunning to not want him.

"Tum-ti-tum. Yes, that'll do."

Stroll back outside all relaxed and find… that Jennifer-not-his-girlfriend tart all done up to the nines and slobbering all over him? Aargh! Storm up like a demon.

"What the hell is going on?" He looks absolutely aghast. Clearly he didn't expect us both to be in the same place, the two-timing rat. The elegant Jennifer turns with a snooty sneer and laughs openly at my inappropriate dress. She is in top-to-toe designer-wear.

"Whoever's this then Aaron, darling?" He's still practically wearing her. God, I am so stupid? He was just trying to get into my pants. Again! Oh! I can't take any more of this.

"Carly, it's not what you think…." Oh, what an original line. You'd think an ac-tor could do better than that!

"Jennifer and I were just … "

"SMACK!" Hit him straight across his rugged jaw. I have never been so angry in my life.

"Jennifer and you can go straight to hell! Preferably right now! GOODNIGHT!"

He's stunned.... just long enough for me to make a very sharp exit straight through the restaurant and out the front door. Can't really see as I'm slightly upset but I shall just keep running anyway. Scramble into a handy taxi. I'll have to go to the bank for more money. There's no way I'm speaking to that two-timing Yankee git. Hell will freeze over first. You'd think I'd have learned my lesson by now. It doesn't matter which continent they come from. Men just mess up your head!

CHAPTER SIXTEEN
The Last Of The Great Romantics

It's Thursday evening and I'm at home [so what's new?]. Still no word from Siobhan on the Australian dilemma, despite my leaving two messages on her answer phone and one on her voicemail. I really hope she's alright. Jerry is out on a hot date. He's gone to a philosophy lecture at the local library with a Polish mature student called Ivan. It would seem that his single handed bid to conquer the whole of Europe continues. Hope this one lasts longer than Renaldo. I hate to see Jerry upset. He pretends he's not, but I know that deep down, under his self-protective shell of flippancy, he would really love to meet that special someone and have a steady, meaningful relationship. His posturing is just self-defence. He's been let down too many times in the past by men who just want what they can get. Well, haven't we all? I would love to see J. happy He is the nicest guy in the world.

Maybe I ought to try Siobhan again, to see if she's O.K.? No, I've left a message. She will phone when she's ready. Maybe she needs some time on her own to think. Plonk myself down on the settee and start flicking idly through a home shopping catalogue that some company I've never heard of has kindly left on my doorstep. Hmm, clothes, clothes, more clothes? Oh, that's nice? A gorgeous sexy top catches my eye. I'd really like that... But I don't need it and I can't afford it. Bugger! Being sensible sucks. Get up lethargically and trail through into the kitchen. Drop the wretched catalogue of temptation straight into the swing-bin before it can beguile me into spending money that I just haven't got. What do I need slinky tops for? I'm celibate. I don't want to tempt anybody. Who cares what anyone thinks? Mind you it would be nice if... NO! I am not getting it back out of the bin. It shall not lure me. I have will power … and principles. And besides, there are eggshells and other icky stuff in there. It will be covered in yuck already. I'm not touching that.

Bored again, I wander disconsolately across to the lounge window, press my nose against the chilly glass and sigh heavily. There's a couple of youngish-looking women with three squealing toddlers and two prams between them. They're sitting on a bench in the play area of the park happily chatting as the kids run around. Feel a sudden sharp pang of broodiness. I had tried so hard to compartmentalize that feeling, but that could have been me sitting over there now. I would have loved to have kids. If only Jake had wanted... Oh well, it's too late now.

Look away from the cheery scene and flick the kettle on. A nice relaxing coffee, I think...well, a nice relaxing de-caff maybe. And then I'd better get back to the task in hand. Only another ooh? - thirty-two paintings to go. I must have been mad to agree to this. No, I am not going to give in to negativity and self-pity. That won't get me anywhere. I might still meet a nice man, eventually. And I might still get to have kids. I'm not too old yet. No point worrying about it. I'm just rummaging about for my coffee making essentials when...

"Rrrring! Rring-rring!" Huh? Phone? Nope. Doorbell. Wasn't expecting anyone? Hope J.'s date hasn't gone horribly wrong and he's come back early? Nah, he'd just have let himself in. Saunter through to the door and open it to find Giles and Siobhan.

"Oh! Hi guys. Come on in. I've been trying to get a hold of you for days." They've obviously come to some mutually satisfactory decision over the job because they're both sporting big cheesy, self-satisfied grins. Jolly good! Somebody's happy. Wave my jar of Nescafe at them invitingly,

"Coffee? I'm just making some."

Giles,

"Oh right - yes please." Plonks his khaki-cardiganed self happily down on the sofa. Siobhan sits down neatly beside him beaming,

"Yes please Carly." They are holding hands like teenagers. How sweet. Fix three quick Nescafes and plonk them down on the coffee table with a plate of assorted chocolate biscuits. Toss a stray magazine to the floor and snuggle up on the big armchair facing the lovebirds. Indicate the refreshments with a casual wave.

"Help yourselves." Let them get a couple of gulps of de-caff and a mouthful of chocolate before I see fit to ask,

"Well? I take it everything's sorted then?" Both look up smiling and munching. Look at each other questioningly. Siobhan smiles and pats the leg of his beige corduroy trousers encouragingly.

"Go on. You tell her Giles."

"O.K. then. Carly, we've got something to tell you."

"Uh-huh? Thought you might have. Come on then. Don't keep me in suspenders. I could do with some secondary cheer." Giles takes a deep breath,

"Siobhan and I...we're, we're getting married." What? I didn't see that one coming? They've been going out for nearly twenty years? Siobhan sticks a hand out to show me the tastefully small single diamond engagement ring. Breathless with excitement,

"Isn't it beautiful? Giles asked me on Tuesday. We just got the ring to-day. We're going to drive up and tell our parents at the week-end. " I am temporarily speechless. But only temporarily...

"What? But I thought? Oh, that's fantastic! Congratulations!" Jump up and give them both a cuddle, despite the scalding coffee risk to our persons. I can feel my eyes filling up.

"Oh, I'm so pleased for you. About time!" Both beam back at me. Siobhan,

"Giles is going to leave the bank and come to Australia with me." Giles,

"Yes, I thought I could find something out there, you know? I'm not fussy as long as we're together." Oh, how romantic.

"Oh, that's lovely. When do you go? Have you thought about a date for the wedding yet? Oh, I can't believe it." All stand about smiling in a very silly fashion. Siobhan,

"No. We haven't had a chance to think about it yet. The job starts next month. I'll find out all the details tomorrow."

Giles,

"We'll still be here for your big preview though Carly. We wouldn't want to miss that."

Laugh,

"You'd better not. You might be the only people there - apart from Jerry and Ange. My parents will be away on a cruise then. It was booked ages ago, or they would've flown down from Glasgow. And I can't imagine that the public will be in a mad rush to see a bunch of paintings by someone nobody's heard of. For God's sake don't leave me on my own with Shrimpton-Boswick. He might try to console me. Egad? I'm counting on you to protect me Giles." Giles stands tall in his baggy cardigan and C & A cords and assumes a tough-guy expression,

"No problem. You can stand behind me. Your virtue will be totally safe." Siobhan shrieks hysterically,

"What virtue? Ouch!" Smack her with a cushion,

"Cheeky bitch! I'll have you know that I'm practically Julie Andrews. And I'd really like to stay that way. So Giles can keep that big gadgy away from me, if you don't mind. You may marry him after the preview, once he's done his body-guarding duty."

"Oh, O.K. - fine. That sounds fair."

"Erm, do I get a say in this girls?" Both laugh at this ridiculous suggestion. Give him a dismissive gesture.

"No, of course you don't. Do what you're told."

Siobhan -

"No darling, don't be silly. You have to love, honour and obey." Giles gives a put-on confused frown,

"But Siobhan my love, I thought that was your role. There must be some sort of mistake? And I didn't realise it that meant your friends as well."

Siobhan,

"Oh I'm afraid that it does." Smile cheekily,

"Sorry Giles, looks like you're stuck with me, for, oh what? - another three weeks?" He shrugs good-naturedly,

"Oh fine. We're going out to celebrate. Want to come?"

Siobhan,

"Oh yes, Carly, you must." Smile happily,

"Try and stop me. I'll just get my jacket. This is a champagne situation And the first bottle's on me. Leave the flat in search of a cheeky little Krug.

CHAPTER SEVENTEEN
The Psychic Wardrobes Of Life

Food shopping – home – key into the lock and …… What the heck is that smell? It's like hash or something equally odd? Have I left the oven on? Is my precious flat burnt to a crisp? Wander through the hallway to check. No, apparently it's not…but what on Earth have we here? Jerry is perched on a cushion in front of my T.V. Well, nothing unusual in that. But he is wearing a bright pink leotard? And waving some incense sticks about. ??? He has his eyes shut and is saying 'Uummm…" I know I'm going to regret this but I really do have to ask.

"Jerry, what are you doing? Pray tell." Keeps his eyes shut and squeals.

"Pilates! Carly, PILATES!" Fine! I was only asking.

"And the same to you, you old queen." J. opens one weaselly eye in frustration.

"God, Carly, pilates. It's like yoga. It's good for your karma and stuff."

"Will it do anything for my butt?"

"What your butt's going to get is a good swift kick if you don't stop putting me off. Now would you just SIT DOWN!" Well, ooh? Temper, temper? Swirls round on his cushion and stabs me with one beady eye. This is clearly quite serious stuff…

"You were out so I started without you. Join in when you get the idea…O.K.? Ready? Ummmmm." Eh? Eh? Double eh?

"Jerry! Stop making that ridiculous noise."

"Sshh. I've reached another level." Oh yes, you certainly have. Screw my eyes up all the better to interpret his actions. The 'uumm' bit seems a quite vital part? Oh, well, I'd better humour him I suppose. Toss my coat onto a handy chair and assume the position on a spare cushion. We look like a two-person anti-natal class. Well, I imagine we do. I haven't actually ever been to one …but it was on television. Couldn't be less relevant to me. So, O.K.….

"Uummmm?" I'm still waiting? Should something be happening here? It's a bit like sex with Jake, latterly. You know there should be something else. Otherwise other people wouldn't do it so much. Like sex, I must be doing this wrong?

O.K. - that's it! Ten minutes of 'uumm' now. Even Jake didn't want that much… Besides, I should really like to know…

"Jerry, what does this do exactly?" Shushes me away with one hand.

"It's clearing out your karma babe. I told you your cupboards were full."

"My what? But we only tidied my them last week?"

"Your spiritual closets darling. Like I told you the other day."

"You didn't? I would have remembered. You said 'All men are bastards!' It isn't quite the same thing. Besides, in what way will this 'uumming' nonsense sort out my wardrobe of life?" J. stops uumming and spins round to face me, arms outstretched like a fool? He looks like Mystic Meg in tights. Jerry, you've gone too far.

"We're trying to regenerate your karma Babes. Your psychic battery is flat." I wish that my butt was flat.

"You have to cleanse your inner self…" Colonic irrigation? Oh, YUCK! No way!

"…to repel the buffets of life…." And what exactly is a buffet?

"…and to dispel any negative energies Babe…like Jake, or your mortgage…" Oh, what utter twaddle. J. opens his eyes wide and flops back onto the floor. Oh, thank God! He's finished ranting and turned back into J. He must have been possessed by some hippy demon. I should have called a priest straight away.

"Right Carly, that's enough. You ought to be cleansed by now." Oh no! he's still talking bollocks? Do priests come on 999 calls? He's waving a teachery finger at me.

"What you need to do is take action." Nope. You are being too vague. For God's sake give me a clue.

"Oh? Uh – like what?"

"Well, I don't know, do I? What you need to begin your new life is closure on your old one. In order to make a fresh start you have to get rid of all your old hang-ups….like, like?" He's clearly floundering. He hasn't read the whole book.

"My love life, my butt and my mortgage?" His beady eyes light up and he claps his hands madly.

"Ye-es, that kind of stuff! So, what are you going to do Sweetie?"

"Well, I was hoping that you might tell me – being the expert on spiritual hoovers and stuff."

"God! I've only been doing it for a week. I just got a video from Smiths." Oh, great! Bang goes another lifeline.

"Admit it, why don't you, Jerry, you fraud? You just wanted a pink leotard?"

CHAPTER EIGHTEEN
Dress To Impress

In a slightly premature fit of pre-nuptial enthusiasm Siobhan has dragged Angie, J. and I to an exclusive designer bridal boutique in search of bridesmaid and wedding dresses. Well, she didn't actually drag Jerry as such. He insisted on coming and suggested the shop. After all, fashion is his thing. It would be entirely sexist to exclude him. So Angie and I are to be bridesmaids and Jerry is to be a hyper-trendy usher. He is presently insisting on a morning suit with extra long tails and a top hat. Siobhan is trying gamely to dissuade him from the hat.

"Really Jerry, I had envisaged you cutting a dash in a silk cravat and waistcoat with your hair all waxed just so." She indicates the appropriate direction for J.'s wedding hair to wax in with an impressive swoosh of one hand, narrowly missing his left ear.

"That, Jerry, would look fabulous. Now for the waistcoat, something stylish..." J. Shudders,

"Now Siobhan, let's be clear, I am wearing nothing that even vaguely resembles old people's wallpaper or a footballer's wedding. Have you got that? Hmm? Good! I'm thinking distinguished, debonair, sophisticated." Ange and I wander casually along behind them as they happily debate the relative merits of ivory silk over ruched taffeta. Ange has a faraway look in her china doll blue eyes as she lovingly fondles the beautiful fabrics and sighs over the endless array of bridal dream come true outfits. An unfortunate choice of location for someone desperately in love with a man who can't marry her because his wife wouldn't let him. She is doing her best to fake enthusiasm for Siobhan's benefit but it's not very convincing. I'm quite pleased to be a bridesmaid. I've never done it before and the dresses are gorgeous, like something out of a fairy tale. But Angie's done it five times. Always the bridesmaid and all that.

Jerry is trying to foist a Russian-style faux fur trimmed dress with an elaborately beaded bodice onto Siobhan who is resisting his wiles bravely.

"Oh but Siobhan, it's simply divine. You absolutely must try it on."

"No Jerry, no. It's not really me, is it?"

"Oh but…"

"No, I thought more something along the lines of this. What do you think?" She picks out a plain cream pure silk off the shoulder number and holds it up for our approval. It's certainly much more her than the 17th century Moscowvite in panto look. J. is not impressed. Throws his hands in the air and addresses himself to the ceiling,

"A nothing dress? I bring her to a veritable Mecca of innovative design and decadent beauty and what does she want? A nothing dress? Sheesh! It breaks my heart." Try to shut him up quickly before he upsets Siobhan,

"J.! It is Siobhan's wedding. Don't be such a big fashion bully." Ange sighs soppily and gently strokes a silky sleeve,

"I think it's just beautiful."

Siobhan adopts a decisive tone,

"I like it Jerry. I don't want anything too fancy."

Jerry,

"Well, you've certainly achieved that. It's bereft of any personality whatsoever." Oo-er? This could degenerate rapidly into a full-scale row? Try to intervene,

"But Jerry, it's so well cut. And you must admit it's very good quality. And it does go rather well with Siobhan's skin tone." Jerry sniffs condescendingly and eyes the dubious frock,

"I suppose so… maybe."

Siobhan,

"Well, I like it. It's in my size. I'm going to try it on." She stomps off huffily in search of an assistant... J. waves a dismissive sulky hand,

"Fine, fine. Just you go ahead. Commit couture suicide. See if I care." He folds his bony frame elegantly onto a handy uncomfortable-looking chair to wait and admires his fingernails distractedly. Meanwhile Angie is still wandering about like a lost soul wistfully fondling tiaras and satin shoes and stuff. Plonk myself down beside Jerry on a matching uncomfortable chair. Eye Angie worriedly. She was on the verge of a breakdown already. This cannot be helping.

"O.K. Angie?" She discreetly brushes a single tear of misery from her blushered cheek and plasters on her best fake smile to reply in an over-bright tone,

"Oh! Yes, fine, fine." She holds up a stunning tiara to show us,

"Look. Isn't it gorgeous?" Murmur in unison,

"Oh yes, lovely."

"Yeah, yeah - fab." She carries on rifling through some magazines. Jerry folds his arms and nods discreetly in her direction, whispers,

"She's taking this well, all things considered, don't you think?"

"I think Jerry, that she's just putting on a brave front. I mean, does she look like she's enjoying this to you?" Cocks his head to one side to consider,

"Um, no. No, not really. We'll have to do something."

Snort,

"Like what for instance?" J. screws up his face in search of inspiration,

"We should...? We should....? - No, I really haven't got a clue." Both sit in concerned contemplation of Angie as she faffs about with miscellaneous bits of wedding paraphernalia.

At last Siobhan swooshes imperiously out of her cubicle, followed by the obsequious assistant, who is bombarding her with the standard 'buy it' kind of compliments. Never take an assistant's word for anything, particularly when there's a big bucks sale involved. However, the dress does look simply fabulous. The plain classical lines really suit her and are highly flattering to her somewhat ample figure. It subtly hints at her curves, giving the impression of a stunningly voluptuous goddess - as opposed to, well? - cuddly. It must be by the same designer as the magic pink twine dress. Oh, I need a dress like that!

Siobhan is twirling happily in front of the massive floor-to-ceiling mirror,

"What d'you think then Carly?"

"It's absolutely gorgeous! Get it! Get it! Sorry J., I know it's unthinkable - but you were wrong." Siobhan turns to Jerry and raises a questioning eyebrow,

"Jerry?" J. sucks his face in huffily. He hates to admit to ever being wrong. Grudgingly, he waves a fake-casual hand at the gorgeous frock,

"Well, perhaps if you get a decent head-dress and tart it up a bit with jewellery and stuff... it might be O.K." Siobhan raises a sardonic eyebrow,

"Oh? Gee thanks Jerry. You really know how to make a girl feel good. Anyone would think you were straight. " J. squeaks indignantly,

"Oh!? How dare you, you ungrateful trollop!" Siobhan ignores him and turns to look enquiringly at Angie,

"What do you think Ange? You're the casting vote on my bridal committee. Yes or no? Is it me?" Angie is biting her lip and trembling. Uh-oh? A tight little voice,

"It's perfect Siobhan. You look stunning. Giles will be so … Oh, I don't feel very well." And right enough; her face has suddenly gone a less than fetching shade of puce. She turns and bolts off up the spiral staircase to the entrance. Spring up and scuttle after her,

"Don't worry. I'll go." Smile apologetically at the gawping assistant on the way past,

"Sorry. Gastroenteritis. Excuse us."

Abandoned to Jerry's tender mercies Siobhan sighs heavily and vanishes back into her cubicle closely followed by the 'Oh Madam, it's soo you' creature. Jerry eyes the ceiling again and shakes his head melodramatically,

"Really! Some people? Soo temperamental."

I eventually catch up with Ange in a thankfully deserted alleyway beside the shop. She is hunched up against a wall making highly distressing sick noises.

"Angie! Are you O.K.?"

"No! Go away."

"O.K. that was a pretty silly question." Put an arm round her heaving shoulders,

"Come on Ange." She straightens up and turns round. Her mascara has smudged, her make up has run and it looks like her whole face has melted.

"Do I look O.K.? Do you think anyone will notice?"

"No. It'll be fine." Drag my hanky out of a pocket and dab at her ineffectually.

"There, there. You're all right. Come on now." She does a couple of little choking sobs,

"I'm sorry, I'm sorry. God, I am sooo stupid!"

"No you're not. Don't be silly. Stand still till I sort your face." She leans back against the wall sniffling, takes the hanky and gives her face a good wipe.

"What did they say when I ran out?"

"Nothing. I just said you were ill. Gastroenteritis if anyone asks O.K.?" Angie smiles snottily,

"O.K. - thanks."

"Now then, now then, wot's all this ere then?" Jerry appears round the corner looking concerned but still doing a cockney policeman. He likes to hone his creative abilities at every opportunity, no matter how inappropriate the occasion. He's banned from the local funeral parlour for life. But then, he won't need to get in till after that, so that's O.K. He eyes Angie's now make-up free face dubiously,

"Have you finished puking?"

"Yes, thank you."

"Jerry! For heaven's sake, have some tact. Can't you see she's ill?" Indignant,

"I know! I was only asking."

Angie,

"Really, I'm O.K. Jerry. Can I go and sit in Miss Daisy please. I don't think I could face going back in there. It was awfully stuffy. I'm melting."

"Sure. Come on." Jerry ushers her along the road in a gentlemanly fashion. I scuttle back inside to retrieve Siobhan. Poor thing. Abandoned by all her bridal entourage. Not a good omen for the wedding itself.

CHAPTER NINETEEN
Closure At Last

As I am clearing out my life I thought I would start by clearing out my closets. I am surrounded by boxes of miscellaneous stuff. I haven't seen some of these things for years. J. is supposedly helping but it's like being helped by a very small child. He's just making more of a mess. He is truffling intently about in my cupboards and boxes flinging things willy-nilly behind him as, after roughly two seconds, he either loses interest or spies something new to play with. It really is just the tiniest bit exasperating you know. Problem is he's too nosey by half ….too nosey by three-quarters even. He's busily snooping through all my old things; clothes, jewellery, junk-stuff and photos. He has now pounces on a sepia print and is waving it under my nose.

"What are you doing in this one Carls? You look like a total tart – all jacked-up cleavage and shag me eyes. It isn't like you at all." Lean over his shoulder to take a look.

"Oh, I'd forgotten about that. I was doing something for Dave."

"I'll bet you were, you little hussy!" He doesn't understand.

"No, it was a photo shoot. He needed a practice model. He was mucking about with sepia tints and he wanted to try his big lens."

"Oh fnaar, fnaaar!" Oh, get lost, Innuendo Boy.

"So, what's with the slutty expression? Were you turned on by Dave? Was he jiggling his zoom lens thingy about, off camera and stuff?"

"Oh Jerry, do grow up. I was having a laugh and it didn't really matter. It was only Dave. I was feeling a bit slutty and I wondered what my face looked like, you know, when I'm doing a seductive face?" Don't wave your eyebrows Jerry. I'm trying to explain.

"You know how everyone can do that face?"

"What? Even Giles Cardigan-Man?" Euchh!

"… and you know that it works because you can see the other person's face?"

"Ye-es?"

"… but you can't actually see your own face while you're doing it?"

"Uh-huh?" He's looking a bit confused.…

"Well, it would be a bit rude, wouldn't it, to ask a guy to wait while you take a little mirror out to see your own face? Besides, they might think you were being egotistical as opposed to just naturally curious. Mightn't they? Jerry?" Jerry dumbfounded? Amazing! Maybe I shouldn't have told him? If J. is shocked I must be really weird.

"So, exactly what were you thinking about?"

"Oh well, just, you know? I was just looking right through the lens and visualising some really sexy guy, can't remember who, and giving him my best face. You should have been there. Dave was ecstatic. It was really quite fun." I am a secret floosy. Why is J. not laughing?

"Carly, you are crazy. You know you could have got into trouble." What?

"That's rich coming from you, isn't it, Custard-Boy? And it's not like I was naked. It was only my face? And it was only Dave."

"Even Dave has a dick… Or at least I imagine he does."

"I don't want to know about your rude imaginings, thank-you. For God's sake, lighten up." Jerry is staring at the photo. His gob is totally smacked. Good! That's no mean achievement. Jerry is quite hard to shock. Might go for the jacked-up boobs look again. I really could do with a laugh.

…………..

Three hours later – the clearing-out notion has done precisely that…and left me like a limp old dishrag. Even Truffle Man seems to have lost his momentum somewhat, though he is still snooping very slowly. He has donned a colossal bashed old straw sunhat from my holiday in Corfu last year, dangly gold Celtic earrings and a selection of miscellaneous bangles about which the kindest thing you could say was that it was an interesting choice. And I thought that his dress sense was infallible? You can't wear silver and gold jewellery at the same time. Doesn't everybody know that?

I am collapsed on the floor leaning back against the side of the bed watching J.'s game attempts to carry on his mission. I believe it has now become a point of nosiness to finish the search. I can only see his feet now as he has crawled right into the darkest depths of my cupboard. God knows what he's hoping to find in there. He is the Indiana Jones of my closet. How ironic. He has spent all his adult life out of the closet and now he can't wait to get back in? Freud would have made something out of that I'm sure. But Freud would have been wrong. J. is just a noseybonk. I don't think he can help himself. He ought to go to Noseybonks Anonymous and be made to stand up and admit it I can just visualize the scene.

"Hi, I'm Jerry and I've got the stickiest beak in town. I am disproportionately fascinated by tedious trivia of no consequence... Sometimes, well, quite a lot actually, about people I don't even know...and, and..." He starts to falter here, embarrassed by the intense scrutiny of his fellow noseybonks. The group leader does an encouraging 'do go on' face.

"Come on Jerry, you can tell us. No-one's judging you here. You'll feel much better. We've all been there, you know." The circle of reformed noseybonks nod and murmur their communal assent. Emboldened, Jerry grasps the nettle and takes a deep breath. Straightens his skinny frame to reveal his darkest secret. Words tumble forth in a mortified rush. He shakes his head while speaking, appalled at how far he has let himself sink.

"And I buy... I buy Heat magazine, ...and other publications of that nature." God? Oh Jerry! How shameful! He clasps his bony knuckles in front of him steeling himself to carry on...Nods in his notorious hyper mode.

"But I haven't been nosey now for, oh? – at least three minutes."
Impressive huh? The group gives him a huge round of applause.

"Carly, what's this?"

"Huh? What?" I am snapped back to reality by yet another question
from the king of the Nosey B.'s himself. He is waving a delicate white
lacy thing with long wispy straps at me.

"Is it, like, some kind of kinky underwear?"

"It's a bra for wearing under backless dresses. The straps go down
around your waist." He seems quite happy with that answer. It must be
hell to have such an enquiring mind. He is toying with my lacy straps,
clearly miles away. Maybe he is hatching an idea. I must say, it looks
extremely painful. I'm glad I don't have too many of
those...particularly big ones... ouch. Suddenly Jerry snaps his head up
and points a skinny digit aloft. I knew it. Go on then, Jerry - amaze
me.

"You know what you should do Carly? Huh? Huh? Do you?"
Inflict my doubting Thomas eyebrows on his dubious enthusiasm.

"No, you are being far too vague. Do I know what I should do
about what, exactly?" It would appear that he refuses to be squelched
so easily. He is still bouncing about on the floor like a fool. Points his
previously aloft finger at my head willing me to try and get the gist.
???

"You know, you know how you need to get closure on your past
and stuff? Like your life and all that shit?" Nod slowly. I don't want to
be too overly encouraging. I don't know what he might be leading up
to. Or how much trouble he's going to get me into this time. I am
agreeing to nothing till these vital issues are established.... preferably
in concrete or blood or something else of that reassuring ilk.

"Well, Carls I've just thought of how you can do precisely that!"

"Precisely what?"

"God Carly! Pay attention. How to get closure and move on... That
is what you want to do, isn't it?"

"Well, ye-es...?"

"Good! So here's what you ought to do. Firstly, you have to get
everything that's been bugging you out of your psyche for ever."

"Oh fine! Easy-peasy stuff then?"

"But! You have to deal with your old hang-ups on your terms. You don't want to have them scuttling about in the recesses of your subconscious, just waiting to sneak up when you're at your lowest ebb. No Babe. What you want to do is kick their sorry asses right on out of there. Don't you?" My face has now set in my best Clint Eastwood look. But no, I still don't understand? What was the question again?

"J. I have NO idea whatsoever what you're talking about." He sighs dramatically.

"You just need to sort out your chakras Babe. Your karma is such a mess."

"Jerry, you do talk drivel, you know."

"No, really Carls. For instance, you want to get this actor guy out of your head, yeah?"

"My head, my flat and my knickers, yeah, so?"

"So – you finish it! You make some decisive gesture that sticks it right into him."

"There would be a certain irony in that admittedly."

"Then, Sweetie... then you will have clo-sure." Sounds fair.

"What kind of decisive gesture? Isn't slapping him enough then? I thought it was the last resort?"

"No Babes. That leaves you as the victim….the one he cheated on. You want to rub his nose in it."

"No, I don't Jerry! That's horrid!" J. sighs and rolls his weasel eyeballs ceilingwards.

"Why don't you write him a letter telling him where to get off? That would give you a chance to say all the things you didn't get a chance to say at the time. The things you must wish you had said but you only think of later. THAT would give you closure." Uh – maybe? But what would I like to say? 'You are the biggest scumbag on the face of this planet. Darken my door again and I'll kick you down the stairs? Um, no, that's not quite right? But it is fairly accurate. No, this is just too hard. I really don't like being nasty.

"No, I don't think I want to write a letter. I'm not sure what I want to say."

"We-ell, what about sending something significant…as a gesture…something that meant something symbolic that he couldn't fail to understand."

"What? Like a wreath or a horse's head you mean?"

"Well, usually I presume one would return a ring or something like that. But as your encounter hadn't quite reached that footing I'm not all that sure. You want him to realise what he's missing and be gutted? I know! Send him one of your slinky photos, you know, so that he can see what he's missing…Yeah Babe. That would be perfect. What about this one here?" Waves particularly saucy tart shot. Ye gods! You've got to be kidding? I don't want him to see that! …Or do I? It's not like I'm going to have to face him ever again. And it might help my sagging self-esteem?

"O.K. fine! I'll do it. Is that the tartiest one I've got?" Jerry's getting all excited. It usually takes much more persuading than that for me to fall in with his mad and potentially disastrous plans.

"Ooh, ye-es! Yeah, Carly send that one. And write something cutting on the back." Eh?

"Like what, for example?" Rodent boy considers.

"Oh, you know, read it and weep, Casanova. Something along those lines."

"He can't read it Jerry. It's a photograph. What about 'This is what you're not getting!'?" J. squeals.

"God yes, put that. That's fantastic! That'll have him kicking himself."

"Good! That'll save me the trouble of doing it myself. I'll just stick it in an envelope. Where are they? Oh, I think they're in the lounge. Back in a tick." Toddle of in search of my missing envelopes leaving Jerry huddled like a designer refugee among the debris of my previous life…on which I am about to have closure. Who needs ac-tors anyway?

CHAPTER TWENTY
Oh Baby!

Tuesday - 6.30p.m. I'm cleaning my paintbrushes with turps at the kitchen sink when there's a tentative tap on the front door. Wipe my painty hands on a rag and shuffle through to investigate. Siobhan is standing on the doorstep looking woebegone.

"Siobhan? What's wrong?"

"Everything. Can I come in?"

"Yes, of course." Stand aside to let her past. Slam the door shut and follow her through to the lounge. She is standing twitching by the window. Frown in concern,

"Can I get you something? Tea? Coffee? Anything?"

"No thanks. I'm fine."

"No offence, but you don't look it. Is it the move? Or the wedding plans? Are the in-laws squabbling already? Have the mother-in-laws bought the same hat?" She perches herself nervously on the edge of the settee. Her face is a tense mask of misery.

"I wish that was all it was." Now I'm really getting worried. Siobhan is never like this. She's by far the most well-balanced of my friends. Mind you, my other friends are Jerry and Angie. Sit down opposite her on the scruffy armchair.

"Siobhan, you're scaring me? What on Earth's wrong?" She looks up blankly,

"I'm pregnant."

"What? You can't be?"

"I'm afraid I am. I've done a test. I'm six weeks gone." Gibber helplessly,

"But what? How? But Australia?" A single tear slides down her make up free face. Oh dear God? Rush round and sit down beside her. Put a comforting arm round her trembling shoulders.

"Siobhan, it's O.K. Don't worry."

"We were taking precautions. They must not have worked. I'm never late. I thought perhaps the pressure of the move and everything - but two whole weeks? I only got the test to prove to myself that I wasn't.... And I am. " Miserable tears flood down her cheeks.

"But Siobhan, the job?"

"I know. I can't go. We can't go. And Giles has handed in his notice already. Carly, what are we going to do?"

"There, there, it's alright. Now listen, Giles can get another job. With his qualifications and experience it'll take him about five seconds tops. They might even just give him his old job back if he explains. And it's a shame about Australia but you can still go there sometime if you want. And, and well, I'm glad you're staying. I would have missed you. Sorry to be selfish and all that." She sniffs and squeezes my painty hand,

"Oh Carly, I would have missed you too. And you're right - I'm lucky really. I've got Giles. It's just such a shock, that's all."

"Of course it is. It's bound to be. Bugger! We'll have to pay for our holidays now. Siobhan, how *could* you?" She looks up and smiles. That's better.

"Sorry Carls, Convey my apologies to J. and Ange."

"So you should be. J.'ll *definitely* have to sell his body now. *Or* we could all just go to Cornwall or Margate or something instead? What d'you reckon? Excellent cream teas in Cornwall, so I hear. The biggest jammy scones in the world." Shake my head wisely,

"You wouldn't get scones like that in Oz."

Siobhan laughs,

"Oh well then. I just feel dreadful about Giles. I've really messed him about. It was a big thing for him to give up his security. And we haven't even made it to Heathrow. What's he going to say? He'll be *so* disappointed."

"What? Disappointed to be a Dad? I don't think so. Giles was born to be somebody's dad. He's already got the cardigan. Besides, he's great with kids. And you'll be married soon. It'll be great, you'll see. Lovely man, lovely house, lovely baby. It'll be great. Giles'll be Superdad with a big knitted 'SD' on the back of his cardi."

"Of course he will. You're right Carly."

"I know. I always am. It's a curse. - And really irritating, apparently."

"Thanks for listening. I feel much better. I'm being really silly."

"No you're not. And even if you were - you *are* allowed to be. That's what friends are for - listening to your silliness and flinging it back in your face at a later date. Now, just you sit there and I'll make you a nice cup of tea." Siobhan casually picks up J.'s pink leotard which he forgot to take home the other day. He changed out of it prior to leaving to avoid a furore on the No.19 bus home. She yells, as I'm in the kitchen,

"What's this? It's a bit *pink* Carly? Have you been back to that aerobics class with the Hitler woman then?"

"Huh, no way. As if." Pop my head round the kitchen door to see what she's talking about,

"Oh no, that's Jerry's." Siobhan's eyebrows shoot off her face,

"You're kidding?"

"No, really. He's taken up yoga or something. He left it here the other day."

Siobhan is dumbfounded. She waves the fuchsia pink fashion disaster in disbelief,

"Jerry wears *this* to a yoga class? You are having me on?"

"No, not to a class. Just in the house."

"Well, thank God for small mercies. He'd get lynched if he went outside in that."

"How very fascist. He ought to be able to wear what he likes. It's *supposed* to be a free country." Come back through and pop the teapot down in front of her [I do *own* one, I just don't use it very often.] This is a special occasion and worthy of more than one cup. Kneel down on

151

the rug beside the coffee table to pour out. Shove some biscuits in her general direction hospitably. She is eating for two after all.

"So Carls, have you heard from Ange lately? I haven't seen her for a couple of weeks, everything's been so hectic I haven't had a minute."

"Oh yeah, we went to the cinema the other night. I swear to God Siobhan, if she gets any weirder they will lock her up and throw away the key. That Miles is an absolute prick. What the hell does she see in him?" Siobhan scrumples her face up.

"Well, they do say love is blind?" Snort in derision,

"Blind? Deaf, dumb and damn well stupid. I don't know who I want to strangle the most - him for being such a manipulative dickhead or her for letting him do it. And not just stabbing him or something. Ooh! It makes me so *angry*! He's *never* going to leave his wife. He's just making a fool of both of them."

"Yes he is. But it's Angie's business. You can't tell someone something if they don't want to hear it. You have to realise these things for yourself. What about you and Jake? *Three years* Carly? Did *you* notice how badly *he* was behaving?" Stop ranting to think about that,

"Erm, well - no. Not really. I just made excuses for him."

"Precisely! Just like Ange does. She must know deep down that it's not on but she doesn't want it to be true. So she's managed to convince herself. Self-delusion's a wonderful thing. I'm afraid there's nothing we can do Carls."

"We could take out a contract on him? Shove him in front of a bus?"

"No, appealing as that is, she'd still idolise him, even if he wasn't there. What she needs is to see him for what he really is. And unfortunately, she can only ever do that if he's still about to expose himself."

"Siobhan, *please*! I was just going to eat?"

"Not like that! You know what I meant. Expose himself for the user that he is."

"Suppose so. It's just such a shame. She doesn't deserve this."

"Who does?" Suddenly,

"SLAM! Hi Carls, it's only me." Jerry strolls in and spots Siobhan,

"Oh, g'day my little cobber. Are you staying for dinner? Should we fling another shrimp on the bar-b? Crack open a couple of tinnys of four-x? What d'ya say?"

Siobhan blinks and sniffs. Jerry stares at her, dumbstruck by this uncharacteristic weakness,

Try to deflect him before he says something worse,

"Jerry, not now."

"What? What did I say? It was just a little joke. You'd better get used to it Siobhan. I hear they give all the 'poms' a hard time out there. Ooh, lovely. Giles better keep his cardigan firmly buttoned, I can tell you." Try in vain to stop him,

"Jerry, shut up. Siobhan's…? Upset."

"Why? What's wrong? You're off to Oz with Superstud. You've been picked Possum. This time next month you'll be sunning yourself on a billabong, whatever the hell that is?"

"JERRY! Not now!" Finally sussing the fact that something's amiss he plonks himself down on the coffee table beside the teapot. Assumes his agony aunt tone and squeezes her hand encouragingly,

"Come on, my little Emigratee. Tell Uncle Jerry what's wrong. Are you homesick in advance or something? Has Giles been out on the piss with those rowdy bastards from the chess club again?" Siobhan smiles wanly,

"If only that was all it was?"

"What then? Is it *that* time dear? Have you got the painters in? No offence Carls."

Siobhan laughs grimly,

"Sadly no, Jerry, I haven't. And I won't have for another nine, no, seven and a half months." Jerry frowns. He's trying to compute this info and clearly having trouble,

"What? You don't mean you're? No! You *can't* be? Can you? No waaaay!"

Siobhan bluntly,

"Yes. I can. I am. Way." Feel that this may be an appropriate moment to butt in before Jerry says something tactless that I'll regret on his behalf. Like 'God! How *could* you shag *him*?'

"Jerry, come and help me make some more tea. Be right back Siobhan."

J.

"Oh, but I was just going to ask?" Make a subtle 'shut up, not now, she's upset' face behind her back and shove him gently kitchenwards. He does an 'Ooh, right. Gotcha.' face back, winks and weasels off ahead of me. Siobhan watches us glumly.

"Can't you just talk about me in here guys? And then I could join in? I *can* still hear you in there. This isn't exactly a mansion, you know?" Do a jolly false laugh of denial and disappear into the kitchen after J.

Pop the kettle on while I de-brief J. quietly [in the *gossip* sense of the word]. Only one thing for it in such a situation - some more tea and everything will be fine.

CHAPTER TWENTY-ONE
Boomerang Boys & Branches

I am actually outside the flat for a change, but not that far outside it.
I'm having a therapeutic tidy of the communal garden. It is a ruddy
mess. If I don't do it, it doesn't get done and I've been too busy
getting famous. All the neighbours are elderly and rarely lift anything
heavier than a scone, or a domino in the case of male neighbours.
Oldies are quite sexist. Real men don't make scones! Anyway, none of
them are quite up to gardening. But they do like to sit in the sun, so
I'm trying my best to clear a space.

I really quite like gardening, not proper gardening with weeding
and tedious things of that nature, more the tidying or building things
artistic bit. The garden was previously some kind of field. It seems to
be lacking in structure somewhat. I like building little walls and
borders [I had Lego and Meccano as a kid]. Or pruning bushes into
weird fancy shapes. I am presently attacking a very large lilac
monster. And it isn't co-operating in the slightest. I'll just take a little
bit off this side.

"Snip, snip" Ooh! I'm scratched? It appears to be attacking me
back? Oh well, it's not fatal... Tum-ti-tum, Oh, this is sooo
entertaining. Garden therapy – very restful. It is nice to escape from
the more hectic bits of life. Why can't everyone leave me alone? You
don't need to have a man to be happy. At least, I don't for a while.
Why can't all my friends see that? What do they think that I am? I am
not sad, desperate or lonely – like some goddamned stereotype. And I
haven't quite reached my sell-by date yet – that would be when I'm
dead. And much as I would like to have a baby some day, I do not

have the slightest desire to accost the next random bloke who comes along. I shall go to a sperm bank instead! No? No, maybe not? That is just a bit yucky! Maybe adoption instead?

Oh, here comes an aforementioned neighbour. At least they don't sneak up on you. It is my pre-historic neighbour Mrs Simmons – I believe a close friend of Moses or somebody equally deceased. She is a storybook granny with statutory twinset woollies on [in July?], and prerequisite white hair in a bun. She lives alone and gets a little bored. She is clearly out for a snoop. I haven't seen her since Jake left. I wonder how long it will take her to ask what she really wants to know? Probably not all that long. Oldies often think they have the right to be tactless and prying on the grounds that they're so nearly dead. Murder must be less of a threat when you're practically there anyway.

She finally reaches the end of the three-foot long path. Here we go....

"Oh, hello Carly dear." What? Don't pretend you're surprised to see me. I saw you spying out of the window. I know why you trundelled all the way down here so, go on then…amaze me…and ask me about something else.

"Haven't seen your young man about dearie? Is everything all right?" Oh yes. He's just suddenly invisible, why?

"No, you wouldn't have. He's gone."

"Gone where? Oh! You mean...? Oh! I wasn't being nosey." Not much.

"Oh no, no, of course." And you thought it was a scandal that we weren't married? Were we not living 'over the brush'?

"Oh dear, you're being very brave." No, I was brave to live with him, not without him. No, I'm mistaken. That was 'stupid'.

"So, Carly dear, what will you do?"

"What will I do about what?"

"Well, you know? You'll be living on your own?" Is that wrong too then? Besides you live on your own?

"Sorry Mrs S. I'm not quite with you?"

"Well, it isn't right , a young girl like you on her own." Young girl? Me?

"I'm actually thirty-four."

"Are you? Oh! Well, that's still very young. You ought to have a young man."

"Erm, …why?"

"You know, to look after you." Surely she can't mean sex? I choose to think she means putting up shelves and stuff.

"I'm perfectly fine on my own, thanks. I've got power tools."

She stares blankly. I know! I shall distract her with her favourite subject.

"So, Mrs S. how's Thomas these days?" Thomas is her cat. He is almost as old as her. She brightens.

"Oh yes, dear, he's fine. He was off his food for a bit and but he seems much better now…

…………...

After a pleasant cat chat Mrs Simmons wanders back inside and I turn back to sorting out the jungle. Oh well, at least my disastrous life cheered her up. She won't have to watch a soap today. And I won't have to bother to tell anyone else. I'll leave her the pleasure of that. It should take her maybe a day at the most. It's amazing how fast these old dears can move when gossip is in the air.

I am happily clipping my lilac creation when a cheeky voice sneaks up behind me.

"Allo Luv, didn't recognise you there wiv your togs on." Spin round gasping at his nerve. What? Who the heck are you? It is a strangely familiar man, who is nodding enthusiastically at my tight vest. ?

"Remember me? I'm the window cleaner, Luv. I come round today to get paid… But you can have a freebie this week. You know? Payment in kind already, ha-ha!" Eek, go away! But he doesn't. He's too busy leching at my cleavage,

"Fairly made my day, that did. Oh well, best get on, I suppose. By the way, nice top." He gives me a lurid wink and strolls off, to pester the grannies for their pensions no doubt, unless they show him their thermals.

Oh my God? That was a bit embarrassing. Oddly enough, I'd forgotten that he'd have to come back to get paid. I shall bear that in mind in the future when I am tempted to do foolhardy stuff.

....

An hour or so of strenuous bush-styling later, Excellent! Finished. A topiary masterpiece. Ought I to take it to the Tate? It'd probably fetch more than a proper work of art. I hear that such nonsense does. Oh, wait a minute! I've missed that bit there? I'll just untangle it and clip it. [the next bit happens in slow motion] OH? I didn't realise it was holding back that big branch...It's going to hit me...I'd better move. But I'm not fast enough.

"Aaaarrrgh!" Too late.

"SMACK!"

....

Some time later - Uumph! What? What happened? ...I was in the back garden...This is most definitely not my garden! ...It's ? ...It's ...a hospital? Struggle to turn and see. I can hear a voice really far away outside my head.

"I think she's waking up? Carly? Carly, can you hear me? Carly, speak to me Sweetheart." Who is that? That voice sounds familiar? It's? It's? Open my eyes to check. It's Jake looking down at me in a very concerned way? What on Earth?

"She's awake! Nurse!" The nurse comes over.

"She opened her eyes. Carly, speak to me. Are you O.K.?" Try to go for 'I don't know. What's happening?' but it just comes out as...

"Oomph." Total gibberish? My mouth is not working and seems to feel a bit funny, kind of numb and rubbery. What's going on? And my head appears to be somewhat overcrowded with the hammers of hell in full swing. I really shall have to keep my eyes shut. But no, he doesn't seem to want to let me?

"No Carly, sweetheart, try to stay awake. The doctor is just coming. Come on, now." Doctor? Uh-oh? Open my eyes. Right enough, a big man in a white coat is looming over me with a little tiny torch thing in his hand? Eeek! What have I done? And don't point your little thingy at me! We haven't even been introduced?

"Now then, Miss Watson, nothing for you to worry about. Gave your boyfriend here a bit of a scare, so you did.... Now just you look straight at the light....hmmm, hmmm?" What are you doing to me? And he is not my boyfriend. He's just the ratty creep who left me. And he's seeing somebody else!

"Oomph. Oomph! OOMPH!" Oh yeah, that really told him!

"Now then, doesn't appear to be any real damage done...No bones broken this time. You've been very lucky young lady." Oh? Really? Yippee.

"An inch higher up and that branch would have done some real damage." WHAT?

"Oomph? Umph? Brumph?" Struggle to sit up only to be gently replaced on the horrid hospital trolley which it appears that I am on. Oh, damn it!

So, I can only assume that the facial numbness is not a good thing at all. Clearly that very large branch has smashed all my teeth clean down the back of my throat and much as I am dying to know – a mirror would probably be a bad thing right now. I have to meet Shrimpton-Boswick in the next two weeks to finalise arrangements for my exhibition and preview night. I still have ten squillion-zillion things to do. Paintings take two weeks at the very least to dry ...and where am I? Trapped in a surreal version of Casualty with my beer-swilling, tart-sucking ex-boyfriend of the Freddie Kruger variety apparently? Double, treble, quadruple knickeration! How do I get out of here? God? Erm, where have you gone? Always on a ruddy tea break when I need you? Right now I'd settle for a genie in a lamp. Wonder if plastic surgery is very expensive? And could they do it right away? Or will I have to go to my own preview with a face like a sink plunger? Oh God! *What* will Shrimpton-Boswick say? At least it ought to put him off groping me. See? There's an up side to almost everything.

CHAPTER TWENTY-TWO
No Other Choice Left - Plan Z

The next day, I have escaped at last from Ward Alcatraz and scary Dr No. Yesterday I had a charming exchange with the aforementioned quack, who unfortunately had the upper hand.

"No, Miss Watson, you can't leave the premises. We're going to have to scan your head."

"But if you don't let me leave the premises, I'm going to have to smack your nose!" which actually still came out as Oomph, moomph, woomph, lemme go home!" I found myself hustled quick-smart at the point of a huge scary sedative needle into a horrid starchy-sheet bed. I have a previously undiscovered starch allergy and I look like a goddamned sun dried tomato. Wasn't the Cornish pasty face enough? I shall never go back to a hospital again. It's clearly far too dangerous. I shall die at home in peace instead. My phone is off the hook indefinitely. I don't want to speak to anyone, not even J.? And particularly not Jake. I don't know what the hell he wants but I know what he's not going to get!

I have ensconced myself on the settee with a big cuddly security duvet and I'm rifling through my emergency, sanity-restoring stash of Billy Connolly DVDs. When the inevitable traumas of life occur, I can fully recommend this treatment – the C. Plan, no scary needles involved and totally and utterly infallible. Slot in the first one and cuddle up into my duvet. Save me Billy! I'm waiting.

My hero appears onscreen, huge and hairy as ever. He is clad in the most outrageous pair of bright yellow banana shaped boots, which I understand were not off the peg, if footwear can be such a thing? Jerry would be emerald with envy. Clutching his faithful banjo Billy begins,

"And now, The Welly Boot Song!" This'll work. This is what I need. Go for it Billy! Sure fire, cannot fail. Connolly is King! ...I cannot believe that some people are not au fait with the classics?

The Welly-man launches into this poignant little number,

"If it wisnae fur yer wellies where wid ye be?" Right here Bill – still waiting?

"You'd be in the hos-ping-tile or infirm-aree!" Christ no? Not again! Clearly I should have had my Wellingtons on, if I had any. And then the branch would not have hurt my face?

"You would have a dose of the flu or even pleuresy." Or even a face like a Cornish frigging pasty?

"If ye didnae huv yer feet in yer we-llies!" Not working! Not working? Aaargh!

"Oh cobblers!" An unprecedented failure? Please Bill – second verse?

"SING! If it wisnae fur yer wellies.... plinky, plinky, plonk...(etc, etc)

A few sadly disillusioned minutes later.

"When some bugger takes aff his weee-lllieeees!"

Audience,

"HOORAY! HOORAY! CHEERS! UPROAR!" ...NOOO! NO, it's not true? It can't be? When you're tired of Billy, *then* you're tired of life? Hell's teeth, I am done for! Fling a vicious cushion across the room at the banana-footed traitor.

"Waah! Waah! Aaargh!"

. . . .

A little while later - I have cried myself into oblivion and I would like to be able to say I feel better, but I can't, because I don't. I have never felt so bad in my whole life. But why? It doesn't make any sense? Attempt to decipher my befuddled thoughts and emotions. I mean O.K., I admit it, I'm still sad about splitting up with Jake. After all, we were together for three whole years... And I did love him, inexplicably enough.... And it has only been a few weeks? But we didn't get on? I was miserable. And he either didn't notice or didn't care. Neither of which is much of a basis for a fulfilling life-long partnership. It wasn't what I wanted? It wasn't enough!

I'm just being pathetic because I'm concussed, I look dreadful and I am not used to being by myself yet... And it is a bit lonely? Well, quite a lot lonely, particularly in the evenings when I'm not busy working or out doing stuff. Mind you, it was lonely even when he *was* here. He was no company at all. I am getting confused between a perfectly logical and normal need for companionship and an irrational, pink-coloured view of the past. That's all it is. There is no need to worry. I'll get over it... It's astounding how even a short space of time blurs the full horror of a doomed relationship. I suppose some things are much better forgotten.

And it's not as if I miss the sex? It wasn't really that great anyway recently. I would quite like to have sex as, with the right person, it is the most enjoyable thing one could possibly be doing. But that's not what I really need. I would just really like a cuddle... a proper one. Cuddling your friends is not the same. I am so tired inside my head and totally confused about everything. It was horrid to see Jake with that girl, quite nauseating ... But he is not my property so too bad. I'll get over it eventually I suppose.

But what was he doing at the hospital? I can't remember anything much at all, certainly not going there? I was in the garden? The tree hit me... He must have come round for some of his stuff and just happened to come across me... easily done. I can vouch for that after the other week! What about that two-timing actor towrag? As if I didn't feel bad enough? Oh no! I have to go and have the first one night stand of my entire life with a pathological pervert and professional git.

Great, now I'm Miss Havisham, spinster bitch extraordinaire? No, that's not quite right. Maybe our situations are a little bit similar though? Just mine involved two different guys. She got led on then dumped. Jake dumped me and Aaron led me on... Or did he? Did he just want casual sex and I'm too naïve to know? ...I must be a complete muppet. Perhaps it is socially correct to tell nookie lies like 'you're really special' and stuff? Maybe it's only good manners and I've completely misconstrued the point? I have virtually no experience in this field so I can't really tell? It's not like he tricked me into going to dinner? Oh no! Nothing so tedious and mundane, I'll just kidnap her. That'll be quicker? ...And he didn't so much trick me the first time as assault me? The fact that I quite enjoyed it is neither here nor there. I might NOT have. He didn't stop to enquire in advance? ...I believe that is actually a felony? I've been felonised against my will? How DARE he?

In point of fact, I've been molested, stalked and kidnapped all in the same month? This joker could go down for years – in the clink, that is. He's a goddam one man crime spree! ...Perhaps I ought to phone someone official and report him? But no! I don't need to. I have shunned his advances and firmly rebuffed him with my curt closure note and tart picture. He will be torturing himself already so there is absolutely no need to waste the taxpayers hard earned pennies on an ill-fitting outfit with arrows on it and his other legal just desserts. So! I have closure on both of them. AND I am well en route to becoming a successful artist, despite not being full of poo and actually painting or drawing things. Sculpting counts too, it's just not my forte.

So, on the plus side, I have my lovely flat, my lovely friends. I might well even have money soon? And my face will heal up, eventually. So *why* am I feeling like this? I didn't know it was possible to feel this bad. It's like a physical pain in my chest. I feel like I'm dying inside. I thought 'le petit mort' meant an orgasm? Clearly it isn't that at all? I would just like to crawl into a corner and die. Or at least get the hell out of here. But I can't. I've got to work and my preview's coming up.

It's bad if I can't even talk to my friends about it. I can usually tell them anything. But I don't want to talk. I don't even want to think. ....
Maybe I'm going mad? Maybe if you paint too much you go all Van Gogh? And I have been painting... a lot ... So great! I'm a manic-depressive now and not just some pre-menstrual fool? ... Hey! Wait a

minute! When's my period due? I haven't had one for ages? …Oh no! I can't be? … I cannot be up the duff? I only slept with him once? Calendar? Calendar? …Ah! Calendar. Now when was my last…?

`"Oh no! Oh NO!" Collapse onto the floor and lose the plot completely. This can't be happening to me. I am always so careful. I've never done anything like this in my life. Moan quietly and hold my aching head in my hands in order to steady my thoughts. Now Carly, just calm down. It might not be that at all. You could just be late and not up the stick? It happens for other reasons too…like? Like stress and exhaustion and stuff. Yes, that's what it'll be. I've certainly had plenty of both. I shall not panic. I am yoga breathing slowly. I do not need a paper bag at all – except perhaps for my face? In – out, in – out. I am absolutely fine. I shall go to Boots tomorrow, just to make sure. But it is a formality only. There is nothing to worry about.

Sit up slightly, still on my knees and examine the overall situation. Great! So now not only am I traumatised, but I can't even induce the necessary therapeutic oblivion with a sanity saving drink …as I may possibly be up the stick with some scumbag actor's unwanted sperm? I did want kids? But I wanted them to be human, not half-demonic thesp.? That is not a good lineage at all. Oh fan-tastic! This is just way too cruel. My life is just a great big joke in quite appallingly poor taste.

CHAPTER TWENTY-THREE
An Unexpected Twist

The next day – I've been to Boots. Got the required little blue box. It seems quite straightforward. Just pee on white stick and wait. O.K. We can cope with that.

So, now that I've done that I shall have a calming cup of tea. I am not going to sit about watching a stick for five minutes. That would be absolute torture. Kettle on, teabags out. A Camomile situation, I believe. I am fine, I am not panicking at all. La, la, la. Toss my teaspoon into the sink and take my tea through into the lounge, resisting the strong urge to peek into the bathroom. I shall just sit here calmly. There is no problem. Another three whole minutes to go. No point in worrying in advance. Glance down at my stomach. It doesn't look any bigger? It's been, oh what? Five weeks? So when does it start to swell up then? Doesn't look any fatter than before? Give it an experimental prod with one finger. I am unfamiliar with the pregnancy timescale. I haven't had to think of it before. I did want a baby quite badly for a while, but unfortunately I already had a tall one in the house, one who wasn't very good with 'responsibility' and thinking about someone apart from himself.

I wonder if the baby would look like me, or the father? Would it have Aaron's crazy hair? Oh I hope not. What a nightmare? But it does look good on him? Oh, I don't know? Start imagining tiny actors and footballers in prams with crazy hair versus football shirts and tiny beer cans... or beer in a baby bottle. Yuck! The hair would be much easier to explain. At least I would know who the actual father is.

Imagine if you somehow overlapped? It would drive you completely insane not to know.

O.K. – Five minutes. I'm going to look now. And whatever it says [negative], I'm going to behave [negative] in a mature and adult fashion [negative, negative please!] Scuttle into the bathroom. So, is it blue in the little window? No? Oh! So I'm not? Oh? I'm not pleased? Am I crazy? I didn't want a baby now. Did I? … Well, I'm not, so there's no point dithering over it. Toss the tiny science kit into the pedal bin and wash my hands. Lecture myself in the bathroom mirror.

"You're just being silly! You can't have a baby to someone you hardly know. . That's completely ridiculous… blah de blah." Nope! I am not convinced. It would seem that I have disturbed my dormant hormones now? Damn! Hope they go back to sleep soon. It's most probable that they will, as they are unlikely to be disturbed again for some time. I have had a lucky escape. Peer into the bathroom mirror in horrified amazement. Jesus! Just look at the state of my face? It's all different colours now that the bruising has come out. Who'd fancy me looking like this anyway? No-one without a white stick. My knickers could not be more safe.

A tentative 'bang, bang' at the front door. Finish drying my hands. Hmm, wasn't expecting anyone? Toddle through the hall for a look. Open the door casually. Oh? It is a huge bunch of flowers with feet? Oh no. There's someone behind them. I can see a vague sort of shape. The flowers are thrust forward revealing…. Jake? He's never bought me flowers in his life? And he's looking very nervous? And shuffling about?

"Er, hi Carly. Just came round to see that you're O.K. The hospital said that you'd checked yourself out against the doctor's advice… I was, um, a bit worried about you." Worried? What, you? He winces at the sight of my multi-coloured visage. "Are you alright? I mean, obviously you're not your usual self but…. you know?" I am gobsmacked… again. My God! He actually cares? He is still shuffling about awkwardly on the doorstep. Oh, how rude of me.

"Er, would you like to come in? Um, thanks for the flowers. They're lovely."

167

Jake looks encouraged.

"Oh yeah. Fine, O.K." Trundles past me. Well, I suppose he knows the way. Oh, this is weird. Being visited by my ex. In our old house? I'm not sure about this but I couldn't not ask him. And he has come quite a long way. Shut the door and follow him through to the lounge. He is perched twitchily on the edge of the settee and is looking around at the room. ???

"What?"

"It looks...different?"

"It's tidy." Ooh! Oops! That sounded a bit bitchy? It wasn't meant. He has obviously taken it as a dig. Saw him wince.

"Oh... So how are you Carls? How's the head? You shouldn't have checked yourself out." Don't start telling me what I shouldn't do!

"I'm fine. It's nothing. It looks worse than it is." Raises his eyebrows.

"Carly, don't lie. I was there. It was me who found you, remember?" Uh, no?

"Oh, was it? I didn't know. Uh, thanks." He is getting quite worked up now...and louder – much louder.

"You were out like a light and your head was all blood and your blood was all over the path."

"Stop! Enough information, Too much already. You know I don't like to think about blood. It makes me sick."

"Well, I don't like to look at it, especially yours. But I didn't exactly get a choice. What the fuck happened? Did some bastard attack you? Because if they did."

"What? No! I was pruning that old lilac." Looks confused. He knows nothing about gardening and the potential dangers thereof.

"Eh? What lilac? Lilac what?"

"Lilac tree. The one that's been in our back garden for the last three years.... and probably a long time before that. You must have seen it?"

"Dunno. What's a lilac look like exactly?" What? How could you not know that?

"You know? The big tree in the corner with the pinky-purple flowers?"

"Oh, that thing. How could a tree do that to your face? I mean, a skelf or a scratch I could understand, but Carly, my God? What were you doing?"

"Oh right! So it's my fault as usual is it?" Oh, I remember this well. It's all coming back. I'm just a useless imbecile who really ought to stick to painting her nails and…. and typing and stuff? Puts his head in his hands and sighs deeply like he's tired?

"No Carly, that wasn't what I meant at all…. Why do you always twist everything I say? I didn't come here to argue." God no! That's right, he didn't. He brought me lovely flowers and I'm behaving like a bitch?

"Oh I'm sorry. I didn't mean it. … Would you like a coffee or something?" Looks up from his hands and smiles. He ought to do that more often. He actually looks quite handsome?

"Yeah, O.K. That'd be nice." Nice? Hmm, maybe it would? Maybe I've misjudged him? After all, he obviously cares if he's here? Toddle off into the kitchen to put the kettle on and put my lovely flowers into water. Rattle about in the cupboard for the coffee- making stuff. Glance round. He has picked up one of the tickets for my preview. They were in a big pile on coffee table waiting patiently for me to get round to sending them. I was going to do it today. (I was!)

Bring the coffee through and place it on the table in front of him. Sit down beside him on the settee as the armchair is covered in my paperwork.

"What's this Carly?" Waves the ticket. Nonchalant,

"Oh, it's just an exhibition I'm doing this weekend. It's no big deal. Take one if you like." Raises his eyebrows. He looks quite impressed. Puts the ticket in his pocket. ???

"No big deal? The Eglinton Hall? That's owned by that bigwig. Oh, what's his name? Something really poncy?"

"Edgar Shrimpton-Boswick. You've heard of him?"

"Yeah, he's got shares in the a couple of teams up North. He's loaded."

"Has he? No way!"

"No, really. He's a major shareholder. He's like Richard Branson or something, finger in every pie type of bloke."

"He's like Leslie Phillips actually." Questioning eyebrows.

"Who?" Oh, and you were doing so well.

"Leslie Phillips, an old actor. He was usually a cad in the old films. Says 'Oh he-ello' a lot." Jake looks bemused.

"A cad? What the fuck is that when it's at home? Like some kind of villain, do you mean?"

"Sort of... So what have you been up to then?" He looks a bit embarrassed.

"I meant in general, not with that girl." Looks very embarrassed now.

"Oh, her. Look Carly, I'm really sorry. Nothing happened. It didn't mean anything. I was drunk." So what's new?

"You don't have to explain yourself to me. We're not going out remember? You're a free agent. It's your business." He doesn't look too happy at that. He struggles for words.

"But that's just it Carls. I don't want to be."

"Don't want to be what?" He is rubbing one hand through his hair, making it all stick up, a sign of severe stress usually reserved solely for penalty shoot-outs.

"A free agent – I don't want to be. I want ... I want you back. I miss you, you know." Oh my God! What the hell do I do now? He looks up traumatised. He really isn't good at discussing emotions, or even admitting that he's got them. That must have taken some guts to admit. He's waiting for a response ...And I haven't got one.

"Jake, I.... I don't know what to say. I wasn't expecting this." Oh God! Please don't be going to cry. I don't know what to do. He has grabbed one of my hands and is staring at it. I am stunned.

"Look Carly, I realise things weren't that great for a bit there... And maybe I didn't handle things very well. But you do know that I love you, don't you?" WHAT? You've never said that?

"I ...., umm, I don't..."

"Look, I realise this is probably a bit of a shock. I don't expect you to answer straight away but... I'd really like us to get back together. I know things got a bit difficult since I got laid up, and maybe I could have handled it a bit better... but we could put all that behind us..." Oh God! Help me somebody please. Can't think what to do? He glances up to check my expression. He is still holding my hand.

"And there's something else Carly."

"Oh?" Now what? Oh? He has got off the settee and is kneeling on the carpet. Oh no, you are kidding? Takes both my hands.

"Carly, will you marry me?" He takes a little blue box out of his pocket and opens it – the most beautiful little ring in the world, a perfect single diamond. OH!

I can feel my eyes getting bigger and bigger. I can't believe this is happening. It is surreal. Is it some kind of weird concussion dream? Shut my eyes and open them. No, he's still there... waiting for an answer. Bite my lip. Oh God! What do I say?

"I – I just don't know.... I mean, it's beautiful... I just wasn't expecting..... I wasn't..." Oh no! I am floundering. Jake sighs and squeezes both my hands in one of his. He has very big hands. Smiles bravely.

"Well, at least that's not a no.... I expect you need a bit of time to think about it, right? It's a big decision. That's O.K." He snaps the ring box shut and hastily stuffs it in his pocket. His face has taken on a distinctly pinkish tinge. I start to get tongue-tied, embarrassed by his unusually vulnerable state, trying desperately to make things better.

"Umm, yes, that's it. I need to think... I'm sorry, do you mind? It was a lovely thing to do. I just wasn't ready." He stands up suddenly and rubs his hair with both hands - very serious.

"No Sweetheart, that's fine. Look, I'll go now. No, it's O.K., Don't get up, you're not well. I'll see myself out. You'll need some time to think. I'll phone you in a day or so, O.K.?"

"Uh, O.K." Bends over and kisses my cheek. Oh how sweet. I think I'm going to cry.

"See you later Carly. Don't do anything else silly. Don't want you coming down the aisle on crutches now, do we? Bye." He leaves quietly for the first time ever. Oh! He's gone? Married? Us? No way! ... Or maybe? God! Maybe it would be nice. I've no idea what I want.

I am still sitting on the settee stunned when the pesky phone summons me abruptly back to reality. Lean over and pick it up.

"Hello?"

"Carly, it's Siobhan. The most amazing thing just happened."

"Yes, I know. I was here... But how did you know? Are you psychic?"

"What? What are you talking about? Oh, never mind. I've just got to tell you It's Angie." I am suddenly worried. What's Miles done now? She was really upset the last time.... Surely she wouldn't do anything silly?

"What? Is she alright? What's happened?"

"Alright? She is bloody fantastic! Carly, you'll never guess. I think she's about to ditch Miles!"

In Eastenders the music would start now.

CHAPTER TWENTY-FOUR
Dr J. Saves The Day

Wednesday 10.25 a.m. - As I am feeling marginally less suicidal this morning I have decided I'd better return at least some of the numerous messages on my answer phone and my mobile. Ange, Jerry and Siobhan have all tried both numbers so it would be incredibly ignorant not to call them back.

Besides, I have to find out what's happening on the Angie/ Sleazeboy front. Maybe she's already dumped him? I wonder what happened? Siobhan didn't seem very sure. Also, another major consideration - Jerry is so melodramatic and watches so much cheap T.V. that if he can't find me for a whole week he may well do something embarrassing like reporting me to the police as a missing person or something. I do not want some burly policeman kicking in my front door thank you very much.

But I'm forgetting - J. has a key. He could just let them in. Even worse! They might come charging in en masse when I'm in the bath or the shower or something? Dear God! It doesn't bear thinking about. It's quite bad enough that eventually I shall have to show my battered face. I've not the slightest desire to show anything else while I'm at it. Nope! I'd definitely better phone them all back pronto.

Pick up the phone and snuggle up on the sofa in a comfy phoning position. Best to do this in advance if you're planning to be on the phone for a while. If I'm trying to economise on my phone bill I deliberately do the opposite. It works wonders for your bank balance. I'll try Angie first. She's so wrapped up in her own problems right now that I can probably fob her off with the most basic of details. And she won't give me a hard time about Jake being here. Compared to Miles, Jake doesn't look quite so bad. Good grief! I've finally found it! A plus side to Miles? Wonders really will never cease.

I dial her office number in glamorous T.V. land. I'd better not mention Mr Sleazy in case Siobhan has got it wrong… or Jake's proposal. That would be a bit tactless in the circumstances. Oh, this is just too difficult. If she's in a meeting [which she usually is] I can get away with just leaving a message.

"Ring-ring, ring-ring!" An efficient young female voice answers,

"Good morning, Angela Montrose's office. Tanya speaking."

"Oh, yes, hello. Is Miss Montrose available please? It's Carly Watson here."

"One moment please. I'll just check for you." Small pause as presumably she's doing just that. The voice returns,

"I'm putting you through now Ms Watson."

"Thank you." Angie breezes onto the line on an unusually cheery note.

"Carly, hi. How're you? I've been looking for you for days. Didn't you get my messages?"

Guilty,

"Um, yes, sorry. I was in hiding. Not from you, just in general."

"Why? Has Jake been round?"

"What? How on Earth did you…? Um, I mean, why would he be?"

"Carly, I was joking. Why are you being so defensive? A simple 'no' would be fine."

Flustered,

"Well, as a matter of fact he has. He came round the other night."

"Really? What did he want?"

"Erm, I haven't the faintest idea. I don't think he said."

Disbelieving,

"What? He came all the way round there and he didn't tell you what he wanted? Well, what did he say? He must have said something?" Decide to partially confess, as this is proving even trickier than I had anticipated.

"Well, he didn't really get the chance to say very much. I was tidying the garden and I sort of bumped my head. Apparently he took me to Casualty." She shrieks, much to the detriment of my aching headache,

"What do you mean 'apparently'? Don't you know? Have you got amnesia or something? Were you concussed?"

"I wasn't actually conscious. But I was concussed last night … I think."

"Good God Carly! Are you alright? What the hell happened?"

Embarrassed,

"Nothing. I just, um, bumped my head on a branch that's all."

"You must have bumped it pretty hard to be unconscious?"

"Angie I'm O.K. I'm not exactly looking my best but I'm fine. Don't worry."

She puts on her interviewing inquisitor voice,

"So, did he bring you home?"

"No. I discharged myself when he wasn't looking. But enough about me already. What've you been up to?" She brightens noticeably at this,

"Me? Oh well, I'm just great. Never been better in fact." Really? That makes a pleasant change. So, have you done it?

"Oh? Uh, good…" She gushes on,

"Yes, anyway… I've been thinking a lot about Miles and I lately, you know, what with Siobhan and Giles and everything?"

"Uh- huh?" You've dumped him? Please tell me you've dumped him?

"Anyhow, I decided that I simply couldn't go on hanging about in limbo like this any more. You know, with Miles' divorce and all that?" Huh! *What* divorce?

"Absolutely. So what're you going to do?"

"We-ell, I decided to have it out with him once and for all. No more shilly-shallying around the issue. Get everything out in the open. And guess what?"

Cynical,

"What?"

175

"He's made an appointment with a lawyer for next week, to discuss divorce proceedings. He's going to sort everything out at last. Isn't it fantastic?" Oh heaven preserve us! I thought that she was shot of him at last?

"Oh yes, fantastic. I presume then that this means that he's told his wife at last?" Angie goes all quiet and defensive,

"Well…no. Not as such. Not yet. But he's going to. He promised." Oh no! Oh no! This has all the classic hallmarks of disaster…doesn't she *ever* learn?

"Ange, I don't mean to be cynical or anything… But don't you think he'd better tell her before the lawyer does? I mean, don't get me wrong, it's great that he's sorting himself out and all that. But surely there's an order in which to do these things? Some kind of ethical protocol?"

She snaps,

"Oh, I should have known that you'd be like that, finding fault as usual. I wish I hadn't told you now, if you're just going to twist things. Why are you all so determined to think the worst of him? Can't you see what he's going through? Do you think it's been easy for him? Hmm? Do you?" Sigh heavily. I really don't need this to-day…

"Angie, no-one is trying to find fault. And no-one would be happier than me to see you sorted. I'm just saying be careful, that's all. These things have a habit of turning nasty and I don't want to see you get hurt, that's all. O.K.?"

Snippy,

"Well, you needn't worry. I'm not going to be. Miles would never do anything to upset me. The only ones who do that are you lot. I don't know why you have to be so critical. Can't you at least give him the benefit of the doubt?"

Tired,

"Sure, whatever. Look Ange, I'd better let you get on. I'm sure you're busy. I really hope everything works out for you. Give me a call and let me know what happens, huh?"

"Oh, I suppose so. And I have got a meeting in a bit. I'd better at least look at the notes for it. See you later Carly."

"O.K., bye." Hang up wearily and sag back against a cushion, wincing as a sharp pain knifes through my temples. Well, that went well, I don't think. I haven't got the mental strength left to call anyone else. Perhaps just a quick coffee first? I am just putting the phone down when suddenly it takes me by surprise by ringing loudly.

"Eek!" Drop it on the rug in fright. Recover quickly and scoop it back up.

"Hello?"

"Well, about time too!" It's Jerry.

"And would Madam care to tell me precisely what one has done to deserve to be shunned in this outrageous manner? Seven messages? Seven messages I leave you. And do I get a response? No indeed, I most certainly do not! This from someone I'm not going out with? Sheesh? What've you got to say for yourself Hermit-woman? And I warn you it'd better be good."

Laugh happily. J. always cheers me up.

"Oh, I get to speak, do I? You amaze me."

"Me? Well Darling, I'm not the one doing the Lord Lucan, am I? I believe that would be you. So? What the hell's up? Are you hiding from the bailiffs or have you had a secret face lift?"

"Well, in a manner of speaking, yes… the second one."

"You are having me on? You can't have? You're not old enough. Oh, silly me! But of course, you jest?"

"Sadly no. I hit myself in the face with a great big branch and I look like Mick Jagger only worse. I couldn't phone you back. I was trapped in a surreal version of Casualty with a control freak in a big white coat. Why? Did you miss me?"

"Car-leeee! That is not funny! You shouldn't joke about things like that. It might, you know, tempt fate."

"I'm not. It's true and I've got the paper stitches to prove it."

"Oh God! Oh God! Not your face? Is it really bad? Are we talking 'we can probably cover it with a bit of concealer' or a full scale Mr Potato Head? On a scale of one to ten for damage, what would you say? Three? Four?"

"Eleven. No wait, fifty-two. My face is now entirely abstract. I'm going to stand right in the middle of my exhibition as an informal installation piece, and as a warning to little children against the dangers of playing in one's own garden. Are you particularly busy tonight or would you care to come round and gloat in a voyeuristic manner?"

"Um, O.K. There's nothing on the box. Shall I bring a camera? Is there anyone you can sue for a couple of grand? Like the local council or somebody… for dodgy paving slabs or something of the sort? "

"Erm, no. I don't think so, but thanks for your heartfelt concern. I'm truly touched."

"So what's new?"

"Just let yourself in J. I'm not at home to callers this evening. If I answer the door to you, you might turn out to be somebody else."

"Oh, if only. Someone rich, sophisticated and celebrated perhaps."

"Oh well, never mind J. One out of three's not bad."

"Cheeky bitch! Any more of your lip and I won't bring you any grapes, not even of the Haddows variety."

"Oh you're a hard man Jerry."

"Yes, I know. I've been told. Vinny Jones has got nothing on me."

"Don't worry. I haven't got any more lip. I used to have, in the old days, B.T.B.B. - before the big branch."

"Oh bless! Never mind Babe. Dr Jerry's on his way. We'll get plastered and smash all your mirrors. And then everything'll be fine."

"Feel free. I'm not scared. I've had all my bad luck in advance. See you soon."

"Be there in a tick Carls. Byeee." And in a click of hanging up he is gone, hopefully to Haddows, the A & E of emotional trauma. Hurry up J. I think I might need that transfusion now.

…………...

Approximately twenty minutes later I am slumped sideways across the big tatty armchair vacantly staring at the ceiling when the erstwhile Dr J. swans in with his full pick-me-up kit.

"Car-lee! Where are you my little walking disaster? It's Dr. Jerry come to save you from yourself." He appears in the lounge doorway and looks round to see where I am. He's clutching a huge box of Milk Tray and a bunch of flowers of the garage forecourt variety. Better still he has in his possession a cheerily clinking Haddows bag. Hurray! But oddly, he has a strange rectangular shaped bulge under his jacket. Oh well. I expect there is a rational explanation.

Sauntering in he clocks my pathetic crumpled figure and the piece de resistance of my multicoloured face. Stopping dead in his cheery tracks he drops all his booty in shock. Fortunately for all concerned the clinky bag lands safely on the settee. Slapping an overly dramatic palm to either of his concave cheeks he squeaks in a horror-struck voice,

"Carly? Darling, is that you? Dear Lord in heaven, what have they done to you?" Thanks J. That makes me feel sooo much better. Sigh heavily in resignation,

"Unfortunately J., I did it to myself. Mia culpa and all that. So I don't have the luxury of having someone to blame. I expect it'll heal up soon." He raises both eyebrows,

"Yeah, right, in a couple of years. But Darling? Your preview's this week-end?"

Tight little voice,

"I'm actually well aware of that Jerry. I didn't do it on purpose you know."

"But what are you going to do? You can't go looking like that?"

Tearful,

"I don't bloody well know! What do you think? Because I haven't the faintest idea." Give a little exhausted sob of frustration. J. recovers himself immediately at the sight of 'drama'.

"Now don't you worry your little dented head about a thing Carls. Dr Jerry will sort everything out." He starts flustering about plumping cushions and patting my arm gingerly. My *arm* is fine?

Eventually I am settled to his satisfaction on the sofa with several cushions and a king sized duvet tucked round me. Though how this will help my face to heal up is beyond me? I must be 'resting'. And

I'm not even an actor. Jerry smiles encouragingly and adopts a firm but patronising nursy attitude as he gamely piles chocolates and assorted magazines on top of me. I decide to go with the flow, after all it's quite nice to be pampered for a change. And I really do feel quite bad. Must be the concussion. Apparently concussion makes you sick, even quite a long time after the event.

Flop back onto my cushion-pillows as J. rushes off into the kitchen with his tantalising carrier bag, presumably in search of a glass. Shut my aching eyes and sigh peacefully. It's nice to be taken care of, unusual but nice. Thank God for Jerry. I could so do with a drink right now. He is sooo thoughtful. Open my eyes as he hustles back in. With a waiter-style flourish he plonks a glass down on the coffee table beside me.

"There you go my sweet, just what the doctor ordered. Enjoy." Plonking himself down on the tatty armchair he leans forward and hugs his bony knees. He regards me with a saintly little smile.

"Oh, I do so love my vocation. Helping others Carls, that's the thing. In giving do we truly receive." Is that a fact? Fascinating. Give me my drink. Hoi! Wait a minute! It's orange? …and fizzy? What the hell kind of wine is that? Point an enquiring digit at the bubbling liquid,

"Erm, Jerry, what exactly is that? Is it a Bacardi Breezer?" He smiles benevolently [Saint Jerry]. Talks slowly as if I am retarded,

"Why Carly my love, it's your lucozade. To make you better? Come on now, drink up." Aaaaaaaaargh! Nooooo! It's not even booze? Stare mutinously at him,

"My what? But it was in a Haddows bag? J' leans his chin on one hand and nods placidly,

"Uh-huh. I had an old bag in the house. Why? You didn't really want booze did you darling? You can't drink when you've been concussed. Didn't they tell you that at the hospital? Standard head injury procedures. You ought to have been given a little sheet of paper with a list of things not to do? Stick my bottom lip out petulantly, feeling tearful again,

"Well I wasn't. I was just given a whole lot of cheek. Rotters!"
Jerry leans over the table and squeezes my hand,

"Come on, buck up Carls. It's only for a couple of days or so. Then
I'll take you anywhere you like for a drink, O.K.? Deal?" Grudging,

"I suppose…"

"Good! Now drink up your lucozade like a good little invalid and
then I'll show you your special surprise."

"Surprise? What is it?" J. snorts derisively,

"Well, if I just told you I'd have no leverage with which to
blackmail you, would I my little naivette?" Eye him suspiciously for a
second till my innate nosiness overcomes my momentary burst of
rebellion. Pick up the glass and take a cautious sip. I haven't had
lucozade since I was about ten years old. Hmm, quite pleasant
actually? Take a couple of gulps and plonk it back on the table. Jerry
looks on approvingly.

"O.K.? I'll have my surprise now if you please Mr Blackmailer.
Come on, whip it out."

"Oh fnaar fnaar. No wonder you get into so much trouble if you go
around saying things like that."

"Shut up and give me it. Now!" He laughs and stands up.
Unzipping his jacket he pulls out a DVD and tosses it onto my lap.
Pick it up and examine the cover.

" 'Great Artists Of Our Time. An in-depth look at portraiture
featuring a selection of works by Rembrandt, Holbein, Reynolds,
Gainsborough and Van Dyke.' Oh thanks Jerry. Where on Earth did
you find this?"

He smirks,

"That would be telling. I've been meaning to give it to you but I
kept forgetting. Sadly, you're not actually in it. But I thought you
would enjoy the portrait stuff."

"Yes, it's great. Thanks J. You're the best. There's nothing like
seeing the work of someone better than you to make you aspire to
greater heights. I'll watch it later. It'll give me something to do till my
head recovers." Jerry looks smug,

"Oh, good. I'm glad you like it. Now, my dear, perhaps a little cup of tea."

"Help yourself."

"Thank you. I shall. Maybe even a couple of bourbon creams or something. Being a medic is very hard work." He wanders off kitchen wards leaving me to happily peruse my DVD. 'Great Artists Of Our Time. You never know, maybe one day that'll be me.

CHAPTER TWENTY-FIVE
Oops?

Friday morning and as I appear to be exceptionally poverty stricken this week I am rifling in emergency places for loose change; couch, pockets, bottom of my bag. As the first two proved depressingly fruitless I am pinning all my desperate hopes on the bulging string shoulder bag.

Peering into its murky depths I strike gold, well almost. A couple of pound coins glint teasingly up at me. After rifling frustrated in vain for at least three seconds I give up and tip the entire contents onto my bed. Scoop aside the dubious debris and nab the precious coins. [Precious is entirely relative to your bank balance.] Aha! Got you, you little blighters. You shan't escape me now. In you go. Stuff them unceremoniously into the pocket of my scruffy jeans and turn to the annoying task of getting everything to fit back into my bag. Sigh and start to shove the ever-expanding contents in through it's tattered top.

Suddenly something unfamiliar catches my eye - a classy looking piece of thick gold edged card? Eek! It's that bloke's business card, Raymond thingy? I was supposed to give that to Jerry. Oh nooo! I forgot all about it. That was *ages* ago. Oh God! What if J.'s missed out on his big chance to get published because of me? Damn! Damn! Well, nothing else for it. I'll just have to phone J. and confess. Hopefully the good news of an interested publisher will outweigh the bad news that it's very, *very* late and he might be too busy publishing other people now. And it's all my fault.

Toddle through to the phone, a cloud of horrendous guilt floating round my head. Oh well, once more into the breach. It's got to be done. Best get it over with.. Pick up the receiver and dial.

"Ring-ring, ring-ring, click. [answer phone], "Greetings caller, you have reached the residence of Gerald P. Green, philosopher and poet. Unfortunately, however, it would appear that you have reached it at a rather inopportune moment. Kindly be so good as to leave a cordial message at the sound of the tone. Thank you sooo much darling, byeeee. Meep". Hurray! Answer phone. I'm saved from one of J.'s acid rebukes... even if I do deserve it this time. I can tell him the news and then hide till he calms down. Fantastic!

"Hi Jerry, it's me, Carly. I'm very, very, very sorry. I cannot tell a lie. A publisher gave me his card to give to you... and I forgot. Please try to stay calm. If you kill me now, i.e.: before I get famous, then that painting that I gave you for your birthday will be worthless. Protect your investment J. Let me live. Going out now. I'll stick it through your slot on the way past. Bye. Um, sorry. Bye.

Whew! That was close. I'll run straight round there right now and stick it through his letterbox while he's out and the coast is clear. Then? A much needed trip to the art shop, I think, for some ' getting famous really soon' supplies. Now? Jacket? Handbag? Good. Whiz off front door wards. Fingers crossed and I might even get away with it. And live to paint another day.

. . . .

Ten minutes later - I have just left J.'s - done the deed, escaped undetected and therefore unscathed. Jerry is, without doubt, the most darling man on the planet but when roused his tongue could slice straight through solid steel, if his acidic remarks didn't eat through it first. But anyway, it's entirely academic because I've got away with it, scot-free. Well? Apart from a massive guilt trip. Hustle off round the corner of the block. To the art shop... and don't spare the horses.

. . . .

Home - I refrained with great difficulty from buying the whole contents of the shop. It's the painter's version of a top notch sweet shop. Heaven indeed, and all accessible by plastic card. I settled instead for a select few tubes of oil paint, including a big white, [you can never have too much white], a couple of new brushes and some paint thinner. Humming happily I slam the front door shut behind me. I am desperate to try out my wonderful new stuff straight away. I am totally in the mood to paint. Marvellous!

Stroll cheerily into the lounge and chuck my bag onto the sofa. The answer phone's bleeping importantly. The number one is lighted up in red in its little message counting window. Uh-oh? It's probably J. Do I really want to hear this right now? A tongue lashing [even second party] might ruin my unusually good mood? In fact, it's almost certain to. Best leave it till later…

Start to walk away. But what if it's not J.? What if it's something really important? What if Angie's finally flipped and she's teetering even now on one of her designer window ledge's, about to hurl herself to her doom in the murky waters of the Thames below? Or perhaps it's Siobhan and there's something wrong with the baby? She has been overdoing things and stress doesn't mix well with pregnancy? No, no, I'm just being silly. They'll be fine. Hesitate, staring at the wretched machine in consternation. Nope. It's no use. I've got to know. If I don't listen to it, it will annoy me to distraction. Lean over and bravely press 'play'. As it starts a sudden icy chill pervades the room - it's J.

"Well! And you have the nerve to call yourself my friend? Hah! How ironic. I hope that you're proud of yourself Carly Watson. Thanks to you I have missed my big break. Mr Elkstone has, apparently, gone off to Belgium so I can kiss fame and fortune goodbye… And you my dear, you can kiss my perfectly formed ass, you traitorous little strumpet. And after all the things I've done for you. Well, that is IT! No more. Nada. Fini. The next time you feel the need to commit petty larceny don't come crying to Gerald P. Green. For I shall be 'otherwise engaged'. Goodbye!"

Bite my trembling lip. He probably doesn't really mean it. Well, not *all* of it. He's just upset and disappointed... But I hate bad feeling.

I hate to fall out with anyone, *especially* J. After all, he *is* my best friend... correction, was. He'll probably never speak to me again... And who can blame him. I've inadvertently destroyed all his hopes. Oh well, I've done my best. No point phoning him back to grovel. I've never heard him so angry? I'd better just let him calm down for a bit, just a year or so.

Trail disconsolately through to the kitchen and flick the kettle on. I know it was my fault... and he has every right to be annoyed with me. Like me, he has struggled in vain for all these soul-destroying years to fulfil his creative ambitions. If I'd missed the chance of my big exhibition because someone was dumb enough to forget to tell me something I'd be quite cut up as well... But I didn't do it on purpose.

Sigh heavily and spoon some Nescafe into my favourite Basil Brush mug. As predicted his little volley of vitriol has burst my creative bubble in one vindictive fell swoop. Rub my tired eyes with the back of one hand and stare gloomily out of the window at the park across the road. No money, no bloke and now, it seems, no J. How much worse can things possibly get?

....

Actually quite a lot worse. Two days later and still no word from Jerry. It's Thursday evening, around 7p.m. and I am slumped on the sofa pondering his untimely disappearance. Despite my leaving numerous obsequious messages on both of his answer phones it would seem that in J. World, I no longer exist. According to Angie and Siobhan he has vanished off the face of the Earth. Both were highly sympathetic to my tale of woe and immediately called J. to act as intermediaries in this cold war... but to no avail. He has turned into Gerald P. Green, International Man Of Mystery and isn't answering his calls. The girls have been attempting to placate my fast growing fears for his well-being with far-fetched speculations of his suddenly taking a fortnight's holiday to Morocco or visiting his parents in Kent. That is complete and utter cobblers. He goes nowhere without his

186

mobile phone. He knows perfectly well that we're looking for him. He's ignoring us all...

Unless he's sick and can't get to the phone? Or, God forbid, something terrible's happened to him? He could be in hospital...? Or... worse? No! Oh God! I do hope he's all right? And the disappointment hasn't pushed him over the edge into a depression or insanity or anything? ... You know, like he was really sane before... Oh Jerry! What have I done? Just as I have managed to work myself up into a state verging on mild hysteria and am about to start ringing round the hospitals, the doorbell interrupts my rising panic with a peremptory,

"RRRIIIINNNGGG!" Stop panicking for a split second and stare in confusion in the direction of the hall. Who the hell's that?

Fluster through the hall and fling the door open. It's J. looking his most disdainful - i.e. - very. His snooty face puts the entire upper crust to shame.

"I've decided to speak to you. Let me in." He announces regally swooshing past me into the hall. Stand aside gawping like a fool.

"Er, Jerry, why didn't you just let yourself in? Like you usually do? Have you lost your key?" He minces off haughtily up the hall calling back over his shoulder,

"No, I've lost my trust. Besides, it would have been highly inappropriate in the circumstances...after your... behaviour." Slam the door shut and trail after him into the lounge. He has flounced down onto the sofa and struck a dramatic pose, legs crossed gracefully, arms spread wide across the cushions. He's doing a tight little hen's bum with his lips, like someone very hard done by.

"Look J., I said I was sorry. It was an accident. I just forgot. You're not still in the huff? It's been days?" He leans forward and grasps his knees tensely,

"I am not 'in the huff'. I am rightfully indignant at your gross inconsideration and cavalier attitude to my career. That's an entirely different thing. However, I thought that, as I am a practising humanitarian..."

"Huh! Keep practising."

"Pardon? Did you utter?"

"Nothing, carry on."

"As I was saying, as I am a practising humanitarian I feel that it would be wrong of me not to give you another chance."

Ironic,

"Oh? Gee, thanks."

Condescending,

"You're welcome. Besides, I feel that one ought to be philosophical about life's little trials and tribs. Socrates himself had to put up with much worse. And yet he managed to conduct himself in a seemly and civilised manner... Even though the behaviour of others around him was sadly lacking." I choose to treat this petty barb with the contempt most calculated to irritate J. and ignore it,

"They poisoned him, didn't they? For being a big smarty?" Jerry draws an irritated breath,

"They did poison him Carly, yes. But not quite for that reason. His ideas were ahead of his time." Shake my head in mock sympathy,

"Poor him. That is a bit strong."

"Yes quite. Anyhow, like Socrates I have decided to rise above it all and put our petty difference aside. Consider yourself hereby reinstated as my friend." Raise a sceptical eyebrow,

"After a whole two days? Admit it J., you missed me? What happened? Did you get bored?" J. draws a dagger look at my insouciance. Then gives it up and flumps casually back into his cushions,

"Yeah, I suppose, just a bit. Go on then Delilah, make yourself useful and stick the kettle on." Get up and wander off kitchen wards.

"Oh, all right. Don't worry, I won't put any cyanide in it. " I'm followed by a sarcastic snort,

"Oh, har-de-har. How I've missed your rapier wit. " Ignore him - best thing to do. Fling some coffee together and shuffle back through. Plonk J.'s down gracelessly in front of him, splooshing it over the coffee table.

"There you go Jerry-tes, your strychnine. Enjoy." Flop clumsily into the armchair spilling some of mine as well. Knickers! Rub at it quickly but just succeed in smearing it down the front of my T-shirt. Oh well. Que sera.

"So J.? What have you been up to? Anything exciting?" He looks coy and sips his coffee in an 'I know something you don't know' kind of manner,

"Perhaps. That would be telling."

"Come on J. Spill the beans. I'm bored witless. Entertain me. It's your practising humanitarian duty."

"Oh, all right. " Waves a hand in capitulation. Clearly he's dying to tell me something. Wait in anticipation. Jerry leans toward me conspiratorially, even though there is no one else here,

"You remember how I phoned Raymond and he'd gone off to Belgium?" Frown,

"No. Who's Raymond? Oh! You mean the publisher guy?"

"Yes, yes, him." Pull an innuendo face,

"Oh, it's *Raymond*, is it Jerry? Well, aren't you the dark pony?" J. flusters,

"No, no. There's nothing like that. He's not my type. Anyway, it turns out that he'd only gone away for a few days. He was back on Tuesday and he called me straight away."

"Eh? Really? What happened?"

"We-ell! I'm getting to that... If you'd let me get a word in edgeways."

"Ooooh! Get him. So sorry, I'm sure."

"As I was saying, he called and asked me to lunch... And he was ever so nice Carly. Apparently, he just loves my work. He says that I have huge potential."

"For what? Sorry. Only kidding. No, really J., that's fantastic. Well done you. He'll have you between the covers before you know it." Jerry glares,

"Ex-cuse me? What are you trying to infer, you little trollop?"

"Of a book Jerry, the covers of a book. A great big hardback. You'll be famous. Hurray. The drinks are on you." He tries and fails to look modest,

"Well of course, it's still early days. But you never know. He did seem remarkably keen. I took him a selection of my poems to peruse and he's going to get back to me A-SAP." Rock about in my chair in excitement on his behalf,

"Oh Jerry, that's brilliant. I can't believe it. They don't take any old schmuck out to lunch you know? Just the best shmucks. They must really want to take you on." Jerry lets that pass and preens smugly,

"Quite. Am I not a genius?"

Smile,

"Abso-bloody-lutely! Oh well done Jerry. I'm so glad. Wait a minute! Should we not be celebrating?" J. considers this for two seconds and nods,

"Oh yes, yes, I should think so. Come on Carls - to the pub. My treat."

"Fair enough J. To the pub."

CHAPTER TWENTY-SIX
The Reincarnation Of Angie

The next day – at Angie's flat. I am sitting on a very high-tech stool at the black granite breakfast bar watching Angie make coffee. It would seem that the other week was some kind of practice run. This week she really has left Miles. She is like a different person. Wow! She's … ? She's herself again? God, that's amazing! I know you tend to turn into your partner to a certain extent over the years, but when you watch someone else do it gradually, you tend not to notice so much. I'd completely forgotten the old Ange, all bright and breezy and… cheerful.

She is practically skipping about the 'eating space' humming and clinking mugs. I cannot bear the suspense. I only got the edited highlights from Siobhan. I want to know what the hell happened. It must've been something truly horrendous. She's been putting up with the most total rubbish since she met him.

"So Ange, what exactly happened?" She waves a breezy teaspoon in my general direction without looking.

"Oh, you know? I just had enough."

"After how many years?" She glances up and gives me her mock-gimlet eyes.

"It's only been eighteen months." Only? And it seems like so much longer?

"Oh, right … So what happened? Something must have happened. You've put up with him all this time." Ange brings the coffee over and perches elegantly on the other stool.

"Well, it was just, … you know how he kept saying he'd leave her?" Nod.

"Well, he's been saying that from the very start. He kept saying it was difficult because of the kids and everything." Hell's handbags! Say nothing. There really is nothing to say.

"He didn't want to upset them, you know, so he said, about the divorce. He said that it just wasn't a good time." Oh really?

"He didn't mind upsetting you though, did he, the little git?" Oops! That just slipped out.

"I mean, sorry, I just meant…" Gives me a brave but damaged inside smile.

"No, Carly, it's fine. I know you're right. He is a git. I just couldn't see it. I loved him…And I thought he loved me… But clearly he doesn't. I doubt that he ever did." Oh the ratbag! Poor Angie. She adored him. Pat her hand in sympathy… then stop when I realise that I've turned into Siobhan.

"I'm sure he did in his own way Angie. It was just an impossible situation, that's all. You do know that, don't you?" She shakes her less immaculate then usual but somehow more human blonde hair.

"No Carly, you're just trying to make me feel better. I've been a total fanny and he's just used me and I'm…. I'm well rid of him. … If you can manage on your own then so can I." Why? What am I? A nincompoop? The village idiot?

"Thanks very much Angie, for that vote?"

"No, I didn't mean it like that. I just meant that I don't need him, that's all."

"So…?" For the third time….

"…what actually happened. O.K. You had this revelation. But when did you actually tell him?" She perks up at this. This is obviously the fun bit. Good! The toad has had it coming for an age.

"Well, I was supposed to meet him at Juilano's for dinner last night at eight and I was all ready. I was wearing that gorgeous new dress that I got in Slix the other day, remember?"

"Oh yeah, slinky"

"Anyway, I was just running out of the door when he called to say he'd been held up and couldn't get there till nine or nine-thirty."

"What? He didn't expect you still to go?" She nods. Wave my eyebrows in genuine horror. What a clown! [Him not her.]

"Anyway, he says, all casual as if it's no big deal, 'O.K babe, I'll see you then,' and I said..., and I don't know what came over me, the words just came out. It wasn't like me at all." ??? Stop waffling and cut to the chase.

"...so I said 'Oh no you won't Miles because I won't be there. You'd best change it to a table for one. One complete arsehole that is.' And then I just hung up really quickly before he could speak."

"Oh Angie, that's fantastic! How poetic! The justice, not the actual phraseology. Oh well done! That's precisely what he deserved, the complacent little arse. I didn't know you had it in you, no offence."

"Well, you know, neither did I. It must have been a last straw thingy – in the biggest haystack of bullshit in the world. I just thought 'What am I doing wasting my life with this guy who treats me with so little respect. As if I haven't got feelings or needs. Well, enough is enough. He has dissed me for the last time."

"Dissed you?"

"Yes, you know, like on Ricki Lake? 'Don't diss me! Respect!' Like the crazy people say." What crazy people? I've never seen Ricki Lake?

"You know Ange, I think I know what you mean. It was a bit like that with Jake. You can only get so upset... then you just go totally blank and you feel much better and you can deal with it, you know? Like you can think straight again?" Ange nods in empathy.

"Ye-es, yes, that's it Carly. I have reached the point of no return. Anyway, I do feel much better. I mean, I will miss him, obviously – the devil you know and all that. But I hear there are other men out there?"

"Uh-huh, ones who don't treat you like rubbish.... Of course, I'm no expert. It's only been a couple of months... And some of them do! But I expect there are other ones. We'll just have to go and have a look. Girly night out?"

"Absolutely! As soon as .... We'll go and window shop for new men."

"New men as in 'sensitive and non-sexist' or as in 'newly hatched' because I've already been to the 'brand new pubescent men' bar with Siobhan and I'm not bloody going there again." She throws back her head and laughs - properly for the first time in months. Fantastic! The real Angie is back.

"No Carls, preferably not pubescent, just mature, sexy, considerate, sophisticated."

"Oh right, no problem. As long as we're not being fussy."

"I think that's exactly the problem. We haven't been fussy enough."

"Well Angie, that is all in the past." Clink our coffee mugs.

"Cheers Carls! Here's to being fussy."

"Cheers! Abso-bloody-lutely! Here's to being fussy as hell."

. . . .

Later, at home – I am deeply absorbed in a highly complex last minute sorting out of frames and stuff for the exhibition. I am surrounded by an Everest of paperwork and bubblewrap. I'm sitting on the floor checking off numerous lengthy lists.

"Bring! Bring! – Bring! Bring!" Oh, does that phone never give up? Can't it see that I'm busy right now? Reach over and lift the phone whilst still reading. I am just a little bit distracted.

"Umm?"

"Carls? It's Siobhan. Did you get a hold of Angie? Is she O.K.?"

"Oh yes. I went round this morning. She's fine. Are you at work?" Does her 'Du-uh?' voice,

"Like where else am I ever?" Fair point. Siobhan lives in that office. I'm surprised that she remembers who Giles is. Perhaps that's why they never fall out? They only ever see each other for five seconds, or however long he takes, and then they just both go to sleep.

"So Carls, have you got everything sorted for this week-end?"

"Uh, no? That's what I'm doing right now. It'll be such a relief to be finished at last. I must have been out of my mind."

"So what's new? No, really though, well done. I can't believe how much you've done. It's about time you got some recognition."

"And preferably lots and lots of cash." She laughs,

"Oh well, good to know that you're in it for the right reasons and not mercenary at all. By the way, Ange said that Jake came round. What's going on? Is he coming to your preview?"

"Not sure. I haven't seen the Gunner's fixtures list. It might be clashing with something Earth shatteringly important like a semi-final or something. No, no, that's not fair. He was really sweet to me the other day. " There is a deafening silence on the other end of the phone. I haven't told anyone about the proposal. I know what they all think of him. And I don't want to discuss it. It's private.

"Siobhan, I had to give him a ticket. He saw them. But he's never really bothered much before. Said it wasn't his kind of thing…. And you know what he thinks of my work."

"Yes, cheeky git. Just because he's still at join-the-dots."

"Yeah, well, anyway, he seemed quite pleased and he took the ticket so we'll see. I think I'll have an early night tonight. I'm absolutely shattered." Yawn.

"I'm not surprised. Jerry said you've been working thought the night?"

"Yes. But only to get stuff finished. And I have had a nap during the day."

"What? When you fell over? That's not a nap, that's a coma. Just don't you be making yourself ill."

"O.K. Mum. Anyway, I've finished the painting. I'm just sorting out the frames and the paperwork. Should be done by tomorrow hopefully… I still can't believe Angie standing up to Miles at last."

"Yes, it's amazing. I'm proud of you both."

"Both? What have I done?"

"Dumped Jake, remember? Oh, and a tiny little exhibition? Du-uh?"

"Uh, thanks? I think?" Siobhan is mistress of the back-handed compliment.

"Anyway Carls, must dash. Got a conference. Thought I'd just check on the state of play. Go to bed before you collapse. You've probably still got concussion, you know."

"I've still got a face like the back of a bus. That's much more distressing right now." She laughs.

"I'll bring you some concealer. See you." Shout at her disappearing voice,

"Bring me a brown paper bag!" Though why brown I don't know.? Oh, she's gone. …Oh well, better get on with these lists.

…………..

Later - Finished! Finished everything at last! Try to get to my feet and fall over immediately in an ungainly heap. Apparently my legs couldn't wait and have gone to sleep of their own accord – without my knowledge or permission. ???

"Oh! Ooh! Yuck!" Rub my legs. I hate that creepy feeling when the blood goes back in. Five yuck minutes later, stumble through into the bedroom and fall face first across the bed. Ooh! Lovely! You know you're really tired when you're comfy anywhere, and your bed feels like a bouncy castle made of cotton wool. Tug the duvet over my back awkwardly with one hand. Oh fan-tastic! Shall just …go to… ummmm.

CHAPTER TWENTY-SEVEN
A Real Fairy Godfather - At Last!

Saturday - 6.45p.m. The night of my big preview has arrived at long, long last. But still about two years too soon for my face to have healed up. I am staring in the bedroom mirror aghast, traumatised by my fiendish freak appearance. Oh, Michael Crawford would be proud. This is going to take more then some concealer to conceal I might well have to wear a bag. Perhaps I could go for some type of ultra-trendy mask a la Gabrielle's eye cover fashion statement? 'Mysterious, glamorous new artist makes an intriguing debut at The Eglinton Hall.' would look slightly better in the papers than 'Who is this Cornish-pastie-faced fool?' Sadly right now the latter seems quite unavoidable.

Sigh deeply and bury my fragile facial bones in my shaky hands. *Why* am I always in trouble? No-one could be this unlucky by complete accident. Did some ratty old bag look over my cradle and take sudden offence? Did my mum boob with the christening list? She must have. I am indeed cursed.

I have now got two hours to get ready. Not really time for plastic surgery as such. … I could phone an agency and get a body double I suppose? Like the actual famous people have? …Wonder if it's in the Yellow Pages? What would it be under do you think? Emergency services? Well, maybe? That really could not be more apt. Glance round at my new glamorous outfit, a sparkly ankle length skirt and halter top, which is lying slinkily on the bed just crying out to be worn… but quite clearly not by me. Damn! I don't go with my outfit? It was purchased before my pastie moment. It'll only make me look even worse. As in 'the sequins are fooling nobody Sweetie. We can all still see your pizza face'. Imagine if a magazine has a colour photograph? It would be quite bad enough in black and white?

"BANG! BANG! BANG! BANG! BANG!" So? There's some mad git at my front door now, is there? Oh great! Jolly good! Maybe it's a mad axeman who will put me out of my misery. He couldn't have picked a better time.

Trundle through to the hall in my gadgy old dressing gown. Open the door casually. I am way past giving a toss. If it is some unwanted person they can just sod off. But, no. It is the always-wanted Jerry [sometimes on actual wanted posters] with the weirdest companion on earth.

No? I don't believe I have met you before? I think I might have remembered. J.'s companion is about eight feet tall and skinny as a skelf, in neck-to-toe skin-tight scarlet satin. And has, why yes, I do believe they're silver dreadlocks? But the absolute piece de resistance of this startling ensemble has to be the full [oh, it must be theatre?] make-up. Really quite unusual for a man. But Jerry has some quite unusual friends. The newcomer is carrying a fake leopard-skin suitcase? Oh well, I guess he has his reasons. Maybe it's a cutting-edge thing to carry and it's only for his sandwiches and stuff?

"Hi Jerry, - Hi there, Mr er, Mr ....?" The weird guy does a courtly kind of bow. Amazing that he can in those tight trousers? He must have exceptional control.

"I-am-Lorenzo!" Yeah? Good for you. Scarlet-Boy does a flourishy thing with one hand. Jerry nods in hyper-mode like an enthusiastic puppy.

"Yeah, yeah, Carly. This is Lorenzo" He opens both his weasel eyes as big as they can go – which isn't really all that big.

"Lorenzo is about to do you the most humungous favour Carls." Oh my God! No he is NOT! But it seems that L. is not to be deterred. He glides forward masterfully and takes my elbow.

"Come, my sweet. There's not much time." And ushers me smoothly into my own hall. Ooh! Help! I'm getting scared now. Jerry nods wildly in approval and leans his head close conspiratorially.

"Lorenzo here is just the man you need." For what, for Christ's sake? Please let it be something else?

"But? ...But Jerry, I'm going out? You haven't forgotten that it's my show tonight?" Lorenzo quells my futile protests with one look and opens both his arms wide, like some scarlet satin prophet. Intones in a husky liqueur bass,

"Carly! I am everything you need! I have the wherewithal to unleash your hidden self. One hour with me and you shall be reborn!" Oh fuck! Impressive but quite mad. Jerry has bought me a shag? Oh, how kind? I have never even seen a gigolo before? ...At least, would I know if I had? Is this perhaps a weird sort of celebration gift? Like for twenty-first's and graduations and stuff? Could he not just have said 'well done!'? Well, I do not want to unwrap him thank-you very much. How the heck does one tactfully say that? Perhaps he was very expensive? Oh God! Am I being really rude?

The scarlet pimp strides straight on through into the bedroom. Oh nooo, really, you make yourself at home? He drapes himself dramatically on my bed. Eek! Jerry smiles indulgently at us both and turns around to leave.

"O.K.! Well then, I'd best be off. You two will want to be alone." No we WON'T!

"I'll be back to pick you up later for the show, you know? When you've finished." Gives a cheeky wink. WHAT? WHAAAATTT? NO WAY! Grab his skinny sleeve in desperation and hiss.

"Jerry! What the hell is going on?" J. screws up his raisin face and shakes his head in mock-exasperation.

"Oh Carly, don't be shy. You're in the best of hands. He's an expert, for Depp's sake. I couldn't believe what he did for me last week. I feel like a totally new man. I believe I shall just go and get one."

I can't speak. I am stunned! My mind is totally blank, as it has refused point-blank to have that thought. But it has successfully booted all other thoughts straight out of my head. I am frozen? I can't stop J. leaving? Oh holy handbags! He has gone? Aargh! Somebody help me! I have been trapped by my own good manners with a poncy satin-clad slut? ...This is quite bad even for me? Turn my head bravely to check that it is not a bad dream – but no! The scarlet smoothie lies smouldering atop my duvet. He waves a huge enticing finger in my direction.

"So tell me Sweets, is this your first time?" ??? I'm thirty-FOUR?

"Eh? My, ... my what?"

"You've never been transformed by a professional?"

"I've never heard it called that before?" Lorenzo graciously bestows an intimate smirk.

"Oh come now Carly. You can tell me. It is, isn't it? I can tell." Oh Jesus, this has really gone too far. My cheeks are starting to vie with his outfit.... I'll just have to bite the bullet and tell him nicely thanks, but no.

"Look er Mr, Lorenzo, I'm sure you're very...er, good? But I'm not really into this kind of thing...Er, um thank-you very much. No offence."

As usual, I am just ignored. I don't know why I ever speak at all. Lorenzo springs into action, leaps from his lounging pose and tosses his enormous tacky suitcase onto the bed. A quick double flick of the catches and it flies open.... to reveal?

Oh God! Has he got some weirdo sex toys, surely NOT? But no, he has got something else entirely - some bizarre kind of outfit or something. It looks like a black plastic cape? He can't be going to dress up, can he? I thought that he already had. But he also has a humungous black plastic device thingy, which looks a little bit like a hairdryer. He is points it in the air experimentally like a gun? That's not going anywhere near me! So that's what a vibrator looks like? I've only seen them in pictures before, never actually in the flesh. Eek! Wrong choice of words!

What the hell else has he got in there then? Lean closer to snoop past his elbow. My nose is much more powerful than my common sense. It always has been my downfall. Though my common sense gene does seem to be quite Basil faulty sometimes... He has make-up? Even more make-up than Boots? I am too jealous for words! He is clearly a very vain transvestite gigolo. And has obviously been a boy scout. He is so incredibly well prepared? Well, he can still just ging-gang-gooly off!

All of a sudden Lorenzo spins round dramatically, his massive falic dodgy thing in his hand.

"Right Sweetie, where am I going to have you?" In your dreams and nowhere else buddy! He eyes my pastie-face critically, poncy head tilted over to one side (indicating very deep thought). Is the depth of thought directly proportionate to the angle of the head perhaps? How dare he mentally criticize my face? What a cheeky big git? His head is totally tilted. Therefore I must look like total shit? As if I didn't know that already? ...I believe that it's time that you left!

"I think Carly Sweets, we should go for the total works."

"I think you should go for a bus! Preferably right now! Ten minutes ago would be even better." And take your plastic cape and pervy toys with you, you ponce. I have just had enough!

Scarlet man finally notices that I'm not amused at all. Does Jerry get a refund, I wonder? I shall contact Consumer Rights and ask. He puts one manicured hand on a scarlet satin hip and points his plastic penis gun at my head.

"God Carly, what the hell's with you? Is it P.M.T. or concussion or what?" What? Indignant,

"No! I just don't require your services. Comprendez?" Lorenzo eyes my swollen face and gives a derisory half-laugh.

"Ex-cuse me, but I really beg to differ. Look, no offence darling but we've only got two hours to perform something akin to a miracle." Oh? You are so vain!

"Carly my love, we do want you to have star quality tonight, but not really as the phantom of the opera."

"Eh? What are you talking about, exactly?" God! This fellow does talk cobblers? ...And very confusing cobblers at that! Scarlet Man carefully places the tips of his manicure against his temples and does a deep yoga sort of breath. Clearly he is summoning more patience. I am obviously a buffoon. I can think of nothing more to say. Suddenly he snaps his silver mane back and extends one gigantic hand palm forward. He has the other poised creatively by his side.

"Look Carly, my sweet, I was given to understand by the adorable J. that you were in dire need of my personal services..." EEEEK! How *dare* J. tell strangers about my healed-up bits?

".... I am, and I don't want to blow my own horn Babe...." You'll have to if you want it blown. I'm not going bloody near it!

"...the BEST make-up artist in town..." Make-up artist? He is waving both hands now in an aerated manner?

"I do do all the best celebs..." Really? Do you? WOW!

"I only came here tonight as a particular favour to little J. but ... " Little J.? What? Like Tiny Tim? He inserts an insulting derisory snort here and waves an impertinent hand at my face.

"...If you think you can manage without me, ..Then Darling I'll be happy to leave." Leave? Leave? You could fix my face and you're leaving? No, I don't think that you are! You shall help me or you shall die! ...I shall just lock the door and the windows right now. ...Quick! A fast backtrack is called for I believe. I shall go into grovel mode immediately.

"Oh no! Lorenzo I'm sooo sorry! Of course I don't want you to go." He raises one thin artistic eyebrow, how is it again? Sardonically? Yes, I think that it's that.

"Indeed! What? Not even for, I believe it was, a *bus*?" Aargh! I have offended my only possible saviour?

"Erm, no, I, er....I didn't realise who you were..." Uh-oh! WRONG thing to say. I've dented his ego now, a big mistake with any type of man... I believe that my heating must be broken? The temperature has just nose-dived in here. Lorenzo delivers an arctic rebuff through his designer capped teeth.

"Is-that-so? Of course, if you don't move in the right circles. I am quite exclusive in my chosen clientele. Well, *usually* I am." Oh, mi-aow! I really felt that. But I expect I deserved it... Bugger! He is playing hard to get. He folds his scarlet arms and examines his manicured nails. It looks like he expects me to grovel? Well, O.K.! It's clearly worth it. This satin fool could save my life.

"I really am extraordinarily grateful Lorenzo. I'm sure you're a very busy man...with all your important, famous clients and stuff..." He sniffs, but I can detect a thaw.

"It's really terribly good of you to fit me in like this...And at such short notice as well. What's your professional opinion? Can you help me? ...Or perhaps it's just too much to expect you to achieve? Is it outwith your field of expertise?" He jerks his head up indignantly at that to glare. Oh, how predictable. Men do not like to admit to being inadequate.

"Certainly not! I can do anything! I worked on Dr Who, your face will be a piece of cake!"

Hah! Sucker! And good. Cake is better than pizza or pastie. So go on then Smart Boy. Fix me, I dare you.

"Could you really? Oh, how impressive. Aren't you wonderful? You must be one of the most important men in your field." He is almost simpering now. I shall just reel him in...And I didn't even have to touch him at all?

"Well, I suppose you *could* say that Sweetie." Nod encouragingly as if highly overwhelmed by his very presence. He looks ecstatic. Hah! Got you! Oh, how easy. You shall do anything I want. You may be the expert on the outside of the head but I've got your number on the inside of yours.

"Oh no, Lorenzo. I'm sure you're just being modest." As if! I've got him, hook, line, etc. Oh goody! ...And now for my transformation, please.

I am swept into a chair in front of the dressing table mirror and the black cape is swirled around me as in the hairdressers. Lorenzo grasps my shoulders through it and stares intensely over my shoulder at my reflection.

"Cinderella – you shall go to the ball! Prepare for the experience of your life!" I'm ready! I'm waiting! Fantastic!

....

One hour and forty-five minutes later - A tentative knock at the door announces my chauffeur for the evening's arrival. Lorenzo strides through my tiny hall like Gulliver and thrusts the tiresome door to one side.

"Jerraldo darling! Come in and be astounded. You won't recognise her. She looks…incredible... " I heard that! Well, how insulting! Am I usually a minger? "...She is my best creation yet." Why thank-you Dr F.? I can hear Jerry twitching with excitement.

"Oh God, really? That's fantastic! Let me see." I hear him bouncing through into the lounge. I can see them past the slightly open bedroom door, reflected in the hall mirror. Lorenzo indicates an empty armchair with a dismissive sweep of one creative sleeve.

"Wait there. I must give you the full impact." J's eyebrows shoot off the top of his head. Oooh-er? Lorenzo's impressive bass echoes through the tiny flat as it summons me into their presence.

"Carly! My darling, it's TIME!" God! I do like him. He is barking!

Throw open the flimsy bedroom door and ponce through into the lounge. Pause for a second to pose in the doorway. Oh, this is fun! Jerry gapes, Lorenzo smirks in a super-smug fashion [but that's not unusual. Men always smirk at me, the irritating bastards!] He indicates me with outstretched arms.

"Et VIOLA! A vision is born!" Jerry seems to be speechless? A miracle indeed. I don't believe that I've ever seen him that? ..Or should that be heard him? …Or NOT heard him? …But I digress…

I am wearing my own outfit but someone else's face... and someone else's hair. The hair is very big and covered in sparkly glitter, with plaits and coloured silvery extensions to match my spectacular silver-sequined ensemble and ludicrous stiletto silver shoes - even more ludicrous than Angie's torture ones. I shall have men gagging for it in the street…Well, maybe not for it in the actual street? … Or no, maybe they would? Some men would do it in the middle of Tescos given a sporting chance... and no legal or food hygiene restrictions… Well, they will be gagging for it anyway - anywhere they could get it. BUT - they are NOT going to get it! I shall just torture them and laugh… I may well be having a sexual power trip? Good! It is very nice. I might take to dressing like this all of the time. I'm sure it'll be a huge hit in Sainsburys of a week-end. ...Excellent! My life is complete. I wonder what Lorenzo did for Jerry last week? Prob-ab-ly better not to know...

Lorenzo claps his gagantuan hands together and turns to address a stupefied J.

"So, what do you think then, Jerraldo my darling? Isn't she the most stupendous creature you ever saw?" J. tries bravely to recover from his gape.

"Well, no? That was Mel Gibson at some premiere...but after Mel? Yeah Babe, Stu-pendous! Like, yeah! ...I can't wait for him to see you."

"Who? Oh, Leslie Phillips, you mean? Christ! Good point J.! I'd forgotten about him. He'll be feeling me up as soon as I arrive. Well, forewarned is forearmed. If he lays one slimy finger on my sequins he'll be eating his teeth for a week!" Lorenzo nods casually in approval,

"Quite right. Let them drool but no touching. That's a rule I insist on as well." Yeah? Fair enough! Won't Edgah just love you? J. checks his watch and does the ejector seat thing.

"So what are we waiting for? Carly come on! Madam, your carriage awaits." Proffers a super-skinny elbow for me to hold, ever the gentleman. He's even wearing a tuxedo. How sweet! ... But do I want him beside me for my entrance? He's even thin in a Tux? How annoying! He would make a twiglet look fat .... Oh well, who cares? ... He might make me look more curvy, but I hear that voluptuous is in. So let's go! ...And hopefully even make some dosh...

CHAPTER TWENTY-EIGHT
In Danger Of Getting What You Want - Whatever That Is?

Sweep across the road to a sudden halt at bottom of the enormous stone steps, much to the chagrin of the oncoming traffic. Jerry really is the worst driver. If killed in a Jerry induced R.T.A. do I get to wear this outfit forever in eternity? I suppose it might be a small consolation to be the most stunning spectre of all time? Eternal chic Darling, how fabulous. But not yet - pictures to sell, money to make, poncing about to enjoy and all that joie de vivre stuff.

J. leaps out and scuttles round to heave open Daisy's precariously attached passenger door, so that I may alight from my carriage in style. Those hinges are hanging by a thread. Better not catch a rusty old car part on my outfit? I haven't got to ponce about in it yet. It would be a shame if my magnificence was tarnished before I get a proper chance to show off. Lorenzo scrambles out of the cramped back seat with uncharacteristic lack of aplomb, as one of Daisy's seatbelts has ensnared him by a shiny satin ankle.

"Hey Jerraldo, your car won't let me go." He tugs at the strap ineffectually in a vain attempt to restore his fast escaping dignity... which has finally scented freedom and scooted off down the street. The malicious belt tightens it's grasp. It's shiny old material tentacles are multiplying with the speed of particularly virulent bacteria and have taken over almost one whole leg. J. turns and chortles over to the rescue.

"Sorree. Daisy has impeccable taste, but she really is such a slut. I think she likes you Lorenzo. That's definitely a sign of affection, don't you think?" Lorenzo is not at all amused.

"Affection? She's a venus fly trap on wheels. Get her off my goddamn pants before she fucks with my crown jewels." Jerry does a fake sneer and casually drawls.

"And I thought you liked old bangers? Must have been another vicious rumour on the scene." Lorenzo narrows his kohl-rimmed steely gaze.

"Well, I did like you Jerry.... But you can go off people you know?" Oops! This is getting a trifle out of hand. J. - offended to his skinny core,

"You bitch, Lorenzo! I'm not old!" Time to intervene I believe,

"Excuse me Gentlemen, do you think that you could settle your childish differences today? I'm going to be more than fashionably late here." They both turn and glare at me instead. Well, really? J. morphs back to reality with a toss of the head,

"Sorr-ee!" Lorenzo just sucks his cheeks in huffily,

"Yeah, well, just get this fucking thing off me." J. sighs, hard-done-to, and stomps over to release him.

J. crouches down, his head level with Lorenzo's impressive satin crotch and wraps his arms round Lorenzo's legs to remove the offending, overly familiar car part.

Stand back against a handy wall, trying to keep out of the way of numerous inconveniently wandering pedestrians. They're not going anywhere, you know. They have all been let out of some holding area and will no doubt be rounded up later by officials when their daily round of annoying the innocent is complete. Don't tell me you haven't seen these people. I know that you have. There's not a person in the land whose hasn't had their fingers burned [or their toes trampled] in a so-called chance encounter, 'meaning to walk past you' indeed. Sometimes, for very special missions they are all issued with prams, sometimes even double-buggies, and allowed to infiltrate the busy city streets. I think the purpose of this could well lie at government level. By the time you've been pummelled and squashed all day, your rage at nameless politicians and their creative use of your exorbitant taxes is, to say the least, weakened. Not that I'm saying these alleged pedestrians are government issue. Of course not. Would they do that?

Anyway, back to the ongoing seatbelt fiasco. The boys are both too engrossed in their Houdini experience to notice two badly but predictably dressed old ladies approaching stage left. They are tourists let loose from the SAGA bus for a quick peek at the big smoke. Both old dears eye my sequins with delightedly scandalised faces and do that 'you're meant to hear us, but we haven't got the bottle to say it to your face' loud whisper thing.

"Look, Betty. A *prostitute*. Oh my!" Betty clutches the loose skin at her neck in ecstasy. What a gem to tell the Luncheon Club. Not wishing to disappoint my public, I give them my best cheap slapper smile. It would be a shame to deprive them of their harmless amusement. Lick my lips saucily and give them a big wink. Hah! They're not so sure now. How's your general knowledge of lesbo prossies girls? Yep! That's roughly what I thought. A little information is dangerous and all that. Both turn their helmet-permed heads away from the sight of my shameless person.

"Well, really Edith, Did you see her? Brazen little hussy!" But Edith is in no state to reply. She has clocked the lads and is in deep shock. She squeezes out a croak of disbelief,

"Betty! LOOK! The disgrace." J. is still scrabbling around on his knees on the edge of the pavement.

"Is that why they call them kerb crawlers Betty?" Fan-tastic! Betty clutches a mock crock handbag to her vast woolly bosom.

"Stay back Edith. I know what their game is." Jerry and Lorenzo look round at the sound of raised voices, and Betty spears them with a triumphant horror glare from her reptilian old eyes.

"They're a couple of those, what do you call it, Edith? HOMOS! Yes, that's what they are all right. I've seen Crimewatch you perverts! Don't think I don't know your game!"

Jerry and Lorenzo both do 'WHAT?' faces. Double up with laughter at their indignant expressions. Oh! That was superb! Snort in delight as the gruesome old bags cackle off up the street, at the fastest of their very slow speeds, to the deafening tune of,

"Would you credit it Edith? In the middle of the street as well. Disgraceful. Ab-sol-utley disgraceful."

"I'm telling you Betty, it's Sodom and Gomorra."

"I know! Have they no shame? Whatever is the World coming to?"

This has clearly made their night. I expect they'll be back down next week to play Spot the Heinous Criminal again. Jerry and Lorenzo are left doing the goldfish to their retreating crimpelene backs. Lorenzo places the tips of his manicure onto his scarlet hips, whilst stabbing death rays out of his eyes. A bit of a waste of time really. They're nearly there as it is.

"WELL! Horrendous old trouts!" Lorenzo booms. "Homos indeed?" Jerry is frozen, dumbfounded, in his crouching position, his lips still inches from Lorenzo's trousers,

"But? But how could they have known that? Were they witches or psychics or something? I mean, they didn't even see my face?"

"Haah! Jerry, can't you see yourself? They thought that you were 'making lurve'. How hysterical. As if you would in the middle of the street." Clutch my sequins in pain as laughter cramp sets in. The boys are completely aghast.

Lorenzo,

"They shouldn't be thinking those things at their age! The dirty old scrubbers." J. scrabbles testily with the recalcitrant seatbelt at the edge of the kerb muttering,

"Do they think that we're all in the gutter? Horrid old bags." I refuse to respond. It's too easy. J. carries on,

"And did you *see* what they were wearing? Like, did you? Well, all that I can say is YUCK!" Ooh! Vicious.

"Don't worry J. They thought I was a cheap hooker – exactly the look I've spent the entire night achieving."

"Ahem?" Lorenzo slaps me with an eyebrow.

"Oh yeah, exactly the look Lorenzo has spent the entire night achieving."

"Thank-YOU. Anyway Darling, I don't do cheap. Exorbitant hooker if you please." J. smirks grubbily and does his Beavis laugh.

"You look like a hooker Carly, he-he, he-he." He is frighteningly good at that laugh. Lorenzo sighs and shakes his silver tresses in misunderstood martyr fashion, at this lack of respect for his creation – i.e., me.

"Oh, come *on* you two. Let's get this show on the tarmac." He hustles us into a Wizard of Oz people chain [unfortunately one person short.], up the intimidating steps to the ancient portico strung with twinkling, exclusive looking lights,

"Carly Darling, fame here you come."

…………..

Inside the hall it is all very high class. You can tell by the tone of the hubbub, not even the slightest bit raucous. A low-key murmur from about fifty squillion people? I mean, how impressive is that? Clearly they are very well bred. Good. Perhaps they can afford me.

Exclusive designer black tailcoats are swirling with huge golden trays of champagne [in proper glasses no less] and those revolting little canapé things. I once ate a Stilton one through waiter misinformation and hold the whole canapé world responsible. I couldn't even spit the vile thing out, as there was no suitable spitting place in sight. I had to eat the stinky little yuck. Blaagh! Never again!

The Red Sea crowd parts and reveals a scary sight - Edgah in full pick-up mode. Oh God! He weasels closer into full greasy focus. Eek! He looks even more creepy than usual? [Quite a feat]. He is undressing me with his vulgar beadies. Oh no! I shall pretend I am wearing armour-plated, non-see through undies. That should fend his vile imagination off. He slimes towards me, his clammy gropers outstretched.

"Cahlee dar-ling, you look simply divine." Yeah? Well, you can stop looking now. He flicks his pale, rheumy eyeballs over my heaving bosom. It is heaving with terror, as is my stomach. He wets his lips with a darting lizard tongue. Aargh! I have been visually assaulted. His socially unavoidable suit sleeve is snaking ever nearer to my bare shoulders. No! No! Don't you touch me. Yet again, I am trapped by my own good manners like a bunny in headlights. Damn! Where is my resolve? How was I supposed to get rid of him again? ... Oh no! Don't touch me...AAAARGH!

In a scarlet flash, Lorenzo sweeps an imposing rescuing arm round my waist and whisks me to his side [as in old style dancing]. Bravely, he inserts himself between Edgar and I, and honours the former with a derogatory smile. My satin saviour stretches a huge hand towards the thwarted groper.

"Good evening, Lorenzo Constantini. Carly my love, do introduce us all." Edgar gives a tight little twitch of his expression, which could scarcely be classed as a smile. I struggle to keep a straight face,

"Oh! Er, sorry Lorenzo, um...darling?" I indicate Edgar with a casual wave of my jewellery.

"Lorenzo, Jerry, ... Edgah, umm, I mean *Edgar* Shrimpton-Boswick."

Lorenzo crushes Edgar's fingers in an overly enthusiastic shake.

"I hear you've been looking after my little Carly, Edgar. She's been telling me all about you." Edgar looks more than a little alarmed now. Guilty conscience perhaps (in advance)?

"She has? She didn't tell me about...er, I mean, I didn't realise she had a, er, that is, a 'friend'." J. leans forward and nods confidentially, whilst extending a debonair mitt,

"Oh ye-es, she has. She's got quite a few, actually. Gerald Anstruther-Smythe at your service. How the hell do you do?" Gerald who? His surname is Green? Edgar struggles to control his face, proffers his mangled hand nervously and grimaces.

"Erm, delighted, Ay'm sure." Yeah? Right! Sure you are. He eyes Lorenzo's propriatorial hold on my waist and his impressive if oddly clad stature and gives a little humourless laugh. Clearly this wasn't in the plan. Thank God I'm not alone here. J. drapes a casual skinny arm protectively round my shoulders leaving no socially acceptable body parts left for Edgar to commandeer... and no room behind me to stand in which to do so. Brilliant strategy boys. Did you plan that pincer movement? And have you used it anywhere else before? Hmm, probably best not to know. It was suspiciously slick for a first time – thank heavens!

Edgar does not look amused. His visage says quite clearly 'I've paid a fucking fortune for the right to feel her arse'. Well, tough luck Shrimpton old boy. It isn't up for grabs [in any way what-so-ever!]. And that wasn't in my contract, I'm sure. He edges out a last ditch sour sentence from the middle of his grimace in the face of our firmly fake-smiled trio.

"So, wouldn't you boys like to take a, heh-heh, little stroll around. Don't worry. I'll look after Carly for you, ha-ha." I can feel my eyeballs expanding in horror.

No, you ruddy well *won't*! I have a death grip on both of my bodyguards clothing. Abandon me and you'll have to do it naked. Not that either of them would actually care? Edgar waves an encouraging paw at the melee.

"Plenty of pretty ladies here tonight lads y'know." Gives the boys a matey 'fuck off' wink. He is clearly used to getting his own way. Must be a rich git thing? Lorenzo,

"No, that's fine, man, thanks. We'll take a stroll round with Carly. She's gonna explain how the subliminal references in her latest pieces reflect modern day plutocracy. This is a whole new direction for her. Isn't is Sweetheart?" Nod dumbly. I am amazed beyond belief, as is Edgar who has gone a rather un-fetching shade of puce. Jerry cottons onto the escape plan and stokes the inferno further.

"Yeah, yeah. She's going to reveal her inner self at last. Isn't it just tooo exciting for words?" Clearly it is as Edgar has lost the power of speech – a perfect moment to make good our escape. Lorenzo has the same thought and drags me off with a cheeseboard smirk at Edgar and a final parting shot. He drawls nonchalantly,

"Yeah, catch you later Ed." Ed? Oh fan-tastic! How could I have misjudged you Lorenzo? You are indeed Gabriel himself! [The angel, not the singer].

Clutch my fake lover's sleeve, smiling gamely and step out into the fray. We must look like a set of those little cut out paper dolls? Lock our faces onto best behaviour mode.

…………...

About an hour later, [I think? I have had quite a lot of bubbly]. I felt it was safe to let down my guard as Edgar has long since sulked off into the melee [in an extremely posh puff of smoke – class A?]. Lorenzo is taking advantage of my mentor's absence to allow himself to be admired by random adorees. I don't think they actually know who he is? He has a famous; rich look about him, which seems to inspire shallow groupies. Maybe they think he's in a band or something? Oh well, que sera. We all have our crosses, I suppose.

Jerry is trying to look convincingly 'arty'. He has one elbow supported by his other hand and is resting his bony chin on an empty champagne glass in the hand attached to the aforementioned elbow. He is giving one of my perfectly harmless studies of a nude male figure the full benefit of his deep, screwed up face. The figure in the painting is facing a window in an otherwise empty room. Jerry indicates this with one finger of his champagne glass hand,

"Does it symbolize the futility of naked ambition and the desire to find hope in the bleak commercial climate of modern times?" Raise my pencilled eyebrows. What have you been drinking when I wasn't looking, my harebrained little compadre?

"Is that what it says to you, Jerraldo my dear?" J. nods pseudo-wisely…. encouraged…

"Uh – huh." I have to ask…

"In what way exactly? Could you define it for me in actual terms Jerry? I like to gauge the reaction of the spiritually aware to my message."

"We-ell, it's obvious, isn't it. There he stands, as Mother Nature intended. He has cast off the unwieldy shackles of so-called civilisation, like…umm, like mobile phones and MacDonalds and designer labels, yeah...?" Or any labels even.

"… and he's looking up towards the light in the hope of the rebirth of society and a renewal of traditional worthwhile values … and stuff… yeah?" WHAT?

"Yeah, if you like…" Shake my head.

"…. I just thought that he had a nice bum, J." Jerry snaps his weaselly noggin round and harpoons me with one eye.

"What? Are you taking the mick?" ME?

"No, Jerry, really. It doesn't mean anything. It's just some guy who modelled for me, that's all. Sorry to disappoint you. There was no deeper significance." He sucks his lips right in.

"Well fuck Carls, don't tell the punters. You'll never sell anything. Do you have to be so goddam honest?" I am lost? What does it matter what it means? It's just an image that's all, open to personal interpretation.

"Why Jerry, do you think they're that shallow? Must it have some pretentious significant message. Won't a nice image of a naked guy do?" J. sucks his whole face in to consider.

"Well Carls, for me, hell yes. Especially a naked guy like that... But punters? No, they want something inspired by genius to bum about to their friends. Like 'Ya, I got an original MacLean, dontcha know. The guy's the new Leonardo…blah, blah…'. It's all hype Carls. You've just got to play the game… Don't you see?"

"Uh NO? That totally sucks! I've worked damn hard for years training to draw and paint properly. I'm not about to prostitute my art for cash. Jesus Jerry, how can you even suggest it? It's just like 'The Emperor's Clothes'. No-one wants to admit there's nothing there in case they might just look stupid… Like they don't look stupid when they spend megabucks on crap. There is no fucking higher message. THEY'RE JUST PICTURES – O.K.!"

Jerry is doing an 'Eek! What have I unleashed' face, therefore I must be ranting now? Well, really! He ought not to wind me up so. He'll be telling me next that The Turner Prize is art? I shouldn't have bothered to do all those paintings. I could have flung down a row of old twigs. Well, fuck it! Silly old me!?*!?*!

I suddenly notice that I have attracted a ring of fascinated spectators to my rant. Well, really! Am I not even allowed to have a real opinion either? Turn and indignantly enquire of the public at large,

"What's *wrong* with you all? Don't you *like* sexy naked men? Well? WELL? They have valid aesthetic merit, as well as very nice arse... , Jerry, stop that!" But Jerry does a 'ha-ha-ha, just her little joke' laugh, puts a cheesy arm round my waist and whisks me out of earshot, before I can do myself any more damage. I am about to explode – tick-tick-tock.

"She's an artist, you know..." J. informs the crowd over his shoulder as we depart. They all nod and murmur, quite happy to be entertained by the spectacle of my madness.

".... Feels the strain of living up to a myth, you see? It's a lonely world, that of the true artist. Her angst is engrained in the very core of her work. Can't you see it?... Of course, you'd have to be able to recognise the genius of the understated message to appreciate Carly's painting fully... Not everyone can see it, dontcha know, only the truly creative. Come Carly, let's get you a glass of water, my love...I know, I know. It's all been such a terrible strain..." He continues unnecessarily loudly,

"... We can't expect *everyone* to recognise your vision. Don't worry darling, those with real creative insight will appreciate the deeper artistic significance of the symbolism." The crowd bustles round my paintings nodding and waving their champagne in an inspired attempt to look truly creative.

Glower at them as J. drags me away, muttering,

"Feel free to wave your chequebooks too, you shallow bastards. No wonder all the great artists went crazy, dealing with these flipping plebs!"

…………...

Several yards away J. releases his grip on my waist. We are well out of earshot now. I am still fuming. I need a victim…and have the desperate desire to shout,

"What did you have to do that for Jerry?"

"Your own good, you silly little cow. Do you want to blow this gig completely? If you do, just go right ahead!" He waves a sarcastic floppy hand in the direction we've just come from.

"You're lucky I was there to save you from yourself. I think I managed to salvage the situation rather well. Now they think you're some kind of angst-ridden visionary. You're bound to make a packet. They'll all want a genuine Watson… Hmmm, Carly, Couldn't you maybe change your surname or something? A 'genuine Watson' just doesn't have that glamorous ring."

"Are you crazy J.?" Jerry tosses his head, offended,

"Why, whatever do you mean? I just *helped* you, you ungrateful little trollop! Well really, some people! You know your problem, Sweetie? You just don't…. Oh?" Jerry stops mid-sentence and swivels his head to see something behind me,

What? What's he looking at? ….Oh. Ho-hum. An aesthetically pleasing waiter has materialised behind me and is proffering his offering in J's general direction.

"Champagne, Sir?" J. smirks and takes some,

"Why, I don't mind if I do… Thank-you so much." Oh GOD! Anything in trousers? J. smirks coyly at the waiter's departing back.

"What a nice man."

"Yeah, yeah, sure." I have calmed down. My rage was interrupted by that little interlude. Grab Jerry's sleeve,

"Oh, come on J. I want to find Angie and Siobhan. Where can they be?" Attempt to peer over shoulders and scan the hall. No, can't see a thing. This joint is massive.

"Let's look over here, Jerry."

"O.K. – if you like." Stroll off in search of the girls. Check out all my paintings on the way past to see if they have sold stickers on them yet. J. takes my arm and waves a conversational hand at the paintings we're passing.

"Y'know Carls, hic [way too much champagne] you're just exactly like whatshisname, that French guy." Raise my eyebrows.

"No Jerry, you've got me. Too vague. At least give me a clue. Did he limp or paint curvy ladies?"

"We-ell, how the fuck should I know? I don't know him socially. I thought he was dead? Anyway he used lots of *colours* and stuff."

"As opposed to the artists who didn't?" Oh Jerry, give it up, please. I'll pay you. He sucks his entire face in ... [Oops! Offended Jerry alert!]... for at least two whole seconds. Then his weasel chops light up. He has spied our sexy waiter again. J. foists his still-brimming glass into my startled hands and trundles off waiter-wards.

"I'll get us some more champagne Carls."

"Why? Are we stocking up?" Oh, he's gone? Oh well. At least everyone's happy...And Angie and Siobhan are bound to turn up eventually. I shall go and mingle with my guests.

…………...

Much entertaining mingling later - I am sure that I have charmed lots of rich dudes and secured potential sales. Excellent! A job well done. I'll just nip to the loo and check that my face hasn't gone all shiny. It's like a sauna in here? These people will just keep breathing all over the place. Don't they realise it's only necessary until they've signed the cheques?

...Oh! There they are. I have lost Lorenzo and Jerry but I've found Angie and Siobhan. They are both suitably dolled up to the nines or tens [but not as dolled up as me]. They're with Giles who, to the eternal smacking of all of our gobs, has morphed into a designer style suit? Good grief! He's actually quite sexy wearing that? He must have found a phone box at long last? Siobhan is proudly clinging to his arm. Good! I'm pleased for her. She deserves it. Angie has three gorgeous guys fussing over her.

"Oh Carly, there you are.." She gives me a big showbizzy hug.

"...God Carls, you look fantastic! You must meet Michael, Jason and David from work. I've told them all about you." Really? You mean one of them's for me? Oh wow! …Erm, why were you shagging Miles the Creep when you had all of these hotties at your daily disposal? The hunks give a chorus of deep, seductive,

"Hi there!'s" and extend friendly hands. Ooh! Well 'hi there!' yourselves, you big sexy beasts…Were you planning to extend anything more vital? Oh, does my make-up still look alright? Lean over carefully on my tottering high heels to whisper discreetly in Angie's ear.

"Where the hell have you been hiding them? And why are there three of them? Was it to give us more choice? What will we do with the spare one? I don't want two at once. That's not just greedy, that's obscene?" Angie smirks and nods at the tallest Greek god,

"Oh no Carls, Jason's for Jerry, y'know?" No way? God! He hides that well? Angie looks round at the crowd,

"Where is Jerry anyway?"

"Oh, I lost him… I'll just go and find him. He'll want to be found for this."

Teeter off in search of J.

Oh, who's that? Turn my heavy coiffure to snoop past the shoulder of a miscellaneous suit. Looked just like Mel Gibson? Surely not? If it is I hope J. doesn't miss him. He'll be spitting if he does.

"Oomph!" I have walked into someone. Impossible not to in here really. It was foolhardy not to be looking in this crowd. Look up, apologetic,

"Sorry. I wasn't…Oh! It's you!"

"Carly, hi. I was looking for you. You look… amazing." Yeah? Thanks. What the hell are you doing here? It's the bain of my life actor bogey-man. At least I think it is? Perhaps there are actually lots of him. Perhaps he was a multiple birth or a clone or a sodding alien or something. Any of these options would explain quite a lot, particularly the last one. He's on a fucking planet of his own – planet weird-boy! …But clearly he doesn't know that he is an alien. He thinks he is actually God. What is that complex called again?

He's laughing at me. So what's new? Oh, what are you smirking at now? I didn't ask you to come here and snigger…What? Is my make-up all smudged?

"What? What's so funny?"

"I was just thinking that you're like a little rabbit." Smirk, smirk. How could he know that?…Oh bugger! That's right, he does. Raise a snooty chin at him,

"I *beg* your pardon?" So that's what you think of me, is it? What a cheek to my bedroom prowess!

"Well, only when you wriggle your nose up like that." My nose? What about my nose? …. Oh! So then you didn't mean…? Oh, well thank goodness for that!

He tilts his head to one side to smile at me,

"It's really rather cute." Give him the full benefit of my extremely evil black eye [although it's probably much less scary under all my make-up]. I am not cute! I'm a Cornish pastie, so bog off you sarcastic pig. He does an un-required sexy whisper,

"I really liked that photo you sent me." What? Don't you understand anything? You weren't supposed to like it? You were supposed to be utterly crushed. Sarcastic,

"Did you? Oh, I'm so pleased…Excuse me. I have to mingle now."

"Oh? ... Oh, O.K. Right, fine. I'll just have a look around?" Yes, why don't you do that? Have a look in the traffic outside.

I escape and scuttle off Jerry-wards. Where the hell is he? He must be here somewhere? I want to get back to the sexy guys, I cannot believe my luck…oh, there's Jerry he. He has that waiter trapped against a wall. …still clutching his huge tray of glasses in front of him in desperate polite self-defence. J. has one skinny arm placed strategically on the wall beside his poor victims head and is leaning inappropriately close to his ear.

"Jerry! Put that man down! I want you." Jerry swings his head round in surprised consternation and the waiter takes his chance to escape. J. notices a second too late to intervene. He looks a trifle miffed.

"Carly! What are you trying to do? We were getting on really well."

"Well, don't bother. Angie's brought you a real man... Oh, do come on, J. They're all waiting ." Grab his sleeve impatiently and drag him off before he can scare anyone else.

....

Later still – an excellent evening. I am having the best time. I am having a harmless chortle with Michael from Angie's work. I am not going to do anything but there is no harm at all in having a spine-tingling chat with a convenient sexy straight man. It's quite acceptably pleasant in fact. He is telling me funny stories about media land. He is sophisticated, mature and interesting. Well at last! Where have you been all my...

"Carlee! There you are. I've been trying to find you for an age." Oh knickers! Shrimpton – B! I don't think the B. is for Boswick at all? Your timing really does suck Edgah? Find myself whisked away from my friends and my new potential love interest before I have a chance to protest. ??? Where is Lorenzo? But it's alright. Edgar seems to be in business mode now.

"You *must* meet the Washingtons Darling. Jack is a personal friend of mine and one of our most valued buyers. He's just over from the States for a few days on business, and he's an avid collector of up and coming young artists... Ah, Jack! Here we are...This is Carly Watson, one of our most exciting new discoveries. Carly – Jack Washington." A dignified grey-haired gentleman turns and looks down at me so I proffer a nervous hand. He looks intimidatingly rich and important. Smile in an attempt to look professional,

"Um, hello Mr Washington, ... Pleased to meet you.." He grasps my hand with both of his and smiles charmingly. Oh, quite human really?

"Miss Watson, Hi! The pleasures all mine. I am very impressed with your work, young lady. Think you could rustle me up a commission or two? "

"Oh! Er, thank-you and yes, yes of course." Aaargh! Aaaargh! Success!

I hear very little of the ensuing conversation as I am stunned. I'm not used to things going right. Just smile and nod a lot in an enigmatic fashion. Toddle off in search of the Ladies as the excitement and champagne combine. I'm singing inside my head with happiness. What a fabulous evening. I can *not* believe it. It's going so well that I am in serious danger of losing touch with reality and being overwhelmed by the surreal euphoria of unexpected success.

La-la-la...Uh-oh? There is that crazy Aaron. I'll just scoot round here and then he won't see me...Uh-oh? Too late, he already has. But if I'm quick I could still pretend that I haven't seen him. I'll outflank him with a tactical escape ploy. I can just sneak off down this corridor...Hah! Can't catch me you crazy American.

....

Ten minutes later - Despite my best-laid outflanking tactics, superior strength has prevailed. I have been rounded up and herded into a secret hidey-hole under the stairs. Yes, that's right, you've guessed it, by the impatient slutty actor with the vaguely disturbing rabbit fetish. And, as usual, it appears that he's in a bad mood.

"Carly, what the hell are you trying to do here?" Uuh? Sell some pictures, why?

"You've been ignoring me all evening..." Have I? Oh, boo-hoo! Go away! Apparently total silence is not the desired response. His face is doing that twitchy thing and I don't think he's impressed. Well, oh deary me! I've had enough of his antics. Predictably enough, he starts ranting,

"First you give me the come on... and then you run away? In fact, you always do that. Running away really does appear to be your forte, doesn't it? That's when you're not jumping out of windows or hiding in bathrooms, of course...." Give him a contemplative look. I think that I really hate you. Why won't you leave me alone? But oh no, he's too busy having his daily rant,

"…and *then* what do you do? Send me sexy photos and provocative notes and invite me to your show? Are you some kind of a tease?" Provocative? It wasn't meant to be provocative, you ridiculous man! It was meant to cut you to the quick!

"But I didn't invite you to come here. You came here all by yourself?" Aaron frowns and does his 'you're an imbecile' tone. He must do that character quite a lot He really has perfected the voice. He smacks his hand angrily off the nearest wall

"Oh yeah, Carly, you did. You sent a ticket with the photo, remember?" No, I didn't! How did that get in there? Unless? Oh no, he wouldn't have, would he? …But he must have! Oh my God! The treacherous little weasel!

Turn round totally seething.

"Jerry! Get over here NOW!" Jerry turns, glass in hand. Does his 'Oops! I'm discovered!' face and skulks off into the crowd. *Bastard!* He's supposed to be my friend? Aaron glares grimly after him then turns back to me,

"Looks like your boyfriend is busy right now." My boyfriend? Jake? He's not…Oh! Oh, you mean Jerry? Oh, ha-ha! No way?

"Jerry is not my boyfriend. He's just a friend."

Aaron snorts sarcastically,

"Yeah? Sure Honey. Whatever you say." He looks at me like I'm something he's scraped off his shoe. Don't give me that face!

"He isn't! He's gay for goodness sake!" Aaron raises one of his eyebrows in a highly smackable, mocking sort of way,

"Was he gay before he met you, or did you drive him to it, huh?"

"Oh, you are such a pig! You think you're so smart, don't you? Just because you happen to be on T.V. and lots of crazies want to steal your pants ….And boil your ruddy rabbit! You think that you can just waltz in here and do or say whatever you like?..." Going up by an octave or two now,

"…Don't you *Mr* Stanford? Well then, don't you? Well, you bloody well can't! …And let me tell you for nothing right now that I AM NOT IMPRESSED! So why don't you just bog off back to Jennifer, or one of your zillion other sluts or America even…. And just

222

LEAVE ME ALONE! ….. I've got my knickers on for a change and you are not getting anywhere near them. So just take the hint, why don't you? You're not completely irresistible you know? In fact, I've never met anyone quite so resistible in my entire life!" There! Consider yourself told!"

He is looking…what's the word I want? Menacing? Yes. I think that that pretty much covers it. He goes very husky,

"Have you quite finished Carly?"

"Yes, yes I have. You can go now." Dismiss him with a rude wave of the hand and turn my snooty face away. Coming in here and giving me a hard time for something I didn't even do? Well! Well, really!

There ensues a small pause, punctuated by male and very pissed off breathing. I believe he may well still be there? I can feel the glare in the side of my hairdo? He puts an elegant tuxedoed arm in front of me so that I'm trapped in the corner. Oh knickers! Why do men always pin you to walls? …And they always do that whisper-in-the-ear thing? I really have had enough of this now. Aaron leans closer,

"Well, don't you worry Carly, I'm going to. And this time I will not be back to force my unwanted attentions on you. I had no idea you found them so repellent. And certainly not the other week there – a creditable performance indeed! You should consider acting. You certainly had me fooled…" Oh, you cheeky bastard!

"…And as for your in-depth analysis of the workings of my degenerate mind, I'm afraid that I have to correct you on a couple of points there. Firstly, I just go to work and do my job, just like anyone else…." You are not just like anyone else. You are, without doubt, a total fruitcake!

"…the fact that I work in the public eye does not automatically make me into some kind of egotistical, ill-mannered sexual deviant. That isn't compulsory with the job. I can't imagine for a second where you'd get such a ridiculous idea. …You, however, appear to fall into any or all of these categories…" Spin round to gasp in horror. I *knew* he thought I was a prostitute! Prod him in the tie indignantly,

"How dare you say that to me!" He smacks the wall again furiously.

"Be quiet! I haven't finished!"

"Oh!" You insufferable git! He waves a lectury hand in my face,

"Before you go round pre-judging other people Carly, might I suggest that you take a tiny little look at your own behaviour, hmm? Do you think that being attractive gives you the right to behave like some cheap little cocktease? " Oh! Do NOT say that horrible word! He glowers impatiently, clearly waiting for a reply.

"Huh? Well? Do you? Do you get a kick out of this? I told you how I felt about you, I told you I wasn't seeing Jennifer... but for some bizarre reason lodged in your warped little mind, that just isn't good enough? What do you want, my fucking references? Shall I send you my goddamn C.V.?"

Oh, this is too much! I'm not listening to any more. This is total bullshit! Try ineffectually to push him aside,

"No, don't bother! If that's what you think!" I can feel my bottom lip trembling like a toddler. There is NO WAY I am going to cry in public. And at my preview night for God's sake? This guy is the most evil pig in the world! He even makes Jake look quite appealing? Still incensed, Aaron leans right down to glare into my burning eyes and drops his creepy voice even further.

"Would you like to know what I actually think? Hmm? Would you?" Eek! God, you would make a good villain! And no, not really. But as usual, I don't get a choice.

"I think that you are the most infuriating little witch I have ever come across..." Pardon?

"... and I really can't decide whether to take you home and fuck you senseless or just put you over my knee..." Jesus Christ! Help! Help! He's a ruddy psycho! ... No, I am not scared! I'm NOT! He's hardly going to hit me in here. Draw myself up to my full five foot four and a quarter and attempt to quell my traitorous, quivery face.

"Well *Mr* Stanford, that's absolutely fascinating. Thank-you for sharing that with me. But I'm afraid I'm a little busy just now. Do you think that it might be possible at all for you to just Fuck Right Off ?"

He is momentarily speechless. Slip my head under his designer suited arm and click hastily off into the relative safety of the busy bit of the room on my ludicrous stiletto sandals.

I won't look back. He'll be quite happy now that he's got that off his chest and totally humiliated me. Well, that's fine. We have closure! My face will no doubt stop scorching in a couple of years… So, back to business - where are the rich punters? Oh, there's Edgar. I'm actually relieved to see him. Maybe he's not so bad after all. At least he's got decent manners and isn't utterly out of his mind…

Edgar spots me approaching and extends a dampish palm in greeting,

"Oh, there you are Carlee, my Dahling… And where have you been hiding, you naughty little thing? Whatever shall we do with you, eh?" Oh, please don't mention spanking. I've had quite enough of that from the mad Yank.

Edgar slips a practised sleazy arm round my bare shoulders and trails a clammy palm up and down my back. Oh YUCK! He's pretending to be in ushering mode. And I am still far too shocked to fend him off. So, I'm everyone's favourite slapper, am I? Well, fantastic! Lucky old me. I'm in the wrong profession it seems. I could have been extremely rich by now… and only equally pummelled and groped. God! That careers advice sucks?

…………..

Some time and some poncing about later - I am trying my very hardest to look like a serious artist. You know, the kind you might actually pay? I am in a deep and meaningful debate with a random potential picture purchaser when I am verbally accosted from behind.

"Well, hello there Luv. Got your clothes on again? Well, wonders will never cease. Same time again at your place next week? I'll pop round and give you a good seeing to."

"Oh, fine." Whatever. Window cleaners, they seem to turn up everywhere.

Suddenly,

"AND WHO THE FUCK IS THAT GUY?" A familiar angry voice in my ear. Jump in fright and spin round.

"I heard every fucking word he said, you dirty little slut. Can't I leave you alone for a minute without you dropping your goddamn knickers! I ask you to be my wife and *this* is how you carry on?" It's a pissed and really pissed off Jake in his very worst Fat-Boy-Fat guise.

"Jake, stop it! I don't even know the guy... Let me go, you're hurting my arm!" And I'm not even going out with you? To think I might have taken you back. What kind of a muppet am I?

Jake raises his voice belligerently and people are starting to stare. No, just go ahead and ruin my evening why don't you? ... Are there any men here who don't hate my guts? He is practically breaking my arm.

"You Carly, are coming home right now!" No, I don't think so.

The potential purchaser attempts to intervene in a gentlemanly manner,

"Now look here old chap, that's really not on!" Jake looks round aggressively and locks eyes with him. His face takes on an evilly suspicious glint.

"And who the fucking hell might you be? Want to make something of it, do you? Eh?"

"Oh, no! I was just saying..." The polite guy tails off awkwardly, the fear obvious in his voice.

"Well, just fucking don't, alright? She's coming with me... Carly, come on, we're leaving." Clinging onto the last shreds of my dignity I try to discreetly prise off Jake's hand, one huge finger at a time. I shall have big ugly bruises now, to go with my black and blue face. I will look like a goddamn Dalmatian ...So a Cornish pastie isn't enough? Sigh deeply in frustration, give up on the dignity completely and roar at him,

"Jake, let's get one thing straight. There is no way in hell I'm going anywhere with you in this state. So just let me go and GO AWAY!"

"You'll do what you're told, for a fucking change, now get...."

Sense a sudden blur of movement beside me,

"SMACK!" Oh! He seems to have gone? Oh no, he's just down on the floor?

"Touch her again and I'll break your goddamn neck, you asshole!" Oh God, what's happening now? ... I have apparently been saved by Aaron, or Public Enemy No.1, as he really ought to be known. I thought that he'd gone?

We are surrounded by voyeuristic spectators, like the Indians do to the cowboys, or vice versa. The crowd has formed a flashbulb wagon train circle and the room is starting to spin. Oops! And I'm not even drunk? Maybe it's extremely delayed concussion?

"It's alright Carly, I've got you. Come on, I'll take you home." Oh, O.K. – I'll go with the Yankee tart. Find myself scooped up yet again by the Prince Charming rabbit nose guy. Oh, who cares? Do what you like....You probably will anyway. Think I will just shut my eyes.

Bedlam, bedlam in the hall ....

CHAPTER TWENTY-NINE
After The Storm

Mmm, it has gone very quiet. What's happening now? Frosty air on my face wakes me up to find that Aaron is carrying me along a dark, empty street. Put my head down against his chest and shut my eyes. Oh fine, I am kidnapped again. I'm getting quite used to this. Think I quite like the Stone Age approach. Wake me up at the cave. Or maybe I could just enquire…

"Em, where are you taking me now?" He has a very grim serious face. Ooh-er? Is he still angry with me? He carries on marching along without looking down.

"You're coming back to my place for a coffee."

"Oh well, fair enough. If you like. …Hang on though? What kind of coffee? You do mean coffee to drink?" Oh, you just so better had! He screws up his face and looks down at me with a fairly confused frown.

"What? As opposed to which kind of coffee?" Is he having me on? Nod indignantly,

"As opposed to 'please shag me' coffee!" Well, really! The nerve of the man! …And stop with the smirking already.

Deep, seductive,

"Well Carly, if it's on offer?" Don't wave your eyebrows at me!

Splutter,

"No, it certainly bloody is not!" That wiped your smirk off – Ha-ha!

"Fine! So, then my place it is."

…………..

Back at the kidnapper's lair, it is clear that he lied about the coffee. He shows no signs of percolation... But at least he has allowed me to retain my knickers. Now that does make a change. I am cuddled up on the end of the settee and, as usual, he's staring at me with a deep and hard to analyse face. If I wait he might open the batting ... and tell me exactly why I'm here? He leans forward in his chair, as if about to utter something momentous. Go on, then. Tell me? I'm waiting...

"Carly .... would you like a drink?" Um, no. I would like an explanation? ...And preferably now, Kidnap-man.

Shrug,

"Um, fine. Have you any peach schnapps?"

"Think so, I'll just have a look." He toddles off to check on his peach schnapps supply. Sigh and lay back in my cushions. I expect I ought to just humour him, as no doubt the door is still locked.

After a moment or two, he clinks back into the lounge with a couple of huge crystal tumblers. Hands one over politely.

"There you go. Try that."

Snooty,

"Thank-you." He settles himself down in a casual pose on the other end of my settee. He's having a stare at his drink and clinking the ice. He's got a serious frown on his face again. He looks like he's trying to think. And having quite a few problems, I'd say? For God's sake, spit it out man!

He starts talking seriously to his glass.

"Carly, that guy who was dragging you about back there... Who exactly was he?" Oh no! Start with the difficult questions, why don't you?

"Em, he's my ex-boyfriend." He glances up then looks back down at his drink. He's trying to stare it out.

"And does *he* know that? The ex bit, I mean? It didn't look like he did. Is he jealous of that Jerry guy or something?" You are an extremely nosey man...and really quite remarkably obtuse?

"I've told you already, Jerry is gay. And he *was* actually gay before I met him." Aaron smiles up from his tumbler. You'd forgotten you said that, hadn't you? Oops! He's gone all serious again? Oh dear, this man is a schitzo? And has a strange fascination with tumblers of ice? Must be linked to the drawer-rifling thing?

"So Carly, if that other guy is your ex, what the hell was he trying to do?" I am the last person who's ever known that.

"I don't know. I think he was drunk." Aaron nods wisely at his favourite glass.

"Uh-huh, I think he probably was. Or does he usually fling women about?" Think I'll have to take the Fifth on that one. I can't say 'no' as it isn't strictly true, but it wasn't that bad. He wasn't violent, just a bit of a bully. And there were *some* mitigating circumstances... But that is my private business. I really don't wish to discuss it, certainly not with you.

"Er, um ...Aaron, I'd rather not ..." Uh-oh, he doesn't look happy? Aaron leans over towards me. Now what? I'm too exhausted to run. He strokes my hair in a distracted kind of way.

"I take it 'er-um' means he does?" Oh, dear God? How embarrassing!

"Well, not usually, it's complicated... It looked much worse than it was... Look, I'd really rather not talk about this." I examine my fingernails, so that he can't see into my head.

"Alright, what do you want to talk about then?" Shrug again and wave my schnapps at him,

"I think we've heard quite enough about my weirdo life. Tell me about yours instead." He does a funny little laugh.

"What? Are you saying that I'm weird now?" I didn't actually say that ...But oh yes, you certainly are... He's getting a little too friendly here? ... I shall distract him with a racist remark.

"You must be weird. You *are* American, aren't you?" His eyebrows shoot off the top of his face and he laughs in disbelief.

"Oh, you cheeky little .... ?" He leans over and casually pins me to the couch. Bugger! Always pinned against something? ...And that wasn't the intended response. You were supposed to be deeply offended. Don't you get *anything* right? He has gone into laughing, mocking, half-growly mode. This guy has some range?

"Actually Honey, I was born in England. I just grew up in the States." In his enthusiasm he inadvertently spills half of my drink right down the front of my top.

"Eek! That's freezing!"

"Sorry." Has he got a grudge against my entire wardrobe? He grabs my glass from my hand and tucks it out of reach on the rug. ???

"You won't be needing that Carly. It's an English drink, you know."

"Peach schnapps? No, it's not. Surely it's Russian or something? ...Anyway, I wanted to drink it, not wear it. Look! My stomach is soaking wet now." Aaron glances down at my soggy top. You have a very dirty face for an almost English guy. He starts smirking,

"Here, let me help you. You really should take that thing off.." What? He's trying to slide my top up. Shove him in the chest,

"Get off!" Smirk, smirketty – smirk.

"What? I'm just trying to find the rest of your drink..." You're about to find a slap in the face, mate! He eyes my stomach with a dubious, scoundrelly look,

"… it's probably still quite drinkable you know. Shame to waste it."

"Oh, you wouldn't dare! You're all polite and .... half-English and stuff?" Screws up his face in derision,

"You think I'm too *English* to lick you?" Eeek?

"Erm, well I...."

"Oh, am I really? Come here."

…………...

A few well licked minutes later.

"So? Was that to Madam's Scottish satisfaction, then?" Mr Growly sees fit to enquire. Oh, God yes! That was wonderful!

"Em, perfectly adequate, thank-you." Aaron flings back his mad head and laughs.

"Adequate? Carly, you kill me!"

"That could be a potential scenario I suppose, if you really can't manage to behave yourself."

"So then, Carly, tell me. What else can't English men do?" Should I answer that? Oh, why not? He's far too smug for words. Wave a hand airily in dismissive derision.

"Oh, you know, they don't have real sex. They only have stiff upper lips." Oops! Perhaps I have just gone too far? Aaron looks quite horrified now? And maybe a little bit dirty? Ooh-er?

"Right! That's the last straw, you little Scottish slut. You are just so for it now!" Really? Am I? Fantastic! – Yippee!

"Oh, no, no, no, no! Get off!"

Uummmm Oh yes, that is quite nice… Don't really mind if you do that, umm… Of course, I have heard of this foreplay idea. It's a nice change from 'What about it then, huh?' … Seems to be kissing my stomach? Oh fine, I wonder if he's got a plan? Or if he's just a random sort of groper, whichever bit of you he comes to first? Hmm, very interesting technique. Maybe I could spin myself round?

So, what character are you in now? Is it Heathcliff, perchance? Why yes, I think that it is… Oh! Oh, that's lovely! ...So what about this screen kissing thing? I wonder where one puts one's tongue? … This could require several re-takes. And the understudy can just go home now. Their services won't be required.... Maybe we get to dress up? I must remember to thwart him a bit. When thwarted he seems to get cross. Nothing like a good thwarting… and… Aargh! What on Earth have you got there - a ruddy cattle prod? You are not putting that anywhere near me! ...Oh God! What are you doing? Stop that or I will have to hurt you ... No, no really! – Stop it! Oh NO! Think I might have to bite something now? I wish I had my pink candy stick

CHAPTER THIRTY
Artistic Interpretation - 6/6, 6/6, 6/10?

Uummmmm. Oh, this is nice. Where am I? Oh, that's right! I'm in his huge bed again? And...oh! He's awake? ...Oh, alright, you've got me. I give up.

"Mmm, hi there Carly honey."

"Umm, Hi?" Mr Growly?

"Em... Are you laughing at me?" Oh, you are now?

"And why would I be laughing at you?"

"I don't know? You think that I'm mad? ....Oh, no! That's right, I'm the Queen of the Cock-teasers, aren't I?" DON'T laugh!

"I think you might just have lost your title, your majesty." Oh no! You will have to die! ....Oh no! Oh no! Heathcliff's come back?

"Carly! Stop wriggling and come here!" No, no, - no way!

"I will not! I have to go home..." I'm not staying here. You're too scary. Let me go!

"You are not going anywhere..."

"Oh no, no, I think that I ought to." You might just fuck up my head. As opposed to all the rest of me...

"No Sweetheart, you are staying right here."

"I can't! I didn't bring my spare knickers."

He laughs dirtily,

"Didn't you? Oh, well. You won't be needing them anyway." Eeek! You are NOT touching me with that thing again! ...Oh! Well, maybe you are? Uummmmmm ...Oh my God! That's it! Eureka! I've found out when you do the 'uummming' noise? So yoga is akin to sex? ...And he must be in the 'Shaggable Bastard' category... for clearly a cardigan he's not, ... but he's only the first bit, not the whole title?

No, I give up. I don't know what he is? ... apart from very bloody-well scary. I expect he learnt that at R.A.D.A. or something ... or maybe it's a natural gift? Anyway, I think I quite like it ... uummm, uummm, uuummmm…

…………...

The insatiable Yank is finally exhausted… Thank God! He could have killed me... And I don't think I'm insured against this? He's lying sideways with his head propped up by one muscular arm and is fixing me with a stare. What? Was I really meant to applaud?

"So, Carly, what is the problem?"

"I didn't know there was a problem? I thought you were very, umm, athletic?" Don't wave your eyebrows at me?

"Oh really? Why, thank-you Ma'am. I aim to please."

"Oh, well, it was quite …satisfactory." Oh! Where have you gone? He has fallen off the bed laughing. The pig?

" Satisfactory? Oh Carly, you crack me up." I'll crack you right now, you cheeky big beast?

"Well, what am I supposed to call it? I'm not au fait with the terms.... Some of us didn't go to acting school, you know!" He scrambles back up onto the bed.

"What d'you think that we do there, have orgies?"

"I don't know? I expect that *you* did."

"Oh Carly, you really are funny."

"Yes, yes I know. It's a curse. ...But if you didn't mean *that*, then what problem were you talking about?" Oh no. He has gone all serious again.

"I meant with the running away thing.... And why are you covered in bruises? Has that bastard from last night been hitting you?" Shake my head in an explanatory fashion,

"Oh no, no. That was a branch." I'd forgotten for a bit about my face. He couldn't see it before under all of my make-up. This has been well wiped off overnight. Aaron has also gone purple, but with temper rather than bruising.

"Are you saying that bastard beat you up with a branch? I'll fucking well kill him!"

"No, no I did it myself. I was pruning a tree and it hit me." Oh God! I feel such a fool. And I can see that he's a little bit confused now.

"So then, he hasn't been smacking you about?"

"No, not really."

"Look sweetheart, this is serious. What's the hell's going on with that guy?"

"Nothing! Nothing, he's gone. He just keeps coming back, that's the problem ... And he gets a bit worked up." Oh yeah, you are purple now?

"Worked up? What the hell does that mean? Look, if he comes back again you just tell me. And I'll kick his ass down the street."

Smile,

"Will you? Really?" Oh, that's very generous..

"Uh-huh." Oh, that's nice. I've never met an ass-kicker before? ...And with such impressive credentials as well? Uumm, well lucky old me? He lies down beside me and strokes my hair. Oh fine... I'll just stay here and....

Suddenly a very loud...

"PHWUMP!" ...in the hall. Jolt into a sitting position with fright,

"Oh! What was that?" He smiles and snuggles my ear. He doesn't appear to be the least bit interested in the 'phwump' noise? He mumbles distractedly,

"Oh, it's the papers, that's all." Papers? Papers? – My preview! Oh God! I'd forgotten. What a total disaster? Shrimpton-Boswick will kill me. I started a riot in his hall?

Abandon Mr Snuggly on the duvet, scramble down from the huge bed and scuttle off through to the hall. Oh God, please don't let them have used it? There must be more important news? ...Aaaargh! It's on the front page?!*?!*

"Aaargh! Aargh!" My favourite madman runs through to see what's the matter. I'm sitting on the hall rug, papers akimbo, having a little panic to myself.

"Sweetheart, are you o.k.?" Wave his papers at him in a straggly bunch.

"My preview's all over the tabloids? Oh GOD!" There's a huge photograph of the best bedlam scene and Edgar looking aghast. Put my head in my hands and groan,

"Oh no! Maybe he'll sue me?" Fling the wretched papers across the hall... in case that might help in some way. But it doesn't make me feel any better. I still know that my fiasco is in there for all on the planet to read... even gits who don't like you. Well, just how much does that suck?!*?!* Put my forehead right down onto the rug, between my outstretched legs, and moan quietly.

Aaron retrieves the mangled newspaper calmly and sits down beside me on the floor to read.

Oh dear God, must you? I don't want to know the grisly details of the accursed event... and oddly enough, I'd rather you didn't witness my degradation either, thanks. I really, really like you and therefore would actually prefer you to think well of me. Clearly that's out of the goddamn question right now... But I most certainly do *not* require your pity, so throw the flipping scandal sheet in the bin! Aaron starts reading aloud in a newsreader voice,

"A remarkable debut from innovative new Scottish artist Carly Watson .... featuring a quite astounding piece of performance art involving several people including the artist herself." Raise my face from the floor,

"What? - But it was a riot?" He carries on perusing the article,

"The elusive Miss Watson was not available for comment last night, but her unique style of work will undoubtedly be in huge demand. Gallery owner Sir Edgar Shrimpton-Boswick is delighted with the initial sales figures." I am totally, utterly speechless. Aaron is laughing.

"Oh my God, Carly, well done! So how does it feel to be famous?"

"Well, good grief! You ought to know?"

So I can finally have anything at all that I want. ...And do I know yet what that actually is? Why, yes, I believe that I do.

Printed in the United Kingdom by
Lightning Source UK Ltd., Milton Keynes
141031UK00001B/50/P